THE FLIRT

LAYLA HAGEN

Contents

Chapter One

Chad

"Dad, can I have another slice?" Bella asked.

I laughed. My daughter never could only have one piece of pecan pie. It was her favorite dessert—after the beignets from Café Du Monde, of course.

"Sure, cricket." I tilted forward, kissing her forehead.

Bella was small for an eight-year-old. She was dangling her feet in the empty space underneath the counter she was seated on.

As I cut another slice for her, I glanced at the clock. It was only seven thirty in the morning. We still had time before I had to take her to school. Usually we'd stop by my restaurant on the way, as the kitchen always had leftover pies from the day before. But it was best to get out once the staff arrived because it would become total madness.

"Aren't you going to have pie, Daddy?" she asked. Grabbing the slice before I'd even managed to put it on her plate, she quickly began devouring it.

"You know what? I will." I took off my cuff links, shoving them in my pocket, and rolled up my sleeves. I picked up a slice and ate it, just like my little girl, not bothering with a fork, and Bella grinned, making her whole face light up. "Hurry up, beautiful. We don't want to be late for school."

She pouted. "But I want to see the grans before we go."

"All right," I said. "They should be here any second now."

LeBlanc & Broussard was one of the most famous restaurants in New Orleans. We were located on Royal Street, right in the heart of the French Quarter. It had been in my family for generations. My great-grandparents from Dad's side started it, but it had grown by leaps and bounds over the years. Now the restaurant took up half the building. The other half was our offices.

My chef left last month, and it took the team far too long to find someone new, but thank God she was starting tomorrow. My grandmothers had stepped up in the interim, and although they did a great job, the kitchen staff was ready for a change. My grandmothers were forces to be reckoned with. I had enough practice dealing with them, but the restaurant staff didn't.

The sound of the door opening caught my attention. I looked behind me. Joel, one of our sous-chefs, came in from the employee entrance. He startled, but then his face filled with visible relief when he saw it was me.

"Oh, Chad. Hi, Bella. I heard voices and thought your nans arrived early..." His voice faded, and I was trying very hard not to laugh. Joel was six foot seven and in his fifties, yet my grandmothers had clearly put the fear of God in him. "Anyway, I'm going to get things going."

Bella had finished her pie and had crumbs all over her mouth. I grabbed a napkin and cleaned her up, especially at the corners.

"Bella, let's wait for the grans in the front of the restaurant. We don't want to be in Joel's way."

"Okay, Daddy."

I wrapped her in my arms, lowering her from the counter, and then took her hand.

"We'll be in the front, Joel," I said.

"Sure. Have a great day, boss."

My brothers and I were running The Orleans Conglomerate, which encompassed a multitude of establishments throughout the city. But I was closest to the staff of LeBlanc & Broussard because my office was right above.

"Want to sit here?" I asked Bella. We had a few tables outside too.

"Yes." She yawned, rubbing her eyes. My baby girl wasn't a morning person, unlike me. I got up at six o'clock sharp every day and ran on the treadmill before she woke up.

We sat down in the sun. "Can I sit on your lap?" she asked.

"Sure." I liked that she still enjoyed being close to me. Some kids at her school were already pushing their parents away. I was dreading the day my Bella would do the same.

"Good morning, you two," Mom said. She'd come with her mother, my grandma Celine, the two of them walking arm in arm.

"Grans!" Bella exclaimed, jumping from my lap to hug them both.

"We didn't know you two would be here this morning," Celine said. "What a pleasant surprise."

"Just a quick stop on the way to school," I explained.

"All right," Mom said. "We're going inside and getting things started. Isabeau is coming a bit later." Isabeau was my other grandmother.

I looked at Mom questioningly, but she averted her gaze. That was my clue that it had been another crazy morning in the LeBlanc-Broussard household. Then again, that wasn't unusual at all. My parents and both sets of grandparents lived together in a large mansion in the Garden District. Considering they'd once been at odds, this was a feat in itself. Both sets of grandparents had been against my parents marrying, but that was all in the past now. Their house was enormous, and everyone had their privacy. Still, some days were more *interesting* than others.

"Thank you again for filling in," I said, getting to my feet. "The new chef arrives tomorrow."

"Are we sure this Scarlett's good enough?" Celine asked. "I mean, she's only thirtysomething. How does she know the finer techniques of cooking?"

I cleared my throat. "Gran, *I'm* thirty-four."

"Pssh, you know what I mean."

"Initially, she'll be on probation. She wasn't my first choice either," I admitted, "but her references are great."

"She's never been a chef," Celine continued.

I'd had this conversation with her and Isabeau quite a few times, and I was starting to lose my patience. I had the utmost respect for my parents and grandparents, and I understood that this was a family business and all. I didn't like them questioning my decisions. Mom withheld an opinion because she wasn't involved in the restaurant business at all.

"No, but a sous-chef from a Michelin-starred restaurant in Seattle will be a great addition," I said in a measured tone.

"Isabeau and I will be here tomorrow morning when she arrives, anyway," Celine said.

Mom threw me an alarmed look, and I knew exactly what she was thinking. Isabeau was going to scare away the new chef. She could have that effect on people.

"We'll see," I said vaguely.

"What time will she be there?"

"I haven't gotten confirmation yet. I'll let you know." I was absolutely *not* going to let her know. I'd welcome Scarlett personally.

Mom chuckled and hooked her arm through Celine's. "Come on, Mom, let's go to the kitchen. I'll grab a bite, and then I'll go to the gallery."

My mom had never been interested in the family business. She'd been the original rebel. I respected her for always being strong-minded. But then again, everyone was—on both sides of the family.

After they'd each kissed Bella's cheek, we were on our way. I'd found a school close to the restaurant. It was only fifteen minutes away on foot, and today was an especially good day for a walk. The Quarter was always empty and eerily silent in the mornings. Most businesses hadn't even opened up, except for coffee shops.

Bella looked around curiously at all the shops, her eyes wide when we passed the voodoo store. We hadn't taken a stroll around here in a while; the weather had been too unstable.

"What is that?" she asked, pointing at a doll that had several pins sticking out of it.

"I don't know," I said. "Ask Isabeau."

Isabeau had worked as a tour guide for a time on top of running the restaurant business. My ex-wife and I had named Bella after her—it was short for my grandmother's given name.

"Yes, I will," Bella said.

We moved on quickly down Royal Street and turned left onto St. Peter Street. I hurried as we passed the crossing with Bourbon Street farther down. Usually, I tried to avoid taking her anywhere near Bourbon, as it was the more risqué section of the city, but early mornings were quiet here, too, except the occasional drunkard.

"Daaad," she drawled a few minutes later when we saw the school in the distance, "can we go to Café Du Monde after I finish school?"

"We'll see," I said. Keeping things vague was the key to success with the women in my family. If I said "Maybe," she'd take it as a yes, and I hadn't yet checked my schedule. I wasn't even sure if I'd finish in time to pick her up, and I didn't want to make promises I couldn't keep.

"Okay," she replied. "And Daaaad, when I go to Mom's house, can I take Mr. Teddy with me?"

"Sure thing, cricket. If you want, we can buy you a Mr. Teddy to have in your other room too."

"Daddy!" She shook her head so vehemently that her pigtails bounced around. "We can't do that. Mr. Teddy would be soooo offended," She drew out the "*o*" adorably.

"All right. Then we'll just carry him back and forth."

She smiled brilliantly. "Yeah, we can do that."

I was proud of how well Sarah and I were managing this whole co-parenting gig, considering what a shit show our divorce had been. In fact, the same could be said about our marriage. Sarah came from old money, just like me. Her family used to be in the sugarcane business generations ago. But even with our similar upbringings, we had different values. After we got married, she assumed neither of us would work and we'd be *socialites*. That was simply not who I was. I was proud to continue my family's legacy. We were already heading toward a separation when she unexpectedly became pregnant with Bella. We tried to make it work—at least I did... right up until I found out she cheated.

I didn't even want to remember that time in my life. We'd done our very best to shield Bella from it all, and thankfully, she'd never been aware that we'd been at each other's throats. Divorces were ugly. No matter one's intentions, they somehow spiraled, and not in a good way.

The first thing I told my lawyer was, "I don't want this to get ugly. I want it to be as smooth as possible. We'll give Sarah what she wants, and everything will be easy."

His reply had been chilling: "In all my career, I've never seen an amicable divorce."

I was sure our situation would be different. I'd been wrong. But Sarah and I had come a long way since then. We were never going to be friends, but we were civil around Bella. She lived with me during the week and with her mom on the weekend. Sarah had bought a house in Marigny that had a big yard, too, and Bella was happy there.

When we arrived at the gates of the school, she turned to me and posed, holding her chin high and putting a foot forward. "Does my hair look okay?"

I glanced at her pigtails. She was very fussy about them. I styled her hair every morning, and my little girl was getting more pretentious about her looks.

"Yes, you look lovely."

"Dad, you always say that."

"That's because it's true." I kissed her forehead. She threw her little hands around my neck, and I pulled her into a hug. "Have a great day, cricket," I said.

"Thanks, Dad." She stepped back, turned on her heels, and broke into a run. I stayed until she disappeared inside the building, then walked back to the office.

As I turned onto Royal, my phone beeped. My brother Zachary was calling. I answered right away. We had a meeting scheduled later today, but if he wanted to talk before, it had to be important.

"Morning, brother," I answered in greeting.

"Hey, are you at the office?"

"No, just dropped Bella off. Is this about the meeting?"

"No, actually. Mom called me."

"Right now?"

"Yeah. Apparently our grandmothers are insisting on meeting the new chef."

I started to laugh. "Indeed."

"Think that's a good idea?"

"Fuck no. I was going to think about ways to stop that from happening."

"I have a few!" Zachary proceeded to rattle off some options. None of them sounded bad, but I couldn't see them working.

Then again, he did have a way of smoothing things over. There were six of us brothers, and we couldn't be more different. Xander was the most exacting out of all of us—he never missed a single detail. Julian was good at presiding over everything because the man never lost his shit. Anthony was solution oriented. He didn't go into detail like Xander, but he got the job done. And Beckett was always up for anything. He was the best at making sure Xander didn't drive everyone crazy by going into *too much* detail. It was always a fine line.

"Right, I don't think any of that will work," I conceded after he finished presenting his "solutions."

"Honestly, neither do I. By the way, have you met Scarlett yet?"

"No, I wasn't involved in the interviews. But you did, right?" He was the only one of us who took part in the hiring process across all the branches.

"Yes. She'll do great. And as an aside, she's smoking hot."

"How was that an aside?" I hadn't even had time to look her up online.

"Just thought it was worth mentioning."

"Zachary," I cautioned.

"Don't you dare warn me about anything. I know how to conduct business." And that he did. Which begged the question, why did he bring that up at all? I decided to switch topics.

"All right, I'll catch you later in the meeting. By the way, don't bring up this issue with the grans and Scarlett."

"Why not?" he asked.

"Because then it'll turn into a debate about how to handle it."

"But the more opinions, the better," Zachary said.

"Not when we have a business decision to reach. We don't need this on the docket."

"You're right. All right, talk to you later."

After we hung up, I checked the calendar. The call with my brothers was at five, but I could move it to earlier in the afternoon. That way, I could pick up my girl and take her for beignets. That would make both our days.

And then I had to find a way to protect Scarlett from my grandmothers before tomorrow morning.

Chapter Two

Scarlett

"Welcome to New Orleans, Ms. Jones."

"Thank you," I told Charles, my realtor.

My studio was on the small side, but the rent was decent. Besides, I couldn't find anything else with only a six-month lease. After my probation ended at the restaurant, I'd look for a bigger place. This opportunity was just meant to be—I felt it in my bones. Not only was this my first position as a chef, but it was also in New Orleans. I'd dreamed of living here forever—it was a chef's dream; the cuisine so rich and intricate. I couldn't wait to go out and explore the city. I was buzzing with energy.

"All right. Well, everything is set," he said. "If you need anything, call me, but there shouldn't be any issues."

"Sure, Charles. Thanks!" I closed the door behind him and turned around again, looking at my space. It was cozy, and I loved it!

I had so much to do today. Tomorrow morning was my very first day, so I had to get everything in order.

Heading to the section of the room where I'd left my luggage, I inspected the dresser and immediately realized I had a problem. I'd brought two huge suitcases full of clothes for every occasion, and this dresser was far too small. I'd have to find something to put my stuff in. A mobile rack, maybe.

I turned around once. My studio really was tiny. There was a bed and the couch in one corner and a table with two chairs in the other one, right next to a small kitchen. As a chef, I adored large kitchens, but I was going to spend most of my time at LeBlanc & Broussard's, anyway. They assured me I could have all my meals there, too, which was very generous. That meant I didn't have to cook much at home.

As I put the contents of one bag into the dresser and the bathroom, I was starting to get dangerous ideas. Since I obviously couldn't unpack all my clothes today, I suddenly had more free time than I'd thought. I could start exploring the city right away.

I was still wearing the same clothes I'd put on this morning: jeans, a T-shirt hanging off one shoulder, white socks, and Vans. I didn't want to waste time changing. Even though I'd been feeling tired only a few minutes ago, I was suddenly filled with energy. I'd gotten up at the crack of dawn, too excited about my move to sleep. I was super anxious to begin exploring the city and to leave Seattle behind. There was nothing there except heartbreak. Good riddance.

Well, my parents were there as well, but they'd been extremely happy when I told them about this job offer. It was a once-in-a-lifetime opportunity. I wasn't even sure how I got it. A restaurant like LeBlanc & Broussard's could easily employ an experienced chef, and I'd only been a sous-chef until now. But I wasn't going to look a gift horse in the mouth. It was a fantastic opportunity, and I would make the most of it.

I checked my appearance in the small mirror hanging by the front door. My dark brown hair had an unusual curl, and I wondered if that was because of the humidity in the air. Usually, my hair was as straight as could be, but right then it looked unruly. I squinted and pouted at the same time, snapping a pic of myself and sending it to my bestie, Ariana. I felt a little bit silly, but she loved me with all my quirks. She replied quickly.

Ariana: Finally. I was starting to worry. Apartment looks good?

I took a few pictures and sent them.

Scarlett: Yep. Just as advertised.

Everything had happened so fast that I didn't have time to come down here to scout things out, and she'd been worried that I might get scammed or something.

Ariana: That's good. No nasty surprises?

Scarlett: Nope.

Ariana: By the way, I've heard through the grapevine that Simon is giving the kitchen staff a hard time.

My stomach clenched. Simon was my ex. We'd worked together at the restaurant in Seattle. After they promoted him to chef, he started to treat me like I meant nothing to him. And now that I was gone, he was taking it out on the rest of the staff? That was crazy.

Scarlett: Sounds like Simon. By the way, I know my apartment is tiny, but you're welcome to visit any time.

Ariana: Thanks. I'll take you up on it whenever my boss will approve a vacation.

Scarlett: By that time, I'll be an expert on the city.

Ariana: You've been an expert since you were five years old.

I laughed at her comment and grabbed the key, locking the door as I left the apartment. I was only on the second floor, so I took the staircase.

Ariana had known my passion for NOLA since we were kids and had heard all about my infatuation many times. My obsession began when my parents brought me here on my fifth birthday. I might have inherited my strange affiliation to the South from Mom. She named me after the famous Scarlett O'Hara, so no wonder I turned out the way I did.

A few years ago, I started watching *The Vampire Diaries*, which became my addiction. That was closely followed by its spinoff, *The Origi-*

nals, which took place in New Orleans as well. Guess who became even more obsessed with the city. Yup, this girl here. I loved *The Originals* even more than *The Vampire Diaries*. Most fans had a clear favorite among the leading guys—Damon Salvatore—but I was a Klaus Mikaelson girl through and through.

My studio was very close to Loyola University, and I walked with quick steps to St. Charles Avenue. I'd been surprised at how many short-term accommodations there were in the University District before I realized that they must cater to students. It was all meant to be, I swear.

I took out my phone and glanced at the map. There was a streetcar station not far away from here. *Yes, yes, yes!* I was heading straight into the French Quarter on this fine afternoon.

When I arrived at the station, I noticed there was already a line; roughly two dozen or more people were waiting for a ride.

One of them informed me, "It's a bit delayed."

"That's fine. I'm not on a schedule." I made a mental note to inquire if it usually had delays, though, because I never wanted to be late for work. The dark green streetcar pulled in only a few minutes later, and it was packed.

I smiled for no reason at all as I stepped inside. There wasn't a place to sit, but it didn't matter. I was in New Orleans.

As we started down the road, I kept trying to peek out the window between other people, but it wasn't easy. I wondered if it was this crowded in the early hours of the morning, too, but I'd worry about that later. I'd find a way to get to work.

We passed Loyola, and I made a mental note to check if there were tours of the university. I loved the redbrick building. It had charm and style and a lot of history.

Since I couldn't look out the window, I pulled out my phone and decided to read a bit about my employers. I'd only met Zachary LeBlanc briefly in one of the online interviews, but he said we wouldn't be working directly together. Holding on tight to the rail with one hand, I searched online with the other to see what I could find. Every chef worth their salt knew about LeBlanc & Broussard's Restaurant on Royal Street. The history behind the name was very interesting. The LeBlancs had always owned restaurants and pastry shops around the city. The Broussards owned competing establishments, like coffee shops and jazz clubs. The restaurant itself had only carried the name LeBlanc up until the families were united through marriage. The Wikipedia article didn't go into more details, and there wasn't too much published about either of the families that I could find, but it sounded very intriguing.

I did find one list with all the establishments owned by The Orleans Conglomerate. And wow.

They owned more than fifty establishments. Most were in New Orleans, but there were a few others spread throughout Louisiana as well. And there was also a mention that the company was currently run by the six LeBlanc brothers. I wondered how involved they were on a day-to-day basis or if I'd even see them.

As we entered Canal Street, I decided to jump off the car, wanting to explore the rest on foot. Once I stepped onto the sidewalk, I consulted my phone. I was lost without it. Sometimes I got lost even *with* GPS.

According to my map, Royal Street was one street over, which gave me an idea. I could go check out the restaurant tonight, to make sure I knew where it was and I wouldn't run late tomorrow morning, trying to find it.

Although, to be fair, there was no mistaking it. The building was very emblematic. I'd fallen in love with it just from the photos. It was an old building with a terracotta-colored exterior and three levels of black wrought iron railing on the balconies. There had also been multiple fern plants hanging from the ceiling in the pics, but I wondered if they looked so vibrantly green in real life too. I snapped a picture of the entrance to Royal Street as I approached and immediately sent it to Mom.

Somewhere in the distance, I could hear jazz music. God, the city was so alive, and I loved it! Taking in a deep breath, I realized there had to be a bakery nearby, because I could smell the sugar and cinnamon in the air.

Mom called me the next second. I stopped at the corner of Royal and Canal and answered, putting the phone to my ear. "Hey, Mom."

"Scarlett, how are you? We thought you were busy unpacking and getting settled, and we didn't want to disturb you."

"No, I threw in the towel after unpacking one bag. I don't have anywhere to put the rest of my clothes, so I called it quits."

"Is the apartment really that small?"

"As expected, but it doesn't exactly have a lot of storage space. I'll manage. Don't you worry."

"She's fine, darling," Mom told Dad. "Wait, I'll put you on speaker."

"Hey, darling. How are you?" Dad said so loudly that I had to pull the phone away from my ear.

"You don't have to yell, Edward," Mom chastised softly. "She can hear you."

"I can, Dad," I confirmed. "I'm doing well. I figured I'd go out and explore for a bit, since I can't finish unpacking for now."

"All right. We won't be keeping you. Have fun, baby girl. Don't let anyone give you grief, okay?"

"I won't. I promise."

I was stronger now. I wasn't going to take grief from anyone—especially not from someone I thought I was going to spend the rest of my life with. But that was completely beside the point. Dating wasn't on my to-do list for the foreseeable future. I was here to prove to the LeBlancs and Broussards, or whoever ran the restaurant branch, that I was the chef of their dreams.

I was positively grinning as I walked around, snapping pic after pic. I even loved the police department's building—it was impressive. I spammed Mom with all my photos because I knew she'd appreciate them. There were plenty of establishments on this street—bars, restaurants, cafés, the occasional pastry shops that sold beignets. I couldn't wait to head to Café Du Monde. I wondered if the beignets really were as good as I remembered them from when I'd been here with my parents or if I was just building them up in my mind.

When I arrived in front of LeBlanc & Broussard's, I smiled from ear to ear. I could barely believe this was going to be my workplace. I felt like I was in a movie.

The building looked exactly like it had in the pictures. They had a few tables outside too. They'd even set up a few heaters, which was smart. The air was humid and pleasant for an April afternoon, but if you sat dining for very long, you were bound to get chilly.

I peeked inside the restaurant through one of the front windows. It was a mix of more wrought iron and wood. I couldn't even see the kitchen, which made me think it was separated from the main dining area. *Great!* Open kitchens weren't my favorite.

I toyed with the idea of going inside but decided not to. There was no point in introducing myself today. The kitchen would be busy, and the last thing they needed was a distraction. I'd hate it if it were me. But I stayed for a bit and just people watched, taking in the patrons coming in and out, wondering if they were tourists or locals. My gut feeling was telling me it was a mix, based on the way they were dressed.

A stunning man in a suit caught my attention when he pushed the door of the restaurant open. Once outside, he put on his suit jacket and arranged his cuff links. Was it a force of habit, or did they really need adjusting? God, he was truly gorgeous. I hadn't even noticed another man in months, ever since my breakup, but this stranger simply took my breath away.

He had dark brown hair, and though I couldn't see his eyes from where I was standing, I imagined them being vibrant blue or maybe green.

He didn't seem like a tourist. I wondered if he came by often. Not that it mattered, considering I'd spend all of my time in the kitchen and have zero interaction with customers unless someone requested to see the chef. I tilted my head, trying to decide if this guy was the type to complain about his food and ask the chef to personally apologize.

No, I imagined he was polite, determined, someone who didn't take shit from anyone, but he wasn't a jackass. I was tempted to text Ariana and tell her that I'd noticed a man. She'd be so proud of me. She'd tried to get me to go on a few double dates with her in these past few months, but I'd flatly refused.

After the stranger left, I stayed a while longer, taking in several details of the restaurant. The servers moved quickly, which meant the kitchen worked like a well-oiled machine. Who'd been running it while they didn't have a chef?

I unhitched myself from the brick wall I'd been leaning against and walked over to the side of the restaurant, where I could get a better view inside.

"Dani," a male voice boomed to one of the servers.

She stopped in her tracks, looking up at the guy who'd just arrived in front of the entrance.

"Mr. LeBlanc, hi." I stood to attention. Was he part of the LeBlanc family or just a regular patron? It wasn't an uncommon name here in New Orleans, after all.

"My brother said he was still here."

"Oh, you just missed him. He left a few minutes ago," she said.

"All right. He did mention he'd have a short afternoon today."

"Do you want me to prepare a table for you?" she asked.

"No, I'll go upstairs to the office. My brother's assistant has some documents for me."

"Of course. We can send a dinner upstairs, if you prefer."

"That would be great. My usual, please."

She nodded. "Right away."

I rolled my shoulders. Clearly he was in charge of this place. It wouldn't hurt to introduce myself. I walked right up to where he was standing in front of the entrance, making sure to leave a large enough area so people could come and go.

"Mr. LeBlanc?" I asked tentatively.

The guy looked vaguely familiar as he zeroed in on me. Vibrant blue eyes, jet-black hair. I had this uncanny feeling that I'd seen him before, not too long ago.

"Sorry. Do I know you?" he replied.

"I'm Scarlett Jones, the new chef of the restaurant."

"Scarlett, hi. I'm Julian." He held out his hand and shook mine. "We're so very relieved to have you with us."

"Thank you."

"Listen, I'm not actually in charge of the restaurant branch. That's my brother Chad. You just missed him."

"Oh," I said, a bit disappointed. "That's fine. I was just passing by and thought I'd check out the restaurant. My official start day is tomorrow."

"Yes, the whole family knows," he said with a laugh.

"Okay," I replied, unsure how to react.

Julian grinned. "A word of warning: tomorrow morning might actually be a bit crazy."

"I've worked in a hectic kitchen before. Rush hour can get exciting." But I had a feeling I was missing his point. The mornings couldn't possibly be busy because they didn't offer breakfast.

"I bet you've never worked in a restaurant where half the family likes to pitch in whenever a chef leaves."

I blinked and smiled. "No, I haven't. That sounds interesting."

"Ah, well, come tomorrow morning, you might think differently. Then again, Chad is trying to keep the family away, and when my brother puts his mind to something, he succeeds. Usually. Though he's been failing lately when it comes to our grandparents."

Julian seemed to be talking to himself more than to me. I had no idea how to react. This was *not* how I thought the conversation might go.

"All right," I said. "Any tips?"

"Get the grams to like you."

"Who are the grams?" I asked.

"Sorry. Sometimes I think everyone knows all about us. My grandmothers. They'll both be here. If they like you, your life will be easy. Sooo... just get them to like you."

"No pressure," I said.

"All right, I'm going upstairs. If you want to have dinner here, it's on the house."

"Oh, no thanks. I still want to explore a bit of the city tonight."

"Sure. Enjoy."

I blinked, feeling a bit dazed after he left. Who exactly was going to be here tomorrow morning? His grandparents or just his grandmothers? I couldn't wait to meet Chad LeBlanc too. I wondered if he was anything like Julian.

On a whim, I took out my phone and googled his name. The first thing that popped up was a picture, and oh my God, this was my handsome stranger! I couldn't believe it. No wonder Julian looked familiar. Their appearances were very similar.

Laughing, I debated sending this bit of information to Ariana, then decided not to. She'd say it was a sign, but I no longer believed in signs—except perhaps when it was about sweets. When I came across a third bakery selling beignets, I decided it was high time I tasted one.

Chapter Three

Chad

Early the next morning, I was at the office at 8:20 a.m.

"Any of my brothers here?" I asked Shauna, my assistant.

"Good morning. And no. But Julian was here last night."

That was no surprise. Julian, Xander, Zachary, Anthony, Beckett, and I were each involved in running the company, but they were rarely in the building. Out of everyone, Julian was here the most often. They all had an office at whichever business they liked the most. Julian ran the bar branch of our business, and his home base was in his favorite one here in the French Quarter.

He hadn't made the call with my brothers yesterday, so I wanted to catch up with him this morning. I checked my watch as I strolled inside the office. I was meeting Scarlett Jones in twenty minutes. That was enough time to catch up with Julian. He'd been to New York for a meeting yesterday, and I was curious to hear how it went.

My brother answered on the first ring.

"How did the meeting go?" I asked.

"Good morning to you too," he said slowly. "Not all of us are morning people, you know."

"It's almost eight thirty," I pointed out.

"Precisely. And the meeting went well. Before you know it, I'll open a few bars in New York too."

"That's good. I'm happy for you."

It was our joint ambition to expand the family business beyond the borders of Louisiana. It was time to broaden our horizons.

"Listen, I talked to Mom yesterday evening. Apparently, Isabeau and Celine are coming to the restaurant this morning."

I stood ramrod straight. "What? That was *not* what Mom and I agreed."

I'd called her right before I picked up Bella yesterday afternoon.

"It wasn't Mom's choice."

I groaned. This was typical in our family, though. "Right. Then let me call Mom."

"Dude, you called just to wake me up?"

"No," I said. "I genuinely wanted to know how your trip went."

"Right. Oh, and by the way, I saw your new chef last night."

I was about to end the call but stopped, frowning. "Really? How come?"

"She came to see the restaurant. Dude, she's smoking hot."

I closed my eyes for a moment before slowly opening them again and drawing in a deep breath. "Tell me you didn't hook up with her."

"Damn. Of course not. You know I never get involved with anyone working for us."

That was a golden rule in the family, but with Julian, you just never knew. He viewed rules as annoying suggestions, not something to abide by.

"I warned her that this morning might be a clusterfuck," he continued.

"Right. Well, thanks, Julian. Go back to sleep."

I knew my brother meant well, but scaring off our new employee before she even started was not the way to go.

I punched Mom's number, but she rejected the call. I was about to call again, then noticed that she'd sent me a message.

Mom: Sorry, it didn't work. I'm already downstairs with both. They insist on knowing this new chef since, and I quote, "The reputation of our flagship restaurant is in her hands."

My grandmothers had a flair for the dramatic. Isabeau even more so than Celine.

I laughed, shaking my head. *All right, time to go down and give the family an earful so they behave when Scarlett Jones arrives.*

It was extremely convenient to work right above the restaurant. I could handle any issues immediately, especially if it was family. My grans were completely right about one thing—this *was* our flagship restaurant. It was one of the top attractions in the city. Our waiting list for a table was a solid three months, though we did keep two tables free, just in case. I hadn't interviewed Scarlett personally because I wasn't in charge of hiring the kitchen staff, but I liked her résumé, and my guy in personnel, Donald, had been impressed with her.

I quickly went downstairs and could already hear my grandmothers' voices as I went from the kitchen to the restaurant.

"I'm going to give that girl the test myself," Isabeau was saying.

"No, you're not," I said, joining them.

Mom threw me an apologetic glance, but I smiled reassuringly as I sat down with the three of them at a table.

"Listen, I appreciate the two of you stepping in these past few weeks, but I need you to trust me. I've run this place for almost a decade. I'm good at it. Besides, you know how chefs are. They like to have complete control in the kitchen."

Isabeau wrinkled her nose. "I'd like to know who this girl is who will take over."

Celine nodded. "Me too."

Isabeau and Celine couldn't look more different. Because they were so young when we were born, our grandparents insisted we call them all by their first name. After Bella was born, things changed. They weren't ready to be referred to as great-grandparents, but they insisted on her calling them grandparents. Now they accepted a mix of both.

"I gave my approval," I said politely but firmly. "I love and respect both of you a lot, but I cannot allow you to interfere in my hiring process."

My grandmothers looked at each other, and then Celine smiled sweetly. "Darling, we're not interfering. We simply want to meet her."

There was no way I could convince them to leave before Scarlett arrived, so I changed my tactic. I'd simply point the conversation in the direction I wanted it to go. I was very good at that. It was one of the reasons why I'd taken the restaurant chain to the next level.

The front door opened just as I was about to tell my grandmothers to simply be friendly to Scarlett. I looked up and swallowed hard.

Fucking hell. If this was Scarlett Jones, I was in trouble. Even though we were at the farthest table from the door, I could see that she was exceptionally beautiful. Her brown hair was kind of frizzy, but it looked fantastic on her. Her eyes were deep blue. And that *mouth.*

I understood Zachary and Julian's reaction. Of course they'd noticed she was hot.

As I went to greet her, I looked over my shoulder. "I'll do the talking."

"You keep thinking that," Mom said in a low voice.

Life in the LeBlanc-Broussard family was always interesting.

I turned back to the woman in front of me. "Scarlett Jones?"

"That's me."

I held out my hand. "Chad LeBlanc. I'm head of the restaurant business."

She accepted it with a quick shake. "Nice to meet you. Am I late?" she asked, stepping farther inside.

"No, you're just on time."

She was wearing a dark blue dress, and I absolutely refused to let my gaze drop any farther. I kept my eyes right on hers.

She looked at my grandmothers and mom and asked, "Are we already open?"

"No, these aren't patrons. They're my..."

"Grandmothers?"

I cleared my throat. "Right. Julian told you."

"Yes, and I wasn't sure what that meant." Scarlett laughed but averted her gaze, twirling a strand of her hair between her fingers. She was nervous, and all my instincts wanted to put her at ease.

"Between you and me, the warning *was* warranted. My grandmothers can be a bit much, but they mean well."

What am I doing? I was always 100 percent business with my employees, especially a new hire, and yet here I was, openly talking about the family. I broke eye contact because it seemed to cloud my judgment. "I'll introduce you to them, and then I'll show you the kitchen."

"Thank you. Julian said it's important for your grandmothers to like me. Are they part of the kitchen team?"

Fucking hell! I needed to have another word with my brother.

"They used to be chefs in the family restaurants a long time ago. And they've both been filling in here since our last chef quit. But no, they're not part of the daily operations."

She frowned. "Then I don't understand..."

"The business is important to everyone in the family. And this restaurant means a lot to them."

"Okay."

"Don't worry about anything. Just follow my lead."

Her eyes widened and her lips parted, but she didn't say anything.

With great difficulty, I snapped my gaze away from her mouth and pointed toward the table where they were all sitting, three sets of eyes fixed on Scarlett. To her credit, she was walking with her head held high. I couldn't help drinking her in. Her ass was round and perfect, her neck was slim and inviting... and I was losing my mind.

"Everyone, I'd like you to meet our new chef, Scarlett Jones. I already told her that you'd give her a warm welcome because this is our family business."

"Nice to meet you," Scarlett replied with a smile. "I can't say I've ever had a welcoming committee before."

"These are my grandmothers, Isabeau and Celine, and my mom."

"I'm Adele," Mom said.

"We've been holding down the fort until you got here," Isabeau explained.

"And you wanted to see who would take over in your stead." Scarlett replied.

"I have full confidence in you," I told her, more for my grandmothers' benefit. Even so, Scarlett seemed to grow an inch taller as she gave me a wide smile that completely disarmed me. Wasn't she used to people complimenting her?

"Thank you," she said. "That's nice to know."

"You've never been a chef before," Isabeau stated.

"Isabeau," I said in a cautioning tone. "Scarlett has an impressive résumé, and I know she'll do great."

I intended to lead Scarlett directly to the kitchen, but she cleared her throat.

"No one's ever given me the opportunity," she said with a nervous laugh, "but I'm deeply grateful for this one, and I promise not to make a mess of things. In fact, if I feel that I'm not up to the task, I will gladly hand in my resignation. I would never dream of hurting the reputation of LeBlanc & Broussard's. Please don't worry about that."

Isabeau was looking at her with her mouth open. Celine simply blinked. Mom smiled, pride etched on her face. This woman was something else. She'd neutralized both my grandmothers with nothing but honesty.

"Now that introductions are out of the way, I want to show Scarlett to the kitchen," I announced.

"Sure. It was nice meeting you," Scarlett said.

Without thinking, I put a hand at the small of her back as I led her toward the kitchen. She sucked in a breath at the contact, and I immediately jerked my hand away.

What the hell? Why did I do that? I'd never touched an employee before. I was way more professional than that.

Clearing my head, I told her, "You were phenomenal."

Scarlett turned her head, looking straight at me. "You think? Your grandmothers were more intimidating than I expected."

"They can be. Confession: they drive me crazy sometimes."

Clearly my professionalism was nonexistent today. But something about Scarlett simply demanded raw honesty.

I straightened up as we stepped into the kitchen. Joel was here, of course, along with two others from the crew. He fixated on Scarlett. I obviously wasn't the only one who thought she was hot.

"Ms. Jones, welcome. I'm one of your sous-chefs, Joel. I like to be early."

"That's great, Joel. So do I."

Scarlett transformed right in front of me. A few frown lines appeared on her forehead as she shifted into work mode. She clearly felt at ease in the new surroundings, which was exactly what I'd hoped for in a chef.

"Why don't you walk me through the kitchen organization, and then we can discuss the deliveries and other things."

I stepped back as she looked around the kitchen, making it safe for me to check her out.

Her figure was absolutely stunning. She was tall with delicious curves. The dress was perfect for the workplace. There was nothing provocative about it, and yet my imagination was running wild. I took in a deep breath, then looked away. I had to get myself under control.

Ever since my divorce, I'd sworn to myself that I wouldn't even contemplate dating or starting a relationship. I was on year two of my self-imposed celibacy. It wasn't easy.

I was about to head upstairs when I remembered an important point.

"Scarlett, I do have to steal you for a bit. I need you upstairs in HR."

"Sure," she said. "I'll just drop my bag here. Do you think they need ID or something?"

"It's possible."

She rummaged in her bag, taking out her wallet. "I'll be right back, Joel."

He nodded. "Sure thing, boss. Okay with you if I start the prep?"

"More than okay."

Joel smiled, looking at me. "I already like her."

Scarlett blushed. I pinned her with my gaze as I replied, "So do I."

I led her through a narrow door connecting to the staircase. I didn't touch her back again. Being close to her appeared to be more than I could handle. Hell, even looking was enough to set me off. The cleavage of her dress was decent, but my imagination was anything but.

"That kitchen is amazing," she said. "I can't wait to get to work. Where's the office?"

"On the third floor. When did you arrive?"

"Yesterday. I got situated and then decided to come out and explore a bit. Mr. LeBlanc—"

"Chad," I said.

She bit her lower lip. I drew in a deep breath, looking away.

"That doesn't feel right," she whispered.

"There are six of us LeBlanc brothers, plus my dad. Most of the time, I don't even reply when someone calls me Mr. LeBlanc."

She laughed. "Fine, then, Chad."

Hearing her say my name had an uncanny effect on me. I felt a stirring below my belt, and that was not okay. This was absolutely spiraling out of control.

"I'm so excited about this job," she gushed.

"I meant what I told my grandmothers. I'm certain that you'll rise to the challenge."

"I plan to. It's always been my dream to move to New Orleans. Working in a restaurant like this one is more than I could've hoped for."

Even though she was full of exuberance, I detected a note of sadness in her voice. I wondered why that was.

It's none of your business, Chad. None. You've already crossed so many lines, it's not even funny.

When we finally reached the third floor, I opened the door to the corridor for her. She paused slightly, looking up at me in surprise before walking in. Because I'd opened the door for her? She was in for a surprise. We did things a bit differently here in the South.

"I read that you've got a lot of businesses. Do all the executives work from this office?" she asked.

"Not really," I said. "Some of the management is here, but my brothers have their headquarters and teams elsewhere. They come here often, though, so you might run into them. By the way, once you've settled in, I'd like to have you join us for a marketing meeting."

"Why?"

"We like to involve our chef in strategic decisions. You, Joel, and whoever else you want to have designing the menu. We won't get involved in that unless we get bad feedback from customers, but we like to be informed so everything is reflected in our marketing."

"That's so smart," she said and then flashed me a brilliant smile.

I really couldn't spend too much time with this woman or I was liable to lose my mind. Was there any such thing as instant attraction? The answer was clearly *yes*.

Donald came out from his office just then. "Thought I'd heard your voice, Chad. And you must be Ms. Jones."

She nodded. "Yes, I am."

"Okay. We just have some paperwork to go through, and then I'll let you get your day started."

"Wonderful."

He glanced at me. "Chad, I'll take it from here."

"Sure!" I felt oddly disappointed. "Scarlett, it was nice to meet you. I look forward to seeing you at the marketing meeting."

She nodded, averting her gaze. How could she be so beautiful?

Julian's words flashed through my mind.

"Celibacy is a shit idea," he'd told me when I'd shared my plan with him over one too many Sazeracs. "You're going to lose it when you least expect it."

Up until now, I'd managed. Work kept me busy enough, and all the free time I had went to my daughter. And I'd never been truly tempted.

Yet right now I could barely take my eyes off Scarlett.

CHAPTER FOUR

SCARLETT

"Joel, did I mention that I love you?" I told him at the end of my shift.

He grinned. He was like a huge teddy bear, and though I liked the rest of my sous-chefs, too, he'd already become my favorite.

"Not every day will go as smoothly as this one," he cautioned as I yawned.

The kitchen was well staffed, and I had to give credit to the previous chef. They'd done a great job setting this up to work very smoothly. I did want to tinker with the menu, though. The current one was exquisite, but I wanted to put my own mark on it.

"So, can you walk me through what Chad said about me attending a marketing meeting?"

Seeing Chad again today was a shock to my system. He seemed even sexier than the glimpse I'd caught of him last night. I'd texted Ariana to fill her in, and as expected, she told me "it's a sign".

That was just my luck. Then again, it was quite all right because I was certain that I wouldn't run into him very often, aside from these marketing meetings. After all, I was in the kitchen day in, day out, and he was on the third floor. Management schedules usually weren't compatible with those of chefs anyway. I officially started at ten in the morning and finished at nine in the evening from Monday to Friday. The restaurant offered brunch exclusively on the weekends, and another chef presided over that. I counted myself lucky that the shift ended at 9:00 p.m. The pastry chef stayed until 11:00 p.m. when the kitchen closed. After I left, patrons could only order dessert.

"He didn't give you any more details, huh?"

"No."

"Well, beats me," Joel said. "The previous chef was a bit tight-lipped." He grimaced. Maybe there was some bad blood there, but it wasn't my place to ask. "I'm sure Shauna, his assistant, will fill you in if necessary. She's really nice."

"Oh, good." I hadn't spoken to Shauna. So far, I only had Donald's email because he'd sent me copies of contracts and such.

"Where are you heading?" he asked me.

"Oh." I smiled sheepishly. "I was actually thinking about going to Café Du Monde."

"The first beignets since you arrived in the city?"

I laughed, securing my bag on my shoulder. "No, actually. I had some yesterday, but I want to test these ones. They must be famous for a reason."

He winked at me. "Café Du Monde is good, but there are some other places in the city that serve up beignets that are just as good. Well, in my opinion, even better."

"You'll have to share them with me."

"I will. Just be careful when you walk around the Quarter at night-time, especially as the weekend approaches. Avoid Bourbon if you can."

"What? Nooo... I actually planned on checking out Bourbon Street just so I could experience it at night. I walked down Royal yesterday, and I wanted to see more of the city tonight."

He shook his head. "It can get a bit insane in the evenings."

"Then I'll check out Bourbon another time." Dang, that had burst my bubble, but I knew Joel was right.

Most of the kitchen staff was staying until closing time. I smiled at them, saying, "Good night. See you all tomorrow."

There was a chorus of "Bye, chef," and I could barely believe it.

I was a chef in New Orleans. And I had a sous-chef who liked me. I had worked in kitchens where sous-chefs tried to sabotage the chef in order to get their position and was so glad that wasn't the case here. How did I get so lucky?

Then again, as Ariana would say, "You've had the shittiest luck. It's about damn time you had good luck."

I frowned, shaking my head. My best friend could be a bit of a grump. I wouldn't say I had the shittiest luck. I had just encountered difficulties on several levels. But I liked to think it all was a learning experience.

Once I'd left the restaurant, I had to give it to Joel—he was right about the busy streets. Even Royal was a bit insane right now. Yesterday, it had been far more relaxed. But then again, I'd been here in the afternoon. I was tempted to head over to Bourbon just to check if it was less crowded, then decided not to. Joel was a local. He knew what he was talking about, and I wasn't going to take any risks. But I couldn't wait to explore the French Quarter. I noticed a very cute little bar that was more of a hole-in-the-wall wedged between a shop selling tarot cards and one boasting to have "the best pralines in New Orleans."

I could see I was going to be very busy. My free days would be filled to the brim with activities for the foreseeable future, especially my mornings. Tomorrow, I was going to go on a bus tour of the city. It was a super touristy thing, but then again, it was my first time here as an adult, so I wanted to check out the touristy things too. In general, my tastes were pretty simple—what was usually a crowd-pleaser pleased me as well. The one exception was in the kitchen. There, I had *very* specific requirements.

I ran my hand through my hair as I turned to go right onto Toulouse Street and then took a left onto Chartres Street. As much as I was loving NOLA, my hair was not. It was a mess, having turned curly and frizzy after only a few minutes outside.

I stopped in my tracks when I reached Jackson Square. I was going to bring my beignets and sit and watch the church and the goings-on. It looked so different now, late at night. I could swear there was even a little bit of fog surrounding it. That fog might look magical, but it was also the reason for my frizzy hair.

Unfortunately, there was also a sizable line at Café Du Monde. I wasn't expecting it at this hour. When I saw they were open 24/7, I'd thought it was a bit much, but clearly they had enough demand. As I stood in line, I searched for my earbuds. I put one in my left ear but left the other one in its case—I didn't like to be totally shut off from the world.

I was just about to set up my favorite Spotify playlist—with music from *The Originals*, of course, because it fit the mood so well—when a voice reached me.

"Hello again."

Even though I'd only met him today, I'd recognize his voice anywhere. I looked up, and yes, Chad LeBlanc stood in front of me. His eyes were vibrant blue. He was truly the sexiest man I'd ever seen.

And your boss, Scarlett. Remember that, okay?

"Hey!" I exclaimed a bit too enthusiastically.

"After-shift treat?"

"Exactly."

He tapped his temple. "Great minds think alike."

"You often drop by this late in the evening?"

"Only when my daughter gets a craving and doesn't want to wait until tomorrow morning."

I swallowed hard, feeling like complete crap. Holy shit, the man had a family, and I was ogling him. I was certain he couldn't tell, but still, I felt a bit dirty.

"I always tell her it's not good to eat sugar this late in the evening, but I make exceptions," he continued. "This line better move fast. Although, she probably won't miss me. She never does when one of my brothers is at the house."

"How old is she?" I asked.

"Eight. And Julian is definitely keeping her entertained." He checked his phone, laughing.

"Her mom also likes beignets?" *Now, why did I ask that?*

I noticed his eyes clouding before he whipped his head away. "Her mother and I are divorced. Bella lives with me."

"Sorry, I didn't know—"

He waved his hand, cutting me off. "Doesn't matter. Anyway, when her sugar craving is too much, I take a trip to Café Du Monde, and one of my brothers or someone else in the family watches her."

Oh, man. I was in danger of melting. How cute was that?

"She usually tries to negotiate with me to buy her some on the way to school every morning, but she's learned that it's easier to get me to do her bidding in the evening."

I narrowed my eyes. "I can't see you doing anyone's bidding."

"I usually don't. Just when it comes to my daughter."

We stepped forward as the line advanced. At least it seemed to be moving quickly.

"How was your first day? Kitchen treat you all right?" he asked.

"Yes. Everything went surprisingly smooth." I hesitated. "Can I ask why you lost your previous chef?"

"He moved to New York because his wife got a job there."

"All right. Are you buying beignets for yourself too?"

"I wasn't going to, but now I'm having second thoughts since I ran into you." My heart fluttered. *Calm down, Scarlett.* "Can I tempt you to eat your beignets with me? That way, I'll get to hear more about your day."

I flashed an impish smile. "Only if we also get a café au lait."

He grimaced. "I know people get both, but trust me, the café au lait is nothing to brag about."

"I find that hard to believe. Besides, I usually like what most people like." I was talking more to myself now.

Chad frowned slightly but then laughed. I probably came across as a dork.

"Do you trust me?" he asked.

"Hmm... I mean, I only met you this morning."

He burst out laughing, and I was delighted that I'd get to spend more time with him. Was I aware that I should answer no to his question? Absolutely. The man lit a fire inside me, and that was unacceptable.

But what the hell? I was getting beignets and café au lait at nine o'clock in the evening. One more bad decision wasn't going to hurt, right?

Our turn came quickly. Chad ordered eight beignets, then said, "Last chance. You really want café au lait?"

I nodded vehemently. "Yes. I want the full experience."

"Fair enough." Turning to the cashier, he added, "One café au lait as well."

I took out my wallet, but he grabbed my wrist before I could take out my card. "No."

Huh? I raised my eyes at him. My skin was burning where he touched me. *God, please don't let him realize that.* My heart was beating fast, as if I'd sprinted all the way from the restaurant.

"It's my treat."

"Chad, I was going to get them anyway. You don't have to buy them for me."

"But now I'm here, so it's my treat."

I opened my mouth but decided not to argue. "Okay. Thank you."

He let go of my wrist but still looked at me intensely as I put my wallet back. What did he think, that I would stealthily try to pay?

After we got our order, we moved out of the line. He put an arm protectively around my shoulders as we made our way through the crowd, and I sucked in a deep breath. There was no skin-on-skin contact, but my shoulders sizzled all the same.

Oh Lord. I was already in over my head, and it was only my first day.

"Where do you want to go?" Chad asked.

"How about Jackson Square? So far, it's one of my favorite spots in the city."

"Sure."

We walked toward the square at a brisk pace. Luckily, we found a free bench. I took out a beignet before we even sat down and immediately bit into it.

"Ohhhh! They more than deserve their reputation. These are the best I've had until now."

"They're very good," Chad replied, and I realized he was eating one too.

"I thought you came here to buy them for Bella."

He winked at me. "I bought more because she always insists that I eat one with her. She'd be very jealous if she knew I was here."

"Got it. Well, that's one thing I've crossed off my list."

"What else is on your list?"

"I want to taste beignets from multiple places in the city. And I'd love to try king cake, of course, but that's only available around Mardi Gras." I looked at him hopefully. "So, here's to hoping I'll still be here by then."

He narrowed his eyes but didn't say anything. My stomach lurched. *He's your boss, and you're on probation, Scarlett. Don't push it.*

"How come you decided to move to New Orleans?" he asked.

"I've always had a bit of an obsession with the city. My parents brought me here when I was a kid for my birthday, and I've loved it ever since. I've always meant to come back, but..." My voice faded. "I guess it just never worked out. But I love it so far. The culture, the whole vibe in the French Quarter. I can't believe I'm lucky enough to actually work *in* the Quarter."

I glanced at him and realized he was watching me intently. He wasn't saying anything. God, it was unnerving.

I was about to start my second beignet when my phone beeped. I took it out, figuring it had to be Ariana. I hadn't updated her at all today about how everything was going. But then I froze. It was a voice message from my ex. I tried to exit the conversation, but instead I managed to press Play.

"What the fuck did you tell our boss before you left? Everyone suddenly treats me like shit around here." I tried to pause it, but it was dark out and the button was tiny, and I kept missing it. "I hope you get what you fucking deserve, you useless—"

I finally managed to press Pause. My heart rate was so erratic that I felt lightheaded. I dropped the beignet in my lap. Pounding pain was forming right in the center of my forehead.

Nothing like airing your dirty laundry to your new boss.

"Chad, I'm so sorry you heard that. Umm... I'm just going to go." I made to rise to my feet, but the whole of Jackson Square seemed to tilt. I dropped my ass right back on the bench.

"Scarlett," Chad said, "you're not feeling well." He grabbed the beignets, putting them away. "Close your eyes and take a deep breath. It'll help you relax. Hold it in after you've inhaled."

To my astonishment, the technique worked.

I opened my eyes and startled. Chad was kneeling in front of me, eyes trained on me. They were full of concern.

"Better?" he asked softly.

"Yes, much better."

"Are you sure?"

"Positive."

He sat back on the bench.

"Right. So as I was saying, I think it's late." My voice was shaking. "I should go."

He covered my hand with his. "No, you should stay for a few minutes just to make sure you don't feel bad again. Then I'll order you an Uber."

"But the streetcar is right here."

"I'll order you an Uber," he repeated in a commanding tone. "It'll be a company expense, so I won't accept a no."

I wanted to fight him some more, but there was no point. Besides, I wasn't feeling that great.

"Thank you. You're very considerate, and I truly apologize for that message. I tried to stop it, but it's dark out, and I just didn't manage it."

"That was a previous coworker?" Chad asked.

"My former coworker and my ex," I blurted.

He stared at me. "That was an ex? Why the fuck would he ever talk to you like that?"

I gave him a sad smile. "That's not even him at his worst."

Why am I sharing this with Chad? He's my boss, damn it. But after hearing Simon's rant, I felt like the man needed an explanation.

"Earlier, you asked why I moved here. He was part of that decision. We worked together at the restaurant in Seattle. We were both sous-chefs. After the chef left, he was promoted. I was happy for him. A bit sad because I aspired to be a chef as well, but, you know, I was happy that at least one of us made it." My voice broke. "Looking back, we never had a stellar relationship. But after he became a chef, things took a nosedive. He felt the need to show that he was above me in rank in every way possible. That behavior transferred to our personal lives too. Since he had a higher position, he wanted to decide everything that was going on in our lives even though I was paying half for everything. I had a feeling he expected me to suddenly worship him. It got so bad that a colleague told him that his behavior toward me was unacceptable and extremely uncomfortable for the rest of the crew. That's when I realized that I was being a doormat, so... I quit and tried my luck here." I rolled my shoulders back, trying to smile. "And it worked out."

"You've been through a lot," he stated.

"Yes. I'm just happy to have this chance to start over." I looked at the ground for a moment, then back up. "I'm really sorry about earlier. It was unprofessional to play that in front of you, but—"

"Scarlett, stop torturing yourself, okay? It happened. You don't have anything to apologize for. Does he often send you rude messages?"

"Actually, no. Not at all. I'm not even sure what happened that he felt the need to berate me, and I don't want to know. I'll block his number or whatever it is I have to do to stop getting any messages." I paused for a bit as I gathered my thoughts, then announced once again, "I'm ready to go home now."

"You're sure? I can stay with you here for a few more minutes."

"Really, Chad," I said, trying to hide how nervous and ashamed I felt, "it's fine."

"All right, then. Tell me your address," he said as he handed me back my bag with the second beignet.

I hadn't even realized he'd taken out his phone. "You were serious about that Uber."

"Yes." His eyes were even more intense than usual, and that was saying something. I gave him the address, and he typed it into the app.

"Your Uber is going to be here in one minute. Let's walk up there." He pointed toward Decatur.

As I rose from the bench, he put a hand firmly on my lower back, probably to steady me. I didn't need it... but I didn't mind one bit.

"Listen, if that guy gives you any trouble, let me know." The protectiveness he exuded warmed my heart. No one except my parents ever did that for me.

"Why?"

"Because I'll take care of it."

I started to laugh. "Chad—"

"I mean it. No one has a right to talk like that to another human being."

I looked at my shoes. "I know, I know."

"That's your Uber," he went on as a small Volvo stopped in front of us.

He finally took his hand off my back as he opened the door. "Text me when you get home so I know you're all right." He grabbed my phone and called his number so I had it in my recents. Then he said, "I'll see you at the marketing meeting on Monday."

"Oh, that's right. I almost forgot."

Why did my stomach somersault at the thought of seeing him again so soon?

Probably because he was the kindest person I'd met in quite a while. *And smoking hot.*

"Sure. Have a great evening, Chad."

"You too."

After he closed the door, the car moved forward.

I still couldn't wrap my mind around this evening. I truly hadn't expected Chad to be so concerned for me. I'd never experienced this type of care in my life. What did that say about my previous relationship?

Well, it didn't matter, because it was over.

Besides, I'd ended up right here in New Orleans, where my life was getting more fabulous by the day.

Chapter Five

Chad

Bella and I had a tradition—we always ate beignets in front of the TV. Julian left as soon as I'd returned, so now it was just the two of us.

"Daaaaaad. Can we watch *Moana*?"

My insides died just a bit. It had been her favorite movie when she was three. I was certain I'd seen it over a million times. I was surprised she wanted to watch it again.

"Sure, cricket. Let's put it on."

She curled up next to me on the couch, putting her head on my arm. I took her little hand in mine and said, "Your nails are a bit long. Want me to clip them?"

She looked back at me with a cheeky smile. "Yes."

"What's with that smile?" I asked.

"Can you also put glitter on them again, pretty please? Preeeeeeetty please?"

I laughed as I got off the couch. "Sure. I'll bring both."

As a single dad, I was out of my depth when it came to certain things—such as when was it appropriate for her to start wearing nail polish. But I'd given in to this. It was in the kids' section at the drugstore, and the school didn't have anything against it, so why not make my little girl happy? I brought the clippers and the nail polish to the living room, and she clapped her hands in anticipation.

"I'm getting a manicure," she said proudly.

I was a pro. About ten minutes later, we were both watching *Moana* in silence. She was holding out her fingers out to dry.

"Mom doesn't like to do my nails," Bella said matter-of-factly. "She tried once but kept looking at her phone and did it all wrong."

"We'll do it together," I assured her, trying to keep my voice steady. I didn't like to badmouth Sarah in front of Bella. Sarah had confessed to me once that motherhood wasn't at all what she thought it would be like.

I was the one who suggested Bella live with me after our divorce, expecting her to fight me on it, but her reply was cutting.

"Of course she'll live with you. The weekend will be hard enough. I don't want to be a single mom all week. How can I attend all my events? People expect me to be at their parties. I can't just bail."

To this day I got angry when I replayed that conversation in my mind. But Bella was happy, and that was all that mattered.

She fell asleep halfway through the movie, and I carried her to bed, careful not to wake her up. As I closed the door to her bedroom, I went back downstairs and ate the rest of my beignet.

I remembered Scarlett's expression when she first bit into hers. She'd clearly enjoyed it, which gave me an idea. Scarlett wanted king cake, and I had a burning desire to make sure she got it. I didn't understand why, but that was beside the point. I had the ability to do it, so I was going to surprise her.

I picked up my phone and called Beckett. He oversaw the bakery part of the business and had grown it from ten to twenty shops within the past few years. Business was booming.

"Hello, older brother," he answered.

"Hey. Got a few minutes?" It was always difficult to get a hold of Beckett. His social life was insanely busy.

"You know me. I always make time for family."

"I want to order a king cake."

There was a pause, and then he asked, "Now? Dude, I know that since you've become a dad, time runs a bit differently for you, but it's not Mardi Gras."

"I know. If it were, I'd just walk into one of our bakeries and buy it."

"Okay. You want to add it to the restaurant's menu, or...?"

"My chef would like to taste one. It's purely business."

There was a pause, and then he started to laugh. "Well, well."

"Beckett, I want—"

"You *have* to let me enjoy this moment. It's priceless."

"Are you going to make it happen or not?" God, he could be annoying at times.

"Hey, if the family wants something, I make it happen. My favorite baker is going to lose her shit, but I can handle her."

"Okay, thank you."

"Out of curiosity, why didn't you just buy one from Joe Gambino's Bakery?" They were one of the few places in town that sold the cake year-round.

"Because that stuff's crap, and I want her to have the best experience."

"Right. And you still insist that this is purely for business?"

"Can I have one by Monday morning?" I asked, ignoring his question.

"Sure. I'll make a few phone calls and make it happen."

"Thank you, Beckett."

"Hey, you owe me one," he said.

"I sure do. I appreciate it."

I could vividly imagine Scarlett's expression when she saw the king cake. It was going to be priceless.

Beckett kept his word. On Monday morning, my assistant, Shauna, came into my office and said, "This just came from the bakery for you."

"Thank you."

"Should I leave it here?"

"Yes, please."

She put it on my desk.

"Is anyone in the meeting room yet?" Scarlett and I were meeting the marketing team in half an hour.

She shook her head. "Not yet."

"All right, thanks."

She left my office, and I immediately texted Scarlett.

Chad: Good morning, Scarlett. I'd like you to come up to the meeting room 15 minutes earlier, please. I'm waiting for you inside.

She answered a few minutes later.

Scarlett: Sure. I was actually just fretting about, waiting around here for it.

Was she nervous about the meeting? There was no reason for that.

I'll just have to double my efforts so she feels at ease.

I picked up the box Beckett sent, realizing it was a small cake, just enough for two people. I stopped by the coffee station and grabbed a plate and fork before going into the meeting room. It was empty. Perfect! I wanted Scarlett just to myself for a few minutes before everyone arrived.

I'd barely managed to sit down when she came inside. I rose to my feet again and noted she wasn't in her chef's uniform. Instead, she was wearing jeans and a sweater with a V-neckline.

How could this woman be so beautiful? It didn't even matter what she wore, she was just stunning. Her legs were endless. I almost couldn't take my eyes off them—and when I did, my gaze moved to her neck. It was damn sexy and seductive, and I couldn't understand why it beckoned to me so much.

"Morning," she said. "No one else is here yet?"

"No. I have a surprise for you."

Her eyes widened infinitesimally. "Okay."

I nodded toward the chair I'd vacated. "Sit here."

I pulled the chair back from the table to give her space. As she sat on it, I pushed it under her.

"What's this?" She pointed at the box.

"Open it."

I sat next to her because I didn't want to miss her expression.

She opened it and gasped, glancing at me. "This is king cake!"

"I know."

"But it's not in season."

"I know the bakery owner. Happens to be another LeBlanc. I put in a special order," I said.

"For me?" She put a hand on her chest.

Why did she find it so hard to believe? You'd think I'd given her a diamond.

"Yes."

"You want us to add it to the menu or something?"

For God's sake. "No, Scarlett, it's just for you. You said you wanted to taste king cake, and I could bring you one—the very best, no less."

Carefully, she held it up in her hand and bit right into it.

I guess she didn't need the fork after all.

"This is amazing. Soooo delicious." She flashed me a huge smile. She had a few crumbs around her lips and looked fucking adorable. Her smile was out of this world and completely lit her up. Not just her face but her body, too, somehow.

"I've read all about traditions and knew king cake was a must try, and I'm so glad I did!"

"So, what did you find out about the dessert?" I was genuinely curious.

"The French began the custom in the twelfth century for Epiphany, to celebrate the three kings. Sometimes there's a gift inside, like the baby Jesus."

"I don't think he put a gift in there. Maybe next time."

She turned to face me head-on. "Chad, thank you. This is the loveliest thing anyone's ever done for me."

That caught me completely off guard.

What the hell? How is that even possible? I just ordered cake for her.

"I'm glad you're enjoying it" was all I said.

She ate half of it in a span of two minutes without saying another word, then sat back in her chair with a sigh. "So good. I'll eat the rest later."

"You know, that was for two people," I pointed out.

She blinked. "Oh, you wanted some too?"

"We'll never know now, will we?" I was teasing, of course.

She batted her eyelashes. "But your family owns the bakery. I'm sure they'd make a special order for you whenever you like."

"That's debatable," I said. "Beckett only gave in after I told him it was especially for you."

She parted her lips but didn't say anything else for a few moments. Finally, she told me, "Well, if I ever meet Beckett, I'll thank him. How much was it?"

"Scarlett, it's a gift. Something I wanted to do for you."

She looked at me like I was speaking a foreign language. I truly couldn't believe that she was so surprised by this. What kind of idiotic people had she met all her life? Well, if the story about her ex was anything to go by... I had my answer.

"Thank you so much," she said so sincerely that I wanted to jump across the table and hold her.

"So, what did you do over the weekend?" I asked her, needing to change the subject.

"I explored." She lit up and grinned. "The city is so amazing."

I chuckled. "Many people have a thing for New Orleans, but I don't think I've ever seen anyone with your enthusiasm."

"I still can't believe that I'm here, you know? And I spoke to my parents and my best friend, Ariana, of course. They wanted to hear how things were going. What did you do?"

"On Friday evening, I devoured the beignets with Bella. We watched *Moana*, and I painted her nails with this glitter polish she loves." *Why on earth am I sharing this with her?*

She put a hand on her chest. "Okay, that is adorable."

"Anyway, on Saturday morning, I dropped her off at her mom's house and had some time to decompress."

"Sounds like a very relaxing weekend, and—"

Scarlett fell silent as Mia, the marketing manager, and Aurelia, the social media specialist, stepped into the room. She quickly hid the king cake box underneath the table.

"Oh, hello!" Mia said.

"Mia, Aurelia, this is Scarlett. Scarlett, meet the brightest from our marketing department."

"It's nice to meet you," Scarlett said as she beamed at both women. "Look, I'll be honest. I have no experience talking about the menu with the marketing team. So if I'm completely off base, you'll let me know, all right?"

Her honesty was refreshing. Chefs often had huge egos, like her ex. But Scarlett was clearly different, which was a nice change of pace.

"This is all very informal. We like to know what you plan to do with the menu so we can communicate that to our customers properly and entice them into dining with us. And since we're placing advertisements in a wide range of publications, we need to know ahead of time about any changes so we can prep accordingly. We assure you that we don't plan to interfere in the menu at all. We'll meet once more so we can show you the actual ads and get your approval."

"All right," Scarlett said, chewing her lower lip. It took a lot of willpower to glance away. I was obsessing over her lips, and that wasn't good. "First things first, I want to incorporate more shrimp into the menu. A lot of people love seafood, and there's quite a bit I can do with shrimp."

"Do you have anything in particular in mind?" Aurelia asked.

Scarlett got her phone out. "Yes, I made a few notes. I'd like to offer an entrée of a creamed shrimp soup along with a shrimp étouffée for the main course. And I'd also love to offer a veal option…"

For the next half hour, Scarlett talked us through the changes she wanted to make. She was a pro, and the items she was describing were making my mouth water. The grams would be so proud.

Even though I was at the meeting, I didn't actually run it, just listened in as the three of them discussed. I believed in leaving my employees a wide berth and trusting that they knew what they were doing. But I wanted to be in the know about everything.

I cleared my throat after Scarlett finished. "This all sounds great. The shrimp could be problematic, though. All the good suppliers are booked into the next century."

She deflated a bit. "Oh. I didn't think that might be a problem."

"Between now and the next meeting on Thursday, let's figure out if adding more shrimp to the menu is possible at all. Then we'll go from there."

"Sounds good to us," Mia said.

We all stood up. Mia and Aurelia left the meeting room first.

"I hope we didn't scare you," I said once we were alone.

"No, this was quite nice. It's fascinating to hear things from your point of view and how you might present things to customers and advertisers. I've never had this experience before." She checked the time. "I should go down to the kitchen. Must be madness by now."

"Don't forget that king cake," I said, pointing at the small box under the table.

Scarlett laughed. "I wouldn't even dream of it."

She bent down, and I exhaled sharply. Her ass was utter and complete perfection. I had to look away or my imagination would run wild. After she straightened up, her face was entirely red. There was no stopping the inappropriate thoughts running through my mind.

"Chad, this was truly the best way to start the week. Thank you."

I wanted to surprise her every fucking day. She deserved it.

"Damn, I should've sent Mom a picture of the cake when it was intact. She loves it too," Scarlett said.

"I can order one and send it to her."

The look on her face was priceless. "It would make Mom's day. She's just as fascinated with New Orleans as I am. Well, the other way around. I got the bug from her."

"Consider it done," I said.

She looked at me like I'd promised her the moon. "How much—"

"No."

"You don't even know what I wanted to ask."

"I can guess. It's a gift."

"Why?"

There were a million reasons, but all of them were inappropriate. Except one. "Because I want to do this for you."

She looked like she wanted to fight me on it, so I said, "Email me her address, and I'll get Beckett on it this morning. I'm not backing down."

I wanted to come up with an excuse—anything—to keep her here longer. I wanted to know about her family, about what else she'd planned to do in New Orleans. It didn't even matter what we talked about. I simply wanted her here. And that was dangerous. So instead of following that impulse, I stepped to one side, pointing at the door.

"After you. I'll see you on Thursday."

I'd successfully fought my instincts today. But would I be able to on Thursday?

Chapter Six

Scarlett

I blushed for no reason as I went down to the kitchen, clutching my king cake to my chest. I felt as if I was lost in a daydream, and I didn't want to wake up. Chad was the dreamiest man I'd ever met. Not to mention the hottest. Sitting next to him sent all my senses into overdrive.

He's your boss, Scarlett. Remember what happened the last time you mixed work and personal life?

D.I.S.A.S.T.E.R.

After storing the rest of the cake in my locker, I joined the team and immediately brought up the shrimp issue. Turned out they weren't exaggerating about the difficulty of obtaining shrimp. It never even crossed my mind that it might be a problem. Joel informed me that there were a lot of suppliers, but not all of them had consistent quality or the quantity we needed. I could probably reduce the menu to just one course with shrimp, but I wanted to exhaust all possibilities before deciding on that. Over the weekend, I discovered that an Italian fisherman named Genaro was hands down the best distributor in the city. Even though it wasn't my job to find suppliers, I wanted to do this.

"You won't be able to convince him to sell to us. We already tried a few times," Joel said.

"It doesn't hurt to try again."

He smiled. "You're determined, aren't you, chef?"

"Yes, I am."

Finding Genaro's whereabouts was easy. Setting up a meeting with him was another story altogether. The man simply didn't pick up his phone. But that was okay. I had a plan for that as well.

On Tuesday morning, I went to the spot where Genaro's boat was docked. Unfortunately, the man himself was already out at sea. Tomorrow, I'd have to come even earlier.

I hurried back to the restaurant, and to my surprise, I was still the first one to arrive. I quickly changed into my chef's getup and was about to start my day when someone knocked at the employees' door. I opened it right away.

"Miss Scarlett?" the guy asked.

"Yeah, that's me."

"I have this for you." He gave me a small package.

"What is it?"

"A beignet."

"I don't understand."

He shrugged. "Just a delivery for you. That's all I know."

"All right, thank you."

I got a beignet? What is this magic happening right now?

I went back to the kitchen and inspected the box. My heart started to beat faster as I opened it. Indeed, there was a beignet inside.

I took out my phone with trembling hands and snapped a picture. Knowing exactly where this came from, I texted Chad right away.

Scarlett: Thank you. To what do I owe the pleasure?

He replied as I tasted my treat. *Oh, this is great.*

Chad: You said you wanted to taste more beignets in the city. I'm here to fulfill that wish.

I licked my lips, sighing. How could this be real?

Chad: Just so you know, you'll be getting beignets from a different bakery each day.

Scarlett: Even the competition?

Chad: Of course. This is all about finding the best beignet for the lady. And please send me your parents' address.

My stomach fluttered as I sent it to him. I'd forgotten to do that after the meeting. I sighed and decided to simply enjoy the beignet. I wondered if he took pity on me because he'd overheard that shitty voice message. But I didn't think so.

Don't look a gift horse in the mouth. Just enjoy it, Scarlett.

The next morning, I managed to find Genaro. Everyone was right. He was a bit cantankerous, but he was also completely adorable. We hit it off right away. I informed Joel before I even arrived at the restaurant that I'd managed to strike a deal with Genaro. Obviously, I wouldn't be discussing contracts and pricing and so on. But I'd gotten a yes from him, and his admin team was in charge of the rest.

The beignet that was delivered today was even better than yesterday's. I texted Chad before I even finished it.

Scarlett: This is giving Café Du Monde a run for their money.

Chad: I agree. I can just imagine you eating this. You look adorable when you're enjoying food, so go ahead and make a list of what else you'd like to taste.

Oh, oh, oh.

Until now, I'd thought he might just be trying to ease in a new employee. In the back of my mind, I knew this was far too much effort for that, but I figured he liked to go the extra mile. But now it was obvious that we were flirting, and instead of completely changing the tone or the subject, I simply... flirted back.

Scarlett: Careful, I might get feisty.

Chad: That's exactly what I want.

He didn't write anything else, but he was a busy man. He couldn't chat with me all day. I sent a picture to Ariana, who immediately called me.

"Chad is really spoiling you, huh?" She knew all about the king cake, of course.

"Yes. He's... I'm not even sure how to describe everything."

"Then don't. Just enjoy it. Thank heavens your luck is turning around after that moron."

I bit the inside of my cheek. "Have you heard anything new?"

Ariana and I went out together with a few of the restaurant's coworkers a few times, and she'd kept in touch with them.

"Apparently, three staff members quit, citing Simon as the reason. He..."

My heart sank. "What?"

"He kind of thinks you're behind it."

"What the hell?" I snapped. "Who quit?"

"Andreas, Noah, and Elijah."

They were the ones who told Simon that his treatment of me was unacceptable.

"That's... I'm not even sure what to say."

"Nothing. Simon simply never takes responsibility for his actions. You know that. Forget about him. He's in your past. Enjoy that delicious man you've got there, all right?"

"I don't have him..."

She snorted. "It's only a matter of time until you do. I'm sure of it."

Oh, Ariana, I'm starting to hope you're right.

On Thursday, my beignet arrived half an hour before the marketing meeting.

Even though I was seeing Chad in a few minutes, I couldn't help myself and texted him.

Scarlett: This is even better than the other two.

Chad: I figured you'd say that. That's why I saved the best for last. It's my favorite too.

Hmm, something we had in common.

Chad: Are you free?

I sucked in a breath. The honest answer was no because a chef never truly was free, but I couldn't bring myself to tell him that. The dots indicating he was typing popped up on the screen again.

Chad: If you can spare a few minutes, come up earlier. We can discuss the pros and cons of each beignet.

He was *good* at coming up with silly excuses. Even though I should've started the day by making the to-do list for Joel, I simply wrote, **Start with the same tasks as yesterday. We'll discuss the rest after the marketing meeting.**

Guess who ran up the three flights of stairs to the management level in record time? Yep, me. I had a boost of energy from the beignet, too, for good measure. I headed straight into the meeting room, pausing once I stepped inside. It was empty.

A fraction of a second later, I felt Chad behind me. He didn't say a word, but I knew he was there in the doorway. I turned around slightly. I was right.

"Good morning," he said.

"Hi." I was feeling extra shy all of a sudden.

"You have some powdered sugar on your lips."

I blushed instantly and brushed it off. "Better?"

He swallowed hard. I noticed his Adam's apple dip. "Yes."

He did that same gentlemanly thing as last time where he pulled my chair out for me to sit down. Before Chad, I didn't even know people did that anymore.

"So," he said in a serious tone, "today was your favorite beignet."

A smile was playing on my lips. "It was puffier and somehow even creamier, though I know that's not the best way to describe it."

His eyes were still on my mouth. *Do I still have powdered sugar there*

"Your mom should be getting the delivery today."

"Oh my God, thank you. Chad, that's—"

"Don't say it's the nicest thing anyone's ever done for you."

My mouth fell open. "Why not? It's true."

"Because it breaks me every time I hear it."

I jerked my head back. "What do you mean?"

He looked at me intently. "I feel like you're only expecting the bare minimum from people. Usually that happens because you only *got* the bare minimum."

I'd never felt so understood in my life. "Um, I'm not even sure what to say."

"Just enjoy everything, Scarlett, without feeling like you have to pay me back or something."

I wasn't sure how to explain to him that I wasn't used to getting anything without giving something in return. Or having an expectation placed on me.

"I'll try," I said. "I hope Mom gets it after work. That way she can enjoy it this evening."

"What do your parents do?"

"They're both teachers. My dad used to be a nurse, but he had an accident and couldn't handle the job anymore. It was too physical and fast paced, so he got his teaching degree. We had a few rough years during that time. He did try to take on odd jobs, but it wasn't easy."

"I bet it wasn't," he said in a low voice. He opened his mouth again, tilting in closer, but then the marketing team stepped into the room, effectively cutting the sexual tension between us.

"Scarlett, we couldn't believe our ears when we heard that you got Genaro to deliver," Mia exclaimed.

My face exploded in a huge grin.

"I'm impressed." Chad looked at me with pride, and I relished it.

"The man isn't as hardheaded as he seems."

"No, I just think you have a way with people," Aurelia added.

My cheeks heated. "Thank you."

"So, since we have the best shrimp in the city, let's go full steam ahead with the changes you had planned. These are the pitches for the advertisers." Mia put three sheets of paper in front of me. It was copy for Facebook ads as well as magazines, describing flavors, textures, and so on.

"I love this. I read one of the descriptions and can taste the food already." I looked up. "Well done. I couldn't have written it better if I tried."

Aurelia rolled her shoulders back. "I wrote the copy," she said proudly.

"It's fantastic."

We went on through similar copy for all the courses I'd proposed. Chad didn't contribute much, but I felt his eyes on me the whole time.

Half an hour later, the meeting was regrettably over. It was for the best, though, as I had a lot to do. Aurelia and Mia left first once again.

The second Chad and I were alone, I felt my body temperature rise.

"So, no more meetings, huh?" I asked, head tilted slightly.

"I can invent a few if you'd like."

Holy shit. Yep, there was no hiding anymore. We were definitely flirting.

"I know I'd fucking want to," he went on.

"You would?" I whispered.

"Hell yes." He looked away from me and took in a deep breath, then straightened up. "But it's not smart."

"No, not at all," I agreed. We both rose to our feet. "Right, then I'll head to the kitchen."

"Scarlett," he said just as I turned around. I paused, looking over my shoulder. "I'm still waiting to hear about what else you want to taste in the city now that the beignet tasting is over."

I grinned from ear to ear. Wow. We might not have any more marketing meetings, but I had a hunch that I was going to see more of Chad, not less. And even though I knew it was a bad idea, I couldn't wait.

"Why don't you surprise me?" I asked in a flirty tone.

His eyes flashed, and I could only describe the smile playing on his lips as triumphant. "I so fucking will."

Chapter Seven

Chad

"We're not negotiating on this," I said. "My terms are final."

Julian nodded in agreement. "That's our limit."

Danielson, our alcohol supplier, threw up his hands in exasperation. "You can't be serious."

"Yes, we are," I said. "It's your prerogative to try and increase your prices, and it's ours to decline buying from you if you persist."

He just stared at us.

"All right," I said. "This meeting is adjourned."

I stood up from the desk, and Julian followed suit.

Danielson looked from me to my brother and then back. "Fucking hell. No one can negotiate with the LeBlancs, can they?"

"We're your biggest customer," I said. "You should know better than to try to one-up us."

"I'm curious. Who will you go to if I stick to my guns?"

I gave him a sardonic smile. "There is a long line of suppliers waiting to work with The Orleans Conglomerate." I wasn't bluffing. Because we owned so many establishments, we had huge bargaining power. We were making our suppliers rich—we always struck good deals—but I wouldn't allow anyone to take advantage of us.

"Fine, fine. You're getting the same conditions as last year."

I didn't expect him to give in so quickly, but I was pleased. I didn't show it, though. That was one of my negotiation techniques: never show emotions.

"Fantastic," Julian said, and I threw him a warning look. He composed himself, then said, "We'll tell legal to draw up all the papers. Have a good day."

"And you as well," Danielson said through gritted teeth. Though he couldn't be *that* pissed off. His company was going to make a lot of cash.

I walked out of the meeting room, and Julian came with me. The deal was applicable company-wide, but he and I sold the most booze, so we were in charge of this particular negotiation.

Back when Dad ran the company along with the grandfathers and grandmothers, they'd split these tasks among themselves. My brothers and I all interned in the company from an early age, so we learned the ropes without even trying. Now it came easy to us.

"I stand by what I said. You should somehow take over all the negotiations in the company," Julian said. "The guy was shitting his pants."

As we entered my office, I shrugged. "I like to make my position clear. But I always stay respectful."

"Exactly. You don't even raise your voice. You're basically like a stoic wall. And all our suppliers are going to run headfirst into it. Xander is great at the making-a-deal shit too."

My younger brother was very focused and exacting—sometimes maybe even a bit too much. We all were, but Xander took the cake.

"Zachary excels at negotiations, too, when he wants to," I added. Zachary liked to say that he had multiple personalities and applied each according to the situation. Mostly he was like Julian—playing the good cop in negotiations and generally being blasé about everything else. But if there was an emergency, he was the one whose help I wanted.

He credited his ability to respond under pressure because he volunteered as an ambulance paramedic one night a week for the past few years.

"Right, I'll tell everyone about our new deal. I mean, it won't be a surprise. Anthony and Beckett all figured we'd pull it through." He scratched his cheek and said, "Actually, you know what? Let's all meet tonight at the bar. I've got a new jazz band starting tonight. We can celebrate, and you lot can give me your input."

"Sounds like a deal." Even though we owned multiple bars across the city—and even the Quarter, I knew exactly which one he meant. It was where Julian had his office too.

"Sarah is picking Bella up from school, I'm guessing?" Julian asked.

"Yes. And they're going directly to her home."

I looked down from the window into the building's outdoor courtyard. Even though I was on the third floor, I could still see what was happening on the ground floor. Scarlett was sitting at one of the small tables, sipping from a cup. What was it about this woman that drew me in so badly?

She tilted her head to one side, pressing her fingers on the side of her neck. Did she ache there? I could help with that. Fuck, I could help with anything she needed.

Yes, I'd almost kissed her. I couldn't explain what had gotten into me.

"Well," Julian said, "what do we have here?"

I glanced at him. I hadn't even realized he'd come to the window too.

"Scarlett caught your eye, didn't she?"

I cleared my throat, rearranging my cuff links. "I don't know what you're talking about."

"Brother, you're not prone to *gazing* out a window. Besides, the angle of your head was a dead giveaway that you're looking straight at her."

"It's none of your business," I said.

He threw his head back, laughing. "You know, when you first told me about your celibacy idea—"

I'd never live that down. "Fucking hell. I'm never getting drunk around you again."

"On the contrary. You should get drunk more often. Helps you to get loose, share all of your grand ideas with us."

"Julian—"

"Forget it."

"See you tonight?"

"Yes. You'll tell the others?"

"I'll take care of it. You don't worry about anything, except maybe ogling Scarlett." He waggled his eyebrows at me.

"Julian," I warned.

He held up his hands in self-defense. "Fine. I won't say anything else on that topic. You do you."

That was exactly what I intended.

But after he left, instead of going to my desk, I kept looking down. She was on her phone, now slightly hunched over the table, revealing the back of her neck to me. Would that be a sweet spot for her?

I looked away, turning around. I needed to get a grip on myself.

But I didn't. Rather than returning to work, I decided I needed a break, too, and stepped out of my office.

Shauna immediately came up to me. "Chad, I've got some documents for you to sign."

"I'll do that once I'm back."

"You've got a meeting? I didn't see anything on your calendar."

"No. I'm going downstairs for coffee."

She narrowed her eyes. "But... we have a coffee machine here."

"I need a longer break."

Her eyes bulged. Yeah, guess who never took long breaks? Me. I believed in efficiency, and since I scheduled everything between dropping off and picking up Bella from school, I never even had time for breaks.

But now, I wanted to make time.

"The documents can wait," she said. "Enjoy your break."

I headed to the ground level, thankful that no one actually liked to use the stairs, as I didn't want to explain myself to anyone else. I honestly didn't even have a good explanation. I didn't need coffee, but I did need to see Scarlett. Ogling her from the third floor wasn't enough.

Thankfully, she was still in the courtyard when I got there. She looked up from her phone when she heard me.

"Chad. Hi." She glanced around. "Want me to go?"

I furrowed my brow. "Why would I want that?" I walked to the small table, sitting down in front of her.

"I don't know what the protocol is for breaks. The team said I can come out here at any time. I usually drink one cup before lunch rush." Scarlett nodded to her coffee on the table and continued, "I'd love one in the afternoon, but there's no time. Anyway, no one told me what the protocol is if I run into the CEO."

I leaned forward. "Just a hint: they'll probably tell you the CEO never takes breaks."

She licked her lips, and I almost kissed her. "So how come you decided to take one?"

I decided to be completely honest. "I saw you from upstairs."

She parted her lips slightly, and my eyes darted to her mouth before I even realized it.

"Chad." Her cheeks turned pink, and she glanced down at her drink. Then she grabbed her phone. "Oh no, let me just book this before I forget."

"Book what?" I asked.

She smiled again when she looked up at me. "I'm going on a haunted tour of the city tonight. It starts right after my shift."

I stared at her. "In the evening?"

She rolled her eyes, and I wanted to lean over the table and kiss her sassy mouth. "No, in the morning. Of course it's at night. Who would do a haunted tour during the day?"

"Scarlett," I said slowly, "New Orleans is not Seattle."

"I know that."

"I don't think you do. I don't want to sound pedantic or something, but going through the city at night is dangerous, especially in areas like... Wait, you're going to a cemetery?" I asked, glancing at her phone.

"Of course. St. Louis Cemetery is a staple for any haunted tour of the city."

"Jesus. What exactly do people expect to see there? At most, you'll have drunkards or drug addicts."

She tucked her phone away. "You're no fun, you know that?"

I started to laugh.

"What?" she asked.

"I don't think anyone's ever said that to my face."

She put her hand over her mouth. "I'm sorry. I keep forgetting that you're my boss."

"I'm the owner of the restaurant, but not your boss. The chef is the boss in the kitchen."

Her grin was brilliant. "That's right."

I put my elbows on the table, leaning in even more. "Scarlett, there has to be a haunted tour during the day too."

"Chad... I appreciate your concern, but I'm going tonight."

Her determination was admirable—and misplaced. And I knew I couldn't change her mind. So I decided to do something else entirely.

"Do they have another spot? I'm coming with you."

Her eyes widened. "Why?"

I had no explanation. Zero. "I've never been on a haunted tour." That actually was true. "And I don't like the thought of you going alone."

She tilted her head slightly. "I'm going with a group."

"I meant I don't want you to be alone in the group. Who knows what kind of weirdos will join."

"My type of weirdos, probably." She was clearly fighting a smile now. I wanted to kiss this woman more than anything else.

I quickly sat back, as there was a real risk I'd do so right now. "For my peace of mind, I'm going to come with you and keep you safe." She pushed a strand of hair behind her ear, and I wondered if it was a nervous gesture. Was I making her nervous? I hated the thought of that. "Unless you don't want me to come."

She hesitated for a split second. A whiff of her perfume reached me. I had no idea what it was. It smelled like vanilla and cinnamon from the kitchen, but underneath that, I could still smell her, and she was fucking delicious.

"I want you to join me," she murmured. Then she looked at her phone, tapping the screen a few times. "All right, it's booked."

"Perfect, I can't wait. We'll have a great time tonight, Scarlett."

"You promise? Because if you hijack the tour—"

"I promise."

She held my gaze for a few seconds before looking away. The temptation to kiss her intensified.

I wasn't going to be able to fight it tonight.

I was sure of it.

CHAPTER EIGHT

SCARLETT

"Oh, why didn't I bring my makeup bag with me?" I muttered to myself as I checked my appearance in the mirror. The employee bathroom was small, and the light was dubious, but I still preferred to use this restroom rather than the one reserved for patrons. This room was cozy and looked slightly different from the rest of the restaurant, which had been modernized. There were light cracks in the walls that were off-white, almost yellow in color. The sink was old-fashioned, made out of brass, perhaps, or copper. The mirror on the wall had a matching metal edge.

My hair was a complete mess, as usual. I was wearing this morning's clothes, which were nothing to write home about. Then again, I hadn't counted on having company on my tour, and least of all such sexy company.

Shit, maybe I should cancel tonight.

I started to laugh at myself in the mirror. *Oh, Scarlett, this isn't a date.* Chad was simply overprotective. Just like Joel and apparently everyone else in the restaurant. I'd been lectured by at least five people to keep my wallet somewhere that I could feel it or see it all times, which sounded highly impractical, but I was going to do my best.

I applied the lipstick I always carried with me. It was bright red and possibly a bit too much for tonight, but what the heck? Life was too short not to wear lipstick.

I ran a hand through my hair, which I was starting to realize was the way to go in the Big Easy. The humidity messed up my usual styling, but if I ran my hand through it, it simply parted naturally and stayed there.

Be cool as a cucumber, Scarlett. You're going on a haunted tour, and a certain sexy man who keeps looking at your lips like he wants to devour them is joining you. No big deal, right?

It was actually a *huge* deal, but I wasn't going to overthink it.

I was ecstatic when I left the bathroom and ventured out through the employee exit. To my astonishment, Chad was already there.

"Uh, hi," I stammered. Goodness. Under the light of the lamppost, he looked even sexier than usual—with a hint of danger, somehow.

His eyes twinkled. "I scared you, yet you want to go a haunted tour?"

"You didn't scare me," I said playfully, though I didn't elaborate. What could I say? *"I need a proper heads-up to brace myself for your holy hotness"?*

He looked me up and down and then back up before resting his eyes on my face. Wait, no, they were on my mouth again. Probably. It wasn't always easy to tell. I parted my lips to draw in a deep breath, and his eyes widened a little bit. Yep, I was right. They'd been on my lips. I was going to blush if I wasn't careful.

"Where's the first stop?" he asked.

"Hotel Monteleone," I said.

"Of course."

I chuckled. "That's actually on the—"

"I know. On the other end of Royal. We should get going. After you."

I bit the inside of my cheek and asked, "Since I've been warned repeatedly not to go on Bourbon at night... what if we both go? Now that I have my own personal bodyguard and everything?"

He laughed softly. Yes, I was aware that he was my boss and that I was being extra sassy. But out here, out of the restaurant, it was easy to pretend that I didn't work for him.

"Why not? Better to explore it with me than alone."

I smiled as we walked side by side toward the infamous street. When we turned the corner, I was about to remark that it seemed a lot like Royal, but then I noticed subtle differences. For one, there were more people hanging out with their drinks, and there just seemed to be more people in general.

"This way!" He pointed to the right. "And stay close to me."

"Are you afraid someone might steal me away?"

"Fuck yes."

My breath caught. Our gazes clashed. What exactly did he mean? I was teasing him, of course, but he didn't seem to be joking.

"So, what's Bella up to tonight?"

"She's with her mom."

"Right, I forgot."

"She spends most weekends with her."

"And you don't like it?"

"Why do you say that?" Chad asked a bit defensively.

"I don't know. You sounded a bit regretful."

He shrugged, closing the button of his jacket. The gesture was oddly sexy.

"It's great that she's got a good relationship with her mother. But I miss her a lot. I have more time on the weekend to make breakfast, her favorite meal. We're always in a hurry during the week, trying to get her to school on time. I miss when she was in kindergarten. The drop-off time was flexible, and I could make an elaborate meal every morning."

Oh God, who is this man? Sexy god and cute dad all wrapped into one. I was truly melting.

"Your expression changes when you talk about her," I said as we walked past a group of drunkards.

Chad instinctively came closer to me. If he put an arm around my shoulders, I would spontaneously combust. But he didn't.

"Soo... I kind of thought you'd never want to see me again after our beignet evening."

He smiled at me, and damn it, I had to tell him not to do that anymore. He was always sexy and irresistible, but when he smiled, I had to check if I still had panties on. There was a real risk that they'd just melted off.

"Scarlett, it was one of the best evenings I've had in a long while."

My breath caught, and I stared at my feet.

"It was a great evening for me too," I murmured.

The air between us was charged even though he hadn't even come closer.

I looked up, needing to cut the tension. "And I bet this one will be even better."

We moved back to Royal after a few blocks, and it didn't take us long to reach Hotel Monteleone. There was already a sizable group in front of it.

Chad jerked his head back. "All these people are here for the haunted tour?"

"They're very popular."

"Clearly!" He sounded stunned.

"Welcome, everyone. I'm counting twenty-four, so it's a full house tonight. My name is Guillermo, and I'll be your guide."

I walked slowly and stealthily to the front of the group because Guillermo didn't speak very loudly.

I felt Chad at my side the whole time Guillermo told us the stories behind Hotel Monteleone. I was honestly in love with the building. It was huge, and the style was called Beaux-Arts. The white facade looked as if it had been renovated recently. I liked that they treated it with so much care and love.

Apparently, it was a pretty famous spot for ghosts. Some were deceased former employees, like the one nicknamed Red, but apparently a whole lot of ghosts liked to pop in at the bar named Carousel.

"They're peaceful ghosts," Guillermo insisted.

We moved on to several other buildings, mostly on Royal Street. The stories behind some of the haunted places were downright gruesome. When I booked the tour, I'd imagined something whimsical and fun with a touch of magic.

"If you don't like it, we can always bail," Chad said.

"It's not exactly what I thought it would be," I whispered. "But maybe it gets better."

"I have a counter proposal," he stated as we stopped in front of a shop selling diaries and voodoo supplies. No, they weren't diaries—Guillermo informed us that they were *shadow journals.*

"I'm listening."

Chad brought his mouth to my ear, making my entire body vibrate. "Julian asked me to drop by one of his bars. Want to go? You'd love the place."

Oh God. That sounds a bit like a date, doesn't it? This was so far out of my realm of expertise, and I didn't even have a clue. My ex and I had been together long enough that I wasn't up to date with dating etiquette anymore.

"They're playing jazz at his place. Some of the best in New Orleans."

"I see. You're bribing me with NOLA experiences."

"And they serve the best damn Pimm's and Sazeracs."

I hesitated, tilting my head a bit. And I realized that he was closer than I'd first thought. The back of my hand touched his, and a spark spread through my entire body. I swallowed hard. "I'd love to listen to some jazz."

He pulled back, and his smile was downright triumphant. "Great."

I then turned my attention to Guillermo, who regaled us with some more gruesome stories right up until we reached Muriel's restaurant. I'd passed the red building quite a few times and loved its overall charm and, of course, the black iron railing around the balconies. Guillermo told us that the owner still dwelled in it despite passing away some two hundred years ago, and that visitors in the building often reported seeing objects fly.

"Of course, some would say that it might be the result of one too many drinks," he told us.

That made me laugh. I firmly believed that most such sightings were the result of too much alcohol.

I looked at the building intently while he gave us more details. Chad disappeared for a few moments, and once he was back, I said, "I'm going to tip Guillermo and tell him that we're going to leave early. Okay?"

"I've already taken care of tipping him, and I told him we've got plans and they start earlier than we thought."

My mouth fell open. "When?"

"Just now when you were looking at the building."

"Well, it's gorgeous. Deserves to be admired."

He grinned. "I like the way you soak everything in."

"Fine, I'll tell Guillermo goodbye, and then we'll just go."

The guy didn't seem at all mad that we were leaving early. In fact, he came close and winked at me. "If I had that hunk with me, I'd leave earlier too."

Oh my goodness. He thought we were an item? Or maybe he saw the way I shamelessly ogled Chad.

I smiled at him and said, "Good luck with the rest of the tour."

"Have a great night."

"You too."

"Everything okay?" Chad asked when I joined him.

"Yeah, why?"

"You're flushed."

"Yeah, it's just a bit hot around here," I said and hoped he bought it. Oh dear Lord, I was biting off more than I could chew. I was sure of it. "So, where's his bar?"

"Dumaine."

"That's convenient. Are all your establishments in the French Quarter?"

"No, that would be insane considering how many we own. But quite a few of them are. Our best locations are here."

Dumaine was decidedly less crowded than both Bourbon and Royal, but not by much. Clearly New Orleans was in party mode.

"Is the French Quarter like this every weekend?" I asked.

"That's a resounding yes. As long as it doesn't rain."

I glanced to the right and the left, soaking it all in, until we reached a two-story building. It seemed to be the same shade of red as Muriel's, but the iron on the balconies was painted white. The shutters on all the windows were green. I could already hear the jazz music from inside. "Oh, that really is beautiful."

"I knew you'd love it."

As we stepped inside the bar, Chad said, "Yep, there are my brothers."

I recognized Julian at the counter. He was talking to a group of four men.

"Wait, *all* your brothers are here?"

"Yeah, we're celebrating a successful negotiation."

I stopped in my tracks and stared at him. "Chad, won't they get the wrong idea if I show up here with you?"

He grinned from ear to ear. "They sure fucking will, but I'm willing to take the risk for some good jazz and the best Sazerac in town. How about you?"

Chad LeBlanc was bringing his flirty side out to play again. And I was going to flirt right back.

"Sure. Why not?"

CHAPTER NINE

CHAD

I knew my brothers would be stunned to see Scarlett, but even so, their reactions did not disappoint. I had no idea what possessed me to ask her to join me here. All I knew was that the tour was clearly not what she expected, and I wasn't ready for our evening together to be over. So here we were.

Julian just stared at us, mouth agape. He looked so comical, I was tempted to snap a photo of him. Xander and Zachary stood next to each other, each with a Sazerac in hand. Anthony and Beckett were sitting on bar stools, and judging by the volume of their voices, they were already on their second drink.

"Here you are!" Beckett exclaimed. Then he noticed Scarlett next to me and frowned slightly. He leaned in closer to Anthony. "Am I drunk, or is our brother here with a woman?"

"We can hear you," I said.

Beckett looked straight at Scarlett. "Sorry, I didn't want to make you feel uneasy. Julian made my Sazerac extra strong."

Julian gave him a mock salute. "Always the best for the family."

"Hi Scarlett," Zachary said. I'd forgotten they'd met during the online interview.

"Hi!" she replied.

"Scarlett is the new chef at LeBlanc & Broussard," I shared.

Xander narrowed his eyes. They looked so much alike that they could be twins.

"Riiiiight, yes. Isabeau and Celine told us," Xander said.

"I went on a tour of the city this evening. Your brother was concerned for my safety, so he offered to come with me," she explained.

I shot my brothers a warning look. They knew me well enough to know that this was an absolutely shitty excuse. I would never, not in a million years, offer to go on a tour with *anyone*. If I was concerned for an employee's safety, then I'd make the necessary arrangements. But to their credit, none of them—and I mean absolutely none—questioned this, even though both Anthony and Beckett looked like they were about to.

"So," Julian said, "we meet again, Scarlett. Did Chad already tell you that you can drink the best Sazerac in town here?"

"The very best," she replied. Her shoulders had dropped a few inches. Had she been stressed about coming here?

Damn, why didn't I stop to think how unleashing all my brothers on her at the same time would make her feel?

"Hang on," Xander said. "I'm Xander. We need to get introductions out of the way, since the four of us are at a disadvantage. But you two like to keep it that way." He nodded at Scarlett. "They've been doing that ever since we were kids."

Scarlett blinked, looking back at me with confusion in her eyes.

I sighed. "Just to fill you in, Julian is the oldest, and I'm the second oldest. Our younger brothers constantly feel the need to point out that we somehow had more leverage over them growing up."

"Well, we did," Julian said. "I was especially annoying. Made them do errands on my behalf until they were old enough to know better."

I laughed. "And I learned very quickly from Julian. But," I said, pointing at Zachary and Xander, "you two got away with a lot more shit.

They come after me. Not to mention you two." I turned my intention to Anthony and Beckett.

"Well, we are the youngest. And you don't hear us complaining," Anthony said. "I'm Anthony, by the way."

"And I'm Beckett."

"Yeah, and I'm Zachary, and I've already had too many Sazeracs, too, so forgive me if I make you uncomfortable."

Scarlett was grinning at all my brothers. "You're not. This is fun. Well, I mean, I realized the family was tight when I met your grandmothers."

"Yes, we heard about that," Beckett said. Even though he was only a few years younger than Anthony, he seemed almost a decade younger. Perhaps because he still had a boyish curiosity about everything.

"By the way," Xander said, "both grans really liked you."

Scarlett's eyes widened a bit. "But I barely talked to them."

"They have a good feeling about people," Zachary filled in.

"All right, how about a round of Sazeracs for everyone?" Julian said. "We can toast to our new deal."

Focusing on Scarlett, I explained, "We convinced our liquor supplier not to raise prices for the upcoming year."

Julian scoffed. "By *we* he means himself. I was just an innocent by-stander."

I just laughed.

"Chad's got the scaring-the-shit-out-of-our-business-partner act down to a T, so he doesn't need me to chip in much. He's only gotten sharper over the years." My brother placed half a dozen Sazeracs on the counter. "All right, fam, dig in."

Scarlett looked at me with a half smile. "So you go hard on your business partners, huh?"

I nearly snorted into my drink. There was nothing sexual about her sentence, but my mind went completely haywire. The things I'd do to this woman in bed.

I realized at precisely that moment that Julian had been right. My idea of being celibate had been utter and total shit.

"Yeah, he likes to bust balls," Julian said.

Our four younger brothers burst out laughing.

Scarlett brought her drink to her mouth, taking a few sips.

I looked straight at Julian. "Would you mind keeping it a bit professional?"

"No, man, sorry. This is on you. You know how we are when we get together. You brought Scarlett here to meet us at your own risk. You should've introduced her to us in a more formal setting first so we could make a good impression."

"But I am impressed," Scarlett said. "By you all and this drink. I've never even had a Sazerac before."

Both Anthony and Zachary jolted their heads back, obviously surprised by her admission, though I wasn't sure which one. Maybe both.

"Consider this your official welcome to New Orleans, then," I said.

Xander pointed at her. "You can tell us if you ever taste a better drink."

"Xander," Julian said in a warning tone.

"How else will we keep our standards high?" Xander asked.

I shook my head, keeping an eye on Scarlett for any sign that my brothers were overwhelming her. But she seemed to genuinely be enjoying herself.

After a while, the crowd started to shift, and a few couples began to dance. Scarlett looked at them very curiously and said, "I didn't realize you could dance to jazz music."

"Scarlett, this is New Orleans," Zachary said. "We dance to any-thing."

"I haven't danced in a long time," she muttered almost wistfully.

My instincts kicked in again. Fuck, I needed this woman.

"Dance with me," I said.

Scarlett looked down at her drink and then back up. My brothers didn't say anything.

"Sure, why not?" she murmured. "Let me just finish this."

Before I had the chance to tell her that she shouldn't down the whole drink all at once because absinthe is some powerful stuff, she swallowed it all.

"Oh," she said afterward, her eyes watering, "it burned my throat a bit."

"That's... You know what? Never mind." Julian sounded and looked stunned. "We'll make sure you get home in one piece."

"Hey, I can hold my liquor," Scarlett said, already slurring a little.

"Famous last words," Xander replied. "But don't worry. Julian's manning the bar, and Anthony and Beckett are inebriated, but Zachary and I can keep an eye on you."

"That's what *I'm* doing," I clarified.

Xander winked at me. Zachary nodded at him and then clinked his glass to Xander's.

Something was going on, but I didn't have time to dig into it now. I wanted to dance with Scarlett more than I wanted to spar with my brothers.

Taking her empty glass, I put it on the counter next to my half-drunk Sazerac. Then I took her hand. I realized a split second later that she wasn't expecting it, because she shuddered lightly. But she didn't pull it back. I walked us farther away from the bar. I didn't want my brothers lurking. Besides, the area next to the bar was more crowded anyway.

"This music is so soothing," Scarlett murmured.

I pulled her right in front of me, putting an arm around her waist but keeping a comfortable distance. The music was slow and inviting.

"Hm," she said after a few seconds, "maybe drinking that in one swallow really wasn't my best idea."

"Don't worry, Scarlett. I'll take care of you."

She looked up at me, her eyes wide and dreamy. "Oh, I don't think anything will happen to me. That's not what I'm worried about."

"Then what *are* you worried about?"

She cast her glance away, sucking in a deep breath. "This evening. Dancing. You."

Energy shot through my body. "Scarlett... fuck, I want to kiss you."

She gasped, looking up at me. "I thought I was imagining things."

"What?" I jerked my head back, and she laughed. That wasn't how I expected her to react.

"I didn't know if I was making things up or if you were looking at my mouth or being flirty."

"Then let me clear up all doubts. I *was* being flirty, and I *have* been looking at your mouth obsessively."

"Oh."

Even though there were a million colors around us, I could still clearly see her blush.

"I want to kiss you so damn badly."

"Don't do it," she said, "because I'm already imagining how amazing it would be, and I'd rather not know."

"Why?" I asked, pulling her even closer until I felt her hot breath on my neck.

"Because I... this is...," she stammered. "Oh goodness, the Sazerac really was strong. I'm in New Orleans to rebuild my life, Chad."

"Okay," I said calmly, wondering where this was going.

"And, well, I'm recovering from... Seattle. I've promised myself time first before... diving into anything. I don't want to break that promise."

We swayed to the music, and I kept my hand firmly on her waist.

"I understand."

"You do?"

"Yes. I know a thing or two about promises." *And recovering.*

She frowned, and I realized I had to explain. "After my divorce, I realized I didn't want to put my daughter through the highs and lows of dating or knowing that her father was seeing women, so I decided to be celibate."

Her mouth hung open, and she tilted her head slightly forward. "That's got to be hard. How's it going?"

"Very well until I met you."

"Chad..."

"I haven't been tempted, not even once. Until you. You're sassy, fun, and I can't stay away from you."

"That's so romantic," she whispered.

"But don't worry, I will."

"Oh." She sounded almost disappointed.

Did she know how close I was to pulling her into one of these dark corners and kissing her nonstop? Just kiss her for hours until she moaned my name and begged for more. Then I'd take her somewhere else and go through every single fantasy she had, all night long. I would make her come every way there was, then start all over again.

But I couldn't, and neither could she.

Which one of us will be the strong one?

As the song ended, she sighed.

"I want to dance with you to the next song too," I confessed. "I want to dance all night long, but it's best if we don't."

She nodded vehemently. "One hundred percent better. It's a good thing you remembered that. I should go home anyway." She turned slightly, then moved back. "Oh, I can't believe I drank that so fast."

"I'll take you home."

She looked at me in alarm. "No, you stay here and enjoy the evening with your brothers. I'll just grab an Uber."

"I'll take you home," I repeated.

She stood still for a few seconds, closing her eyes, and then murmured, "Okay. I think I can be in a car with you and not maul you." Then she opened her eyes and covered her mouth with her hand. "You didn't hear anything, right? I didn't say that out loud?"

I grinned as my cock twitched in my pants. "I can pretend you didn't say it if it makes you feel better." I leaned in slightly, desperate for more closeness.

"Ah, I just won't say anything else. Not one word."

Laughing, I led her through the crowd, keeping my hands on both her shoulders. When we reached the bar, I realized that all five brothers had been eyeing us all this time. Clearly we hadn't been far enough away.

"I know that expression," Anthony said, looking at Scarlett. "Sazerac went right to your head?"

"Yep."

"I'm taking her home," I announced. A ripple of nods went through the group, but again, I had to give them credit, as not one of them said anything. "Then I'll come back and catch up with you."

"Sure," Julian said. I glared at him. He grimaced and said, "Good night, Scarlett."

It only took a couple minutes for the Uber to arrive, and I helped her into the back seat. She wasn't joking—she didn't say one word in the car. I desperately wanted to know what was going through her mind, but I didn't want to pressure her. Was she doubting her promise to herself?

It doesn't matter, Chad. You have a promise of your own. You have Bella and a failed relationship with her mother. Focus on that. Focus on your daughter.

It didn't take long to reach Scarlett's apartment building. I quickly went over to her side of the vehicle, opening the door and helping her out. Her balance was good, but her eyes were hazy as if she were ready to fall asleep any second.

"Thanks a lot, Chad," she murmured.

"I'm bringing you to your door."

She smiled to herself. "That's also so romantic. Why? Why can't you be some sort of, I don't know, rude and abrasive kind of guy? It would make this so much easier."

I laughed at her comment. "Come on, beautiful. Let's go upstairs."

We went up to the second floor, and when she opened her door, I quickly glanced inside. "This is a studio?" I double-checked.

"Yep. And don't judge."

"I'm not."

"Your tone sounded a bit judgy."

"I'm used to bigger spaces," I confessed.

"So am I, but there weren't too many options that offered a six-month lease." She turned to face me fully. "Thank you for this evening, Chad. It was amazing. The tour, the bar, meeting your brothers, the dance, the kiss."

"What?" I asked, confused by that last part.

"Speaking too much again." She smiled sheepishly. "I already imagined it, and it was delicious. Your hands were all over me, and—"

I lost it. I stepped inside, moving her deeper into the room and closing the door behind us before crashing my mouth to hers. I couldn't stop kissing her. She tasted like Sazerac and vanilla, and I wanted more. So damn much more.

I pulled back slightly, running the tip of my tongue against the contour of her mouth, and she moaned, adjusting her stance making me wonder if she'd pressed her thighs together. Then I kissed her again, moving my tongue slowly at first, exploring her.

I needed some leverage—a wall, a door, anything. But I knew better than to do that. I had to stop while I was ahead, or I was liable to tear off all her clothes right now. I'd drop to my knees in front of her and make her come on my tongue. I desperately needed her. I was so damn close to losing every thread of self-restraint.

She moaned again, and I pulled back a bit, looking down at her mouth. "You're so fucking gorgeous."

"Mm," she murmured, slowly opening her eyes. "This was even better than I imagined." She bit her lower lip. "I guess we could have one kiss, right? It won't hurt anyone."

"No," I said, "but see, here's the thing. One kiss makes me want more, and—"

She put her finger over my lips. "No, no, no. Don't say that, because I'm thinking the same thing. And—"

Feeling her finger against my lips aroused me insanely fast. I lost my control again, cupping her face. She dropped her hand, parting her lips slightly. This kiss was even more demanding than the first one, even more desperate.

And then I couldn't keep my hands just on her face. I trailed them farther down to her waist. She was standing right in front of some sort of dresser, and I lifted her onto it.

"Oh...," she purred, and I kissed her again.

She was at my height now, so it was easier to explore her. I lowered one hand from her waist, putting it on her outer thigh, then sliding it slightly toward her inner thigh. She opened her legs wide, driving me crazy. Then I moved my hand farther up. She shuddered even though she was wearing jeans. I couldn't help myself and pressed my thumb right over where her clit was under all the layers of clothing. Her reaction completely threw me.

She dropped her head backward, a loud moan resounding through the room. She was so on edge. It would take next to nothing to make her come. But this was insane.

I put my hand back on her thigh and rested my forehead against her shoulder. "Scarlett..."

"I know," she whispered. "Let's..." She laughed a bit. "Let's calm down, I guess."

"Yes."

"And maybe help me down. Actually, no. You know what? Take those sexy hands off me and I'll hop off. Otherwise... Well, our track record is short, but it's not really good, is it?"

"No, it's not," I replied with a laugh, then took a large step back.

She drew in a deep breath, and we both startled when my phone beeped.

"Aren't you going to get that?" she asked.

"It was a message," I said. "Probably from one of my brothers."

"Oh my God, that's right. They're waiting for you."

"Scarlett...," I said. I wanted to stay. Damn it, I wanted nothing more, but I couldn't.

"Go. I'm just going to bed, okay?"

I nodded. "I think that's the smartest thing."

"I agree."

"Listen, if you don't feel well tomorrow—"

"One thing you should know about me: I never call in sick. Not even when I *am* sick, unless it's contagious, since I'm dealing with food all day."

"That's a recipe for overworking yourself," I said. "I won't allow it."

She folded her arms over her chest. "Really? One kiss and you think you have some sort of power over me?"

"It was two kisses," I pointed out. "Three, if we're counting the one you imagined."

"No, we are not."

Scarlett smiled. "I was teasing you, Chad. Tomorrow is Saturday. I don't work weekends."

How the hell did I forget what day of the week it was?

"Even better. But just for future reference, if you're sick, do not come to work. I'll hear about it, throw you over my shoulder, and bring you right back home."

"I'd like to see you try."

"No, you wouldn't," I replied.

Her eyes widened. "Hell yes, I absolutely would."

I opened the front door and said, "Good night, Scarlett."

"Good night, Chad."

After stepping out, I glanced down at my phone. I had a message from Julian.

Julian: Told you it wouldn't work.

I usually got cross with him when he challenged me, but right now, I started to laugh. He was 100 percent right.

I might have been able to walk away from Scarlett tonight, but I wasn't sure I'd have the self-control to do it again in the future.

Chapter Ten

Scarlett

On Monday morning, I spoke to my parents on the way to the restaurant and told them about how much I loved my job and the team. I also couldn't help myself and shared a bit about Chad—without too many details, of course. They were surprised but didn't judge me, simply advised me to be careful. I planned to do just that. But for now, I couldn't help rewinding the kiss.

You've got to stop thinking about it, Scarlett.

But I couldn't. And besides, who cared if I played the moment on repeat? I was certain I wouldn't run into Chad anytime soon. After all, I'd already finished my meetings with the marketing team, so there was no reason for me to visit the third floor.

When I was only a few minutes away from the restaurant, I decided to check my emails, since I typically put my phone away once I was in the kitchen.

I was shocked to discover one from Simon.

Subject: (Empty)

You need to get over yourself and fix this mess. How the hell did you turn the whole staff against me? Just because you couldn't cope with me being promoted over you. Fix this or you'll be sorry. You left enough unfinished business in Seattle.

I swallowed hard, quickly deleting the email. *The nerve of him, I swear.* He was short-tempered and neurotic. No wonder the staff wasn't happy. Now that he couldn't take his anger out on me, he probably did it to them.

He could shove his threat up his ass. I left nothing unfinished. I'd triple-checked with the realtor that I could get out of the lease without issues, and there was nothing else I could think of that he could blame on me.

What an ass.

I immediately turned off my phone, focusing on the day ahead.

I arrived at the restaurant at seven thirty, which to some is early, but I liked to be here for all the deliveries. Besides, I'd found a new source for shrimp, and I wanted to personally be here to thank him for working with us. And to make sure I got what I'd ordered.

To my astonishment, I wasn't the first one to arrive. After I changed into my chef uniform, I left the changing room and froze when I heard Chad's unmistakable voice.

"Want another one?"

And then the sweetest little voice replied, "Yes, please, Daddy."

That had to be Bella. Just hearing the two of them took my mind off Simon and his crazy.

Still, I hesitated, looking over my shoulder. *Maybe I should leave.* But I didn't want to hang out in the changing room, waiting for them to go, so I took a deep breath and stepped inside the kitchen, and what I saw filled my heart. A little girl with hair the same color as Chad's was sitting on the counter. Her hair was styled in two pigtails. Chad had his back to me, holding a plate in front of her.

"Good morning," I greeted them.

"Scarlett, hi. I didn't realize it was so late," Chad said.

"Oh, it's not. Don't worry. I just like to come early on Mondays."

"Dad and I always come here on Monday," Bella said proudly. "We eat all the pie that's left from bunch," she said.

I started to laugh because she'd clearly meant to say *brunch*.

"And then the staff wonders where it is," Chad said with a wink.

"Don't worry, your secret is safe with me," I assured them. "So, what are you having?"

"Pecan pie."

"I heard that's delicious." It was the weekend specialty.

"Do you want to eat with us?" she asked. And then she hesitantly added, "There's a slice left."

Chad laughed, kissing the top of her head. "I'm very proud of you for sharing." Then he turned those molten blue eyes on me. "By the way, it means she likes you. She's very protective of pie."

"Thanks for the offer." I walked right up to them and shook her hand. "I'm Scarlett, the new chef."

Her eyes widened. "I'm Bella."

"And I'd love some pie."

Chad gave me a plate, and our fingers brushed as I took it from him. I had to steel myself not to react to the sudden burst of warmth traveling through me. He clearly didn't miss it, because he fixed his eyes on the plate for a bit before looking up at me.

"How was your weekend?" he asked.

"It was great," I replied.

"What did you do?"

"Oh, I did a few more walking tours, and then I bought one of those racks to put my clothes on, since I'm short on storage space. I've been desperately meaning to do that since I moved in, but time got away from me."

"Dad, I think one of my pigtails is coming undone." It was adorable how she held on to the *a*, sounding like "Daaaad."

Chad immediately straightened up, looking at his daughter's hair. "Yep, it is. Let me redo it for you."

I watched in fascination as he pulled off the elastic band, then expertly undid the pigtail and redid it perfectly. How adorable was that? A full-grown man focusing on his daughter's pigtails. I sighed and tried to pass it off as a reaction to the delicious pecan pie.

"I knew there was a reason I didn't go to pastry school. I would just bake and eat the entire time. Now I understand why your brunches are so popular."

"Daddy said you just moved to New Orleans," Bella said, and I nearly dropped my plate. *He mentioned me to his daughter?* "And Gran Celine said she liked you, and she never really likes people."

Chad started to laugh. "She does like people. She was just afraid the restaurant's reputation would suffer."

"She loves this place, doesn't she?" I asked.

Chad nodded. "Yeah. I think she'd still be in the kitchen, running it full-time if she could."

"I see."

So I was a topic of conversation in their home, huh? I was curious to know what was being said, but I didn't think it was appropriate to ask. Not when Bella was here. And even if she wasn't, I had to find some way to function professionally around Chad.

"What kind of pies do you like, Bella?" I asked.

"All sorts of pies. All of them. Everything that's sweet."

"Beignets, too, I've heard!"

Chad's face opened up in a smile.

She grinned. "Yessssss."

"So do I. I have a sweet tooth as well."

"I want to learn to make beignets. But first, I have to learn to bake pie. For the contest at school."

"You said you wanted to dance for the talent competition," Chad said.

"I danced last year, Daddy. I need to do something else this year."

"Okay, then. Baking it is."

"I can show you," I said.

"You can?" she asked.

I nodded. "Of course, I didn't go to pastry school, but I can make a pie."

"Really, Bella. You can ask Nana. Or your grans."

She scrunched up her nose. "Nana doesn't like to cook too much. Her food never tastes good!"

I was so proud that I didn't laugh. Chad was also having difficulty keeping a straight face, but he finally lost it. "Well, you got me there. Mom doesn't love cooking. Neither does Dad. But your grans are very good."

"Yes, but Scarlett is a *chef*." She said the word with wonder.

"Your grandmothers are also chefs."

"But they're not in the restaurant anymore, Daddy. What if they forgot how to do it? Scarlett is a professional."

"If you want, you can come here before school and I can show you," I offered.

Before Chad even opened his mouth, Bella exclaimed, "Yes. I like you so much."

To my astonishment, she shifted closer to me and threw her arms around my torso. Out of instinct, I hugged her back, then gave Chad a questioning glance. I didn't want to overstep any boundaries.

He nodded, his eyes soft. I'd never seen this expression on him.

"Bella," he said after his daughter let me go, "we need to talk about this."

"But Dad, she already said yes."

"I did," I said, deciding instantly to side with Bella.

"We'll think of something," Chad said.

Hmmm... He was being vague. I wondered if he was upset.

"When can we come?" Bella asked. Clearly she knew how to negotiate like her dad.

"I'll talk to Scarlett about her schedule and see where she can fit us in. Are you planning on coming in so early every Monday?" he asked me.

"Yes. I like to make sure I have a smooth start to the week and also check the produce and other deliveries. It should've arrived by now."

"Then we should go," Chad told Bella.

"Can I go to the ladies' room first?"

"Sure. Want me to come?"

"No, Dad. I'm a big girl now. I go all by myself at school."

He smirked. "Right, sorry. You do. You know where it is?"

"Dad, I'm not a baby. Of course I do."

Chad held up his hands in self-defense. It was utterly charming to see this powerful man so disarmed by his daughter. She walked quickly toward the employees' bathroom.

"She's adorable," I said once she'd closed the door behind her.

"I agree."

"She looks like a small doll with those pigtails. You're..."

"What?" he asked.

"You're very cute with her." *Be professional, Scarlett. How do you think calling your boss cute is professional?* Then again, I'd shamelessly rubbed myself against his fingers Friday night, so maybe professional wasn't even attainable anymore.

"Scarlett, I appreciate your offer, but your shifts are long enough."

"Chad, it takes no time at all to bake a pie."

"I'm sure someone from the family will be more than happy to show her. Hell, I can bake a pie with her. I'm no slouch in the kitchen."

"No, but sometimes kids prefer to do stuff with strangers. It's more exciting. Besides, you heard her. I'm a *chef*. You're just a lowly CEO."

"Is that so?" Chad leaned forward slightly but then straightened back up quickly, as if he'd caught himself doing something he shouldn't. "You know, word of this might reach the family. Some people might be jealous of you. Like my grandmothers."

"Oh, I can face them," I replied with sass.

Just then there was a distant sound. "What was that?" I asked.

"Forget it. This weekend," he said. "I couldn't stop thinking about Friday."

I sucked in a breath. "It's been on my mind constantly too. Especially a certain part."

The corner of his mouth lifted in a smile. "Really? Which part?"

"Hm, maybe the guy telling us all about the employee ghosts in the hotel. Oh wait, no. I think the Sazerac. And then there was that hot guy giving me a very, very hot kiss. You know what? I think he wins. That was truly the most memorable part of the evening."

"Scarlett, fuck." *Oh no.* The things my imagination could do with those two words were insanely inappropriate. He swallowed hard. "I promised myself that I'd stay away from the kitchen."

"You did?"

"Yeah. How else do you think I can resist you? Look at me. We've been alone for what, two minutes, and I'm already thinking about—" He stopped midsentence, casting his gaze downward and taking a deep breath. I looked down at his hand. It was rolled into a fist on the counter, as if he were seconds away from touching me. I desperately wanted that, but it simply couldn't be.

So I stepped back.

"Right. Maybe I shouldn't have agreed to pie baking so quickly."

"Mm-hmm," Chad said but didn't elaborate.

"Is anyone here?" a female voice asked. It was vaguely familiar.

"That's Mom." Chad stood ramrod straight. Clearing his throat, he continued in a louder tone, "Kitchen."

She stepped into view along with a guy who was clearly Chad's dad. He looked a lot like him, down to the impressive eyes and stature.

"Oh, you're both here," Adele greeted us, her eyes alight.

Chad's dad waved at me. "I'm Remy, Chad's father." He glanced around. "Where's Bella?"

"She's in the ladies' room," Chad said.

"Okay. Scarlett, I hear your first weeks have gone well?" Adele said.

"Yes. I love working here."

"And I'm so happy my boys introduced you to Sazeracs as well."

I froze. *Wait, what? His parents know about my trip to the bar?* I looked to Chad for help.

He just narrowed his eyes at his parents. "Mom...," he said.

"Oh, right. Um..." She smiled at me. "I didn't know it was supposed to be a secret. Xander came by the house over the weekend, and one thing led to another..."

"He told us that you two paid him a visit at the bar," Remy said in a booming voice.

Chad was staring at his father with a raised brow as if they were having a silent conversation.

"We went on a tour," I blurted.

"We heard," Adele added. She sounded as though she was on the edge of laughter. Clearly she wasn't buying that explanation. Oh, I wanted to just run away, and I wasn't a runner. I liked to face everything head-on, but this was just bizarre.

"Anyway," she said, looking at me, "we just came here because we heard from the pastry chef yesterday that you're getting a delivery of fresh shrimp."

"Yes, we are," I said. "I actually found a new source, and it's amazing."

She winked at me. "We know. That's why we came. We want to sneak some for ourselves at home."

I laughed. "Sure, no problem. They should be arriving soon."

She turned to Remy and said, "Let's wait in the front and not disturb these two."

At that moment, Bella sprinted toward us and said, "Nana, you're here. Papa too."

"Yes. Who's my big girl?" Remy said, lifting her into his arms. She gave him a huge kiss on the cheek. "Do you need to go already?" he asked Chad.

"We can still linger for about ten minutes."

"All right, then we'll take this." Adele opened the fridge and took out half an apple pie, obviously knowing where the leftover desserts were stored. Then she opened a drawer and retrieved forks. "And you can tell us all about your weekend, Bella."

"Yes, come on, pretty girl," Remy said as he carried Bella into the dining room.

The second Chad and I were alone, I realized that the tension between us had never subsided. It was just like before we were interrupted—thick and all-consuming. He seemed to feel it, too, because his eyes zeroed in on my lips, and his pupils dilated.

"Scarlett, we need to talk."

"Okay, sure."

He shook his head. "Not right now with my parents half listening from the front, and I'm about to leave with Bella. I know we already spoke about things on Friday."

I nodded. "And we agreed that we've both made promises. Yet the problem is that I've been thinking about breaking mine the whole weekend."

He was impossibly close now... and then his hand was on my waist. I leaned into the touch. God, how I craved it. I hadn't really realized it until now.

"I've just..."

His lips were hovering over mine now. My entire body was vibrating.

"All right, here are the best shrimp in New Orleans." Genaro's voice resounded from the employee entrance.

Chad and I instantly stepped apart, but his eyes were still fixed on me as I hurried to the door and said, "Yep, I'm here. Let me help you."

"I saved the best for you."

"Why, thank you."

"Don't tell anyone in the city that Genaro is selling you shrimp, or I'll have to fight them off."

"I'm afraid word already spread," I said.

Genaro was probably in his sixties. His white hair contrasted with his tanned skin. He'd confided in me that he came from Sicily and moved to the States when he was a kid, and he was upset that he'd lost his Italian accent over the years.

"Oh no," he said theatrically. "Who knows?"

"Just the family who owns the restaurant. Actually, they're here and would love to take some shrimp home with them."

He wrinkled his nose. "Okay. But I only give it to them if they promise not to tell anyone where they got the shrimp."

"Come to the kitchen." I led him from the entrance, noticing Bella and her grandparents were back there too. Chad was once again focused on me.

Oh, I had to tell him that he couldn't look at me like that in public. Though it wasn't that he was even looking at me in a specific way; I was just simmering for no reason. I had to tell him not to look at me at all.

Adele beamed at him. "Genaro, this is such an honor. I couldn't believe it when I heard you're the new supplier. I'm Adele, by the way."

"Nice to meet you, Miss Adele."

Once Genaro set the box of shrimp on the counter, both Remy and Chad shook his hand.

"Genaro, please tell us how Scarlett convinced you to sell us your shrimp when our previous three chefs failed," Remy asked while I loaded shrimp into a smaller box for Adele.

"Well," he said, "Miss Scarlett here is special. I like her a lot more than any of the chefs you had running this place before."

I looked at him, beaming.

"Don't we all?" Chad asked, eyes fixed on me.

Guess who instantly blushed from head to toe?

Yep, that's right: me.

Chapter Eleven

Chad

"Daddy, please," Bella said when we walked up to the front of her school. She put her hands together, pouting. "I really want to learn how to bake with Scarlett."

I lowered myself onto my haunches until I was more or less level with her. "Cricket, I promised I'd talk to her."

"Today."

"Today," I agreed.

"I really like her."

"So do I," I admitted.

My little girl quickly took a liking to others, but even for her, this was fast-paced. I loved that Bella approved of Scarlett, but I didn't want her to get too attached, as I really wasn't sure what we had between us myself.

"All right, inside you go."

"I love you, Daddy."

She put her arms around me and gave me a kiss on the cheek. I hugged her tightly. My marriage had been a huge mistake, but even so, I didn't regret it. Otherwise, I wouldn't have Bella, and that would've left a huge void in my life.

A school bell rang in the distance, indicating kids should be in their homerooms.

"Come on. Go, go, go," I said.

"Oh my God, I'll be late."

I laughed. I'd never heard her say *oh my God* until now. But she was spending more hours each day with peers and teachers than with me. I was bound to miss out on things.

After she was inside, I hurried back to the office. I had back-to-back meetings the whole day, but I'd promised my little girl that I would talk to Scarlett today, and I intended to keep that promise. But that wasn't the only reason. I was looking for an excuse to talk to Scarlett. I wanted to see her, but I knew she was busy in the mornings.

Once in my office, I checked the plan for the week before diving into the to-dos for the day. I took my first break in the early afternoon. Picking up my phone, I checked all my messages.

Mom had posted a picture in the family's group text, then messaged me individually about it.

Mom: Honey, one of my friends sent me this. You should be able to see it from where you are downtown. I swear, I think it's one of the best rainbows ever.

I almost scrolled past it. Mom had a habit of sending us random things like this—pictures of animals, sunsets, what have you. I didn't have time to stop and smell the flowers, so to speak. But... I knew someone who would be very happy indeed to experience this.

I checked the time. It was three o'clock. Past lunch and before the dinner rush.

Perfect.

I followed my instinct and messaged Scarlett.

Chad: Come to the rooftop in 10 minutes.

Scarlett: Why?

I could imagine her eyes widening, her mouth parting.

Chad: The boss demands it.

Scarlett: You're not the boss of me. You said so yourself.

Sassy, just as I'd expected. My cock twitched, which was totally insane.

Chad: Just five minutes.

Scarlett: Okay.

I knew exactly what I wanted to do. I headed down the stairs and left the building only a few minutes later. Scarlett said she always liked to have coffee in the afternoon, and I was going to surprise her.

I went to my favorite coffee shop on Bourbon Street. Not the street that would come to my mind if I ever intended to open another coffee shop, but this one was good, which was saying something.

"Chad," the owner, Maria, greeted me. "To what do I owe the pleasure?"

"I can't make chitchat today, Maria. Just need two espressos to go." I winked at her because the grin spreading across her face said too much.

"Two?" she questioned. "You have a lady friend."

I tried to act like it was nothing, then decided to throw her off the scent. "How do you know it's not someone I'm working with?"

"Process of elimination," she said as she started the machine. "You wouldn't be getting coffees for your brothers or any business partner. You usually just come here on your own. So if you're making the effort of getting your favorite coffee, it's a lady you like a lot." Maria was too savvy for her own good.

"True, but can you keep it a secret?" I admitted.

She rolled her eyes. "Who would I tell?"

I laughed. "The rest of my brothers."

She waved her hand. "I would never do that. That would only encourage them."

As I paid, I replayed her words. "What do you mean?"

"Well, after your visit at the bar with your new chef, they already have plenty of ideas."

I threw my head back, laughing. "Did they spread the news to everyone we know?"

"No, I actually found out from your mother. She stopped by this morning, too, and we got to talking."

I thought the French Quarter was a small world of its own. Then again, my mom owned a gallery on Chartres, and Celine and Isabeau ran their shop with custom-made perfumes on Decatur. They spent most of their time there—they only closed it if they went on vacation and when they filled in at the restaurant as chefs. And my brothers were spread around the Quarter, too, so the LeBlanc family certainly had enough representation.

"Fine. Can you keep this a secret from everyone?" I emphasized.

"You can count on me."

"Thanks, Maria."

With a wave, I headed back out and hurried up to the rooftop. I had to be careful so the coffee wouldn't slosh out of the cups as I went up the stairs. I didn't put any lids on them because I disliked them. In my opinion, it hindered the experience.

Still, I got up to the roof with a few minutes to spare. I looked around, thinking how we really could do more with this space. I had no idea why we didn't use it. The view was great. You could even see the three turrets of St. Louis Cathedral from here.

"I'm here, I'm here," Scarlett said in a rush.

When she appeared, she was wheezing. She stopped in the doorway, leaning forward and resting her hands on her knees.

"Scarlett, you didn't have to run," I said, but when she straightened up, I changed my mind.

She was red in the face and looked absolutely fucking delicious. Then she saw the cups I was holding and licked her lips. My dick twitched again.

"I smell coffee."

I handed her a paper cup. "This is my favorite coffee in the Quarter. Tell me your opinion."

She sniffed it first. "It smells exquisite."

"I know."

Then she took a sip and closed her eyes. "And I am in heaven."

I'd bring her coffee every day if it earned me that smile.

"Thanks, Chad. How did this even happen?"

"You said you love to have a coffee break in the afternoon but don't have time. Hint: I know the owner. I can make that happen."

She whispered, "It's crazy in the kitchen right now."

"But lunch rush is over."

"I know. Dinner is more complicated. I have to—"

"Scarlett," I said, tilting her chin up. "Close your eyes."

She did as I said.

"Now, take a deep breath."

She inhaled deeply and exhaled. It took all my willpower not to lean in and kiss her. She was trusting me, and I didn't want to take advantage.

"Now, open your eyes and look up into the sky."

She turned around and actually gasped. "Oh, a rainbow. This is stunning. All those red and orange colors, and I think that's even a green streak in between the two reds. This is incredible."

She turned to look at me, smiling.

"I thought you'd enjoy it."

Her shoulders finally relaxed. "Thank you, Chad. This means a lot to me."

"I figured you could use the break."

She nodded and took another sip of coffee. "Where did you buy this? I need to go there."

"It's my secret spot over on Bourbon. I'll take you there. It's three blocks away. Then when you go on your own, always tell Maria to make it strong like Chad LeBlanc likes it."

"You're famous there?"

"Maria knows my family."

She was silent for a few beats, just admiring the rainbow.

"So listen, I've been talking to the pastry chef," she said finally.

"Okay."

She wanted to talk shop now? This was not what I had in mind. I wanted her to relax.

"And she agreed that I can make pecan pie every day this week."

"I don't follow."

"So I can bake with Bella every morning."

If I thought it was difficult not to kiss her before, it was almost impossible to rein myself in right now. "You've actually made a plan?"

She nodded vehemently. "Of course. Let's meet at seven."

"Scarlett, that's going to be a long day for you," I said slowly.

"I know, but did you see Bella's face? She was absolutely thrilled."

"She was. She made me promise to talk to you today, and I was going to," I admitted.

"See? That's one problem solved."

"I want something in return," I said.

She narrowed her eyes. "For me spending time with your daughter?"

"I want you to spend time with me."

"Oh." She licked her lower lip. She really had to stop doing that or I was going to kiss her regardless of where we were and who could find us.

"So I'm making our afternoon date a daily thing," I declared.

"Bold of you to assume that."

"Oh, I like my chances," I said.

She was blushing again, and in her white chef's uniform, it was even more visible than Friday night, especially in broad daylight.

"And I'll supply the coffee as well."

"Now you're not just bold, you're downright demanding."

"Shamelessly demanding," I agreed, tilting closer to her.

"But afternoons are so stressful…"

"We'll meet before lunch, then. Mornings."

"Chad, remember last time we spent time together?"

"This is different," I said. "We'll be here at work. People will be watching."

"But why?" she whispered.

"I can't explain it," I admitted. "It just feels right. Like that's exactly what I should be doing every day before lunch."

Her smile was so damn big as she stared at me.

Then she checked her watch. "Oh, goodness. I need to go back to the kitchen."

She hurried to the door and then turned around, looking at me.

"Chad."

"Yeah?"

"Thanks for the coffee date."

I nodded. This was a coffee, all right, but it sure as fuck wasn't a date. I could do far better than this, but Scarlett was even more gun-shy than I was, and she had good reasons.

You both do, a voice in the back of my mind said, but I chose to ignore it.

I stayed on the rooftop for a few more minutes, enjoying the view and my coffee. My phone beeped, and I immediately checked it.

It was an email, though, not a message.

Subject: RSVP Luncheon Follow-up

Dear Mr. LeBlanc,

As you know, the yearly Jazz & Jambalaya Garden Luncheon is coming up on Saturday. We'd be thrilled to have you there—as a guest of honor, of course. Since it's our twenty-fifth anniversary, it will be a more elaborate affair than usual. Please reply to this email if you're interested.

The Garden Luncheon took place in a mansion in the Garden District. The Broussard part of the family started it twenty-five years ago, and the donations gathered from the guests went to a different cause every year. The entire family were honorary members, but we hadn't attended in years, and I was certain no one would be there this year either.

I almost deleted the email, then thought better of it. I knew one person who'd love this.

Scarlett.

CHAPTER TWELVE

CHAD

The next morning, Bella and I were at the restaurant at seven o'clock sharp. Scarlett was already there in her chef's getup. Was it bizarre that I found her incredibly sexy wearing those oversized white shirts and pants?

Bella was ecstatic. "Look, Dad! I told you she's a real chef."

Scarlett did a full turn, and I realized she'd only dressed up for my daughter's benefit. Did this woman know how incredibly difficult she was making it for me to resist her? Not that I'd been doing a great job anyway.

"Ready to start, Bella?" Scarlett asked.

"But I don't have a uniform," she replied.

"Doesn't matter. I have something for you."

Scarlett took out an apron. It was fucking huge for my daughter, but she said, "I can tie it so it fits you perfectly."

"Okay," Bella said. "Can you please do it now?"

"What did we rehearse this morning?" I asked.

"Oh, yes." She looked up at Scarlett and said, "Thank you so much for teaching me how to bake a pie. It means a lot to me."

Scarlett rolled her shoulders back, and her gaze softened instantly. "It's my pleasure. Turn around and I'll tie the apron. I'll also put the cap on you, if that's okay, so we don't get any flour in your hair."

"Yes, yes, yes," Bella said. "No flour."

I watched them with a knot in my throat. After Scarlett finished tying the apron, she grabbed a cap, then handed it to me.

"Do you want to put it on her?" she asked.

"Sure."

It was easy because Bella had pigtails again today, so I couldn't mess it up too much.

"I brought some hair clips with me," Scarlett said. "The cap will be too big otherwise."

She handed them to me and startled lightly when our fingers touched. A current shot through me at the contact, and I immediately glanced at her. Had she felt it too? By the way she quickly looked away, I was betting that she did.

I secured the bonnet on Bella's head with the clips and then straightened up.

My daughter looked up at me. "You can leave now, Daddy. I can stay with Scarlett."

"You're kicking me out?"

Bella shrugged. "So Scarlett and I can have fun."

"And I'm the fun police?" I teased.

She exchanged a glance with Scarlett, and they both started to laugh. Then Scarlett leaned in to Bella. "Tell me the truth. Is he usually the fun police?"

"Sometimes," Bella whispered.

"Hey, I can hear you," I replied. "And I'm staying. I'll need to drop you off at school, remember?"

"Oh. Right," Bella said, and she genuinely looked sad. She'd enjoyed kindergarten much more than school. I'd asked around and found out that it was a normal reaction with kids. But overall, her teachers said she was adjusting well.

"Well, then, Mr. Boss Man, if you're going to stay, you'll need an apron."

She went into the supply room and came back with a black one. "Why don't you put it around you."

"I'm fine," I said.

"You might get flour on this gorgeous suit."

Bella looked at me with pleading eyes. Ah, the things I did for my daughter.

"All right." I took the apron from Scarlett and tied it behind my back.

"You look great, Daddy."

"Come on, let's start," I said. "We don't have that much time."

Bella looked at Scarlett again.

"Yep, you're right. He *is* the fun police," Scarlett muttered.

I liked this cute conspiratorial thing they had going on. I wished Sarah would do fun things like this with Bella. Mostly, Sarah just took her shopping.

It is what it is, I guess.

Scarlett brought out a step stool from the supply room, and Bella climbed it right away. I'd actually intended to participate in the baking process. I knew how to make a pie, but I mostly made it from memory. Scarlett, being a pro, had a completely different approach.

My girl was taking in every step. After three steps, though, she turned to me. "Daddy, could you take notes? I'll forget all this."

"I have an idea," Scarlett said. "Why don't you video us?"

"Yes," Bella exclaimed. "You're so smart, Scarlett."

"Sounds easier than taking notes," I replied while pulling my phone out of my suit jacket.

I centered the camera on them, holding it high enough so my daughter could easily see what was going on when she watched it later.

Scarlett explained everything in layman's terms so anyone could understand what she was talking about.

"We're only learning how to make the crust today, okay?" she said, their hands full of flour and dough.

"What? No, we're making a pie." Bella's voice was a bit whiny, and I was about to caution her when Scarlett responded.

"Yes, but each day I'll teach you more steps, and by the end of the week, you'll have all of them to make a pie."

"Okay," Bella said, sounding a bit suspicious of Scarlett's plan.

I couldn't believe how easily they were getting along. Scarlett patiently showed my daughter exactly how to mix the water and the flour and how to roll out the crust. I knew I'd be the one who had to do this at home because Bella's tiny hands could never apply that pressure needed. But it wasn't for lack of trying, and my girl was a LeBlanc through and through. When she put her mind to it, she definitely gave her best.

"See, first step achieved," Scarlett exclaimed. "Mischief managed."

Bella looked at her with wide eyes. "Are you a *Harry Potter* fan?" Her voice was incredulous.

Scarlett smiled from ear to ear. "Yes. I love it. It's honestly my second personality."

"What's 'mischief managed'?" I asked.

"It's what you have to say after you use the Marauder's Map so the content hides itself and others can't read it."

None of those words made any sense to me.

Bella sighed, then turned to me. "See, Dad? Adults can like *Harry Potter* too."

"What's going on?" Scarlett asked.

"Dad is a Muggle," my daughter explained. "He hasn't seen any of the movies or read any of the books. And he won't let me watch more than *Prisoner of Azkaban*."

Scarlett bit her lower lip. "Well, as a devoted *Harry Potter* fan, I know the movies and books by heart. I totally agree with your dad. The first three are whimsical, but the fourth one is much darker."

Bella groaned.

"But hey, that means you have something to look forward to every year you grow up," Scarlett went on.

"Are they amazing?"

"I can confirm they are."

Bella turned to me again. "See, Daddy? Scarlett likes them."

"Cricket, we don't have time to go into another *Harry Potter* debate right now. We need to get to school on time, remember?"

She groaned again.

"We can talk while baking," Scarlett told her. "Who's your favorite character?"

"Ron because he doesn't like school either."

Scarlett started to laugh. "Good answer."

"And yours?"

"Harry, probably, because he's brave and has a good heart."

They went on to discuss every single character that appeared in the first three movies. I couldn't stop watching them.

Half an hour later, it was time for us to go. "Baby girl, you have another minute," I told her. I'd given them warnings in five-minute increments starting fifteen minutes ago.

"Okay," Bella said, finally climbing down from the step stool. " Can you take the bonnet off my hair?"

"Sure, cricket." I carefully removed the hair clips and the hat.

"I want to go to the bathroom to wash my hands."

"But you can do that at the counter," Scarlett said, "at the kitchen sink."

"The bathroom hand cream smelled so nice." She looked at me pleadingly.

"Fine, go, but be quick." Tomorrow I was going to give them an earlier quitting time so we wouldn't have to rush.

As soon as she darted out, I turned to Scarlett. "Thanks. It means a lot to me."

She licked her lips, giving me a smile before glancing away. "This was so much fun for me too. Oh, we should probably take the apron off you."

"Sure," I said. I unhitched it at my back and then pulled it over my neck, handing it to her.

As she grabbed the fabric, I touched her wrist and circled it with my fingers. "Eleven o'clock. Are we on?"

She gave me a wry smile. "Well, if the owner commands it."

"He fucking does," I replied.

"Then how can I say no?"

I felt shamelessly triumphant. I was going to see her in just a few hours. "I thought about you last night," I confessed.

Her mouth formed an O. "You did?"

"Yeah. I made a list of all the other places in the city you might like."

She swallowed hard and shook her head. "This isn't real," she murmured.

"What?" I asked.

"I'm dreaming this."

"Scarlett..."

She opened one eye and then the other. "Can I poke you?" she asked.

"Go ahead."

She touched my shoulder. "Oh, right. Yep, you're solid. I'm not imagining this."

"What exactly is so hard to believe?"

"You... Just... everything you do."

I raised a brow. "I stopped following a while ago."

"I can't believe you looked things up because I might like them."

I opened my mouth to ask her why the hell not, but Bella stormed back in.

"I'm ready. My hands smell so nice. What is it?" she asked. She came between me and Scarlett and held her hands up.

I bent to inhale the fragrance. "Jasmine," I said.

"Daddy, can we buy it for home too?"

"Sure. I'll tell your grandmothers you like it. Ready to go?"

She nodded.

As Bella ran out of the kitchen, I zeroed in on Scarlett. "See you at eleven o'clock."

"See you," she murmured, a delicious blush spreading over her cheeks.

―――――――――

At eleven sharp, I stepped inside the inner courtyard holding two cups of coffee. One minute later, Scarlett arrived and looked around carefully, her eyes widening when she noticed me. Why was she surprised that I was here? Was she used to everyone just letting her down?

I held out both coffee cups and said, "Different roasts. You pick."

She grinned. "Oh, this is a game now, huh?"

"You pick it, and then I'll tell you what it is. Actually, no, let's make it even more interesting. You guess, and I'll tell you if it's correct."

"Yes, sir. That sounds great."

Hearing her say *sir* sent another jolt below my belt. I was walking with a fucking hard-on around this woman, and it was driving me insane.

She smelled the first cup and then the other. "Okay. This smells like Colombian, and this is Java."

"Correct on both. You know your coffee."

"I do, though I wouldn't say I'm a connoisseur. I just enjoy coffee and sugary drinks from Starbucks. I mostly consider those desserts." She lowered her voice to a whisper. "Although, I will say I much prefer Maria's coffee compared to what we have in the restaurant."

"I agree with you."

"Why don't you change the coffee machine, then?"

"Because it's efficient," I replied as I sipped the coffee. Scarlett had chosen the Java. "We actually did have one of those manual machines in the beginning, and it was a nightmare. The person in charge of coffee was always backlogged, especially on weekends when everyone wants a million different coffees at brunch."

"Hmm, true," she said. "So... what other surprises do you have in store?"

"What are you doing on Saturday?"

"Exploring the city."

I wiggled my eyebrows. "Perfect answer. I want to take you out."

"Where?"

"As you said, it's a surprise."

"But how do you know I'll have a good time?"

"I have a hunch that I can guess what you like pretty accurately." I looked her straight in the eyes because yes, I absolutely meant the innuendo.

My gaze dropped to her lips. "Fucking hell, I thought this was a good plan."

"What?" she asked, bewildered.

"Meeting you here in our courtyard where anyone could walk in on us. I thought it would make it easier for me to keep myself in check. But all I can think about is pinning you right here against this wall and kissing you senseless."

"Yeah, we do like walls and furniture a bit too much," she said, then quickly stepped away from it.

I laughed. "You think that's going to stop me?"

"Well, no, but a girl can try. You have that delicious spark in your eyes. I thought I was imagining it on Friday, but clearly not."

I moved a bit closer to her.

She smirked. "The wall is giving you ideas."

"It's not the wall. It's just you, Scarlett."

She held my gaze for a beat, then looked down at her cup. She was silent as she kept sipping her espresso until the cup was empty.

"Something on your mind?" I asked.

"Just wondering what you're planning for Saturday."

"I'll give you a hint. You will thoroughly enjoy it."

"Oh, that's not fair. I would probably enjoy anything."

"Even better."

She straightened her head, giving me a shy smile. "Fine, but on one condition."

"Name it."

"No more meeting at work. I'll bake with Bella, of course, but no more time alone."

"Why the hell not?" I tilted toward her, needing to understand her reasoning. And to be closer. I always needed to be closer.

"Because I can't get flustered like this twice a day."

I couldn't help but grin. "Why? I think it's great."

"Chad," she chastised.

"All right. The deal is on. Let's see who breaks first." I leaned in as close as I dared. "I have a hunch that it's going to be me."

Chapter Thirteen

Scarlett

"Darling, I almost forgot. I've made you the most gorgeous sweater," Mom said a few days later as we were wrapping up our conversation. We caught up with each other about twice a week. "It's light, perfect for New Orleans. I'll mail it today."

"Aww, thanks, Mom. I can't wait to get it." It warmed my heart that she had time for hobbies nowadays. She loved knitting. While I was growing up, she'd always been working two, sometimes three jobs. We rarely went on vacation—the one time we did, we came to New Orleans. Maybe that's why I remembered it so vividly.

"Listen, I have to hang up. I just arrived at the restaurant."

"Have a great day!"

"Thanks! I love you."

I was so excited to start every day. I loved baking with Bella. We were having so much fun!

And Chad had kept his promise—in fact, he took it a bit too seriously. The man kept at least five feet between us at all times. But it was impossible not to be aware of his presence. He simply consumed me.

I was getting antsier as more of the week passed by. I kept researching events, googling upcoming festivals. There were always a million things happening in New Orleans, but I didn't think Chad was taking me to any of them. Since he was sticking to his part of the promise, I was doing my best to stick to mine.

After Bella and I proudly finished a pecan pie on Friday, she asked, "Dad, can we eat it too?"

"No, we don't have time. You'll be late for school if we don't hurry."

She pouted. "I want to be late."

"That's not possible, though, cricket," Chad said as I took off her bonnet. She didn't have pigtails today, and her dark hair was absolutely gorgeous.

"I liked kindergarten more," she said. "We played and had naps. Now it's all learning and boring." She looked at me sideways with a playful grin that I'd seen on her dad a few times.

"Scarlett, can you make my hair look like yours?" she asked softly.

I frowned. I wanted to ask, *"You mean like a bird's nest?"* But instead I said, "I don't really have a style, though. It's just an updo."

"I want to look like you."

My heart soared. "I have a hair clip in my bag," I glanced at Chad. He was leaning against the opposite counter. "If that's okay?"

"Sure. Go ahead. I'll cut the pie in the meantime."

While I pulled Bella's hair up in a messy updo, he focused on the pie. Once I'd finished fixing her hair, she looked at me with a grin.

"I'm going to the bathroom to look in the mirror. And wash my hands," she announced.

"Sure, cricket," Chad said.

She really loved that lotion. She used more and more every day. Her hands were almost oily with it, but it made her happy. Bella practically darted out the door.

The second Chad and I were alone, the air between us became thick with sexual tension.

My goodness. I thought that after a week, it would get easier. But it didn't.

Still, we'd done so well until now. He wasn't insisting on coffee breaks, and I wasn't pestering him with questions about our outing tomorrow. But as I watched him carefully setting pecan pie on plates, I couldn't help myself and blurted, "Where are we going tomorrow?"

Chad stopped in the act of cutting a slice and glanced at me with a triumphant grin. His eyes glinted. "I was so sure that I'd be the one who'd fail at keeping up my part of the deal."

"So was I," I confessed, and he started to laugh.

"Hey, not funny," I admonished. "I researched everything happening this weekend, and now I'm even more curious than before. I'd like to know how to dress and also where it is so I can plan my day around that."

He frowned. "Right. I didn't think about that. It's a luncheon."

"Oh?" I asked. "So the dress code is... casual?"

He tilted his head. "Not at all."

"Noted. And where is it?"

"I answered one question. I want to ask one of my own before I answer a second one."

I gasped. "That's not fair."

"No, it's not. But I hold all the cards right now." His gaze dropped to my lips for a split second, and my mouth dried up.

"All right. What is it?"

"I'll think about it later. But promise you'll answer it."

"I promise," I whispered. "So... where is it?"

"It's in a mansion in the Garden District."

Oh, wow. That sounded really fancy.

"What time does it start?"

"Noon. I'm dropping off Bella at her mom's at eleven. I get to make her favorite breakfast, which always makes for a fun morning."

I went from flirty to swooning in three seconds flat. That was adorable.

"I can pick you up at, say, 11:40 a.m.," he went on.

"There's no need," I said quickly. "I can meet you there before it starts."

"Scarlett, why don't you want me to pick you up?"

"Well, since it's in the Garden District, I could do a cemetery tour before. They've got one in Lafayette starting at nine, I think."

He grinned. "You really do like your cemeteries, huh?"

"Hey, I didn't get to do the St. Louis tour because a certain someone hijacked my evening."

"I see. But we had fun nonetheless, didn't we?"

My entire body heated up. "Yes, we did," I whispered.

He put a hand on the counter, looking down as if steeling himself. He was about to tilt closer, I was sure of it, but then Bella ran toward us.

"Dad, I love my hair. Did you watch how Scarlett did it?"

"No, I didn't."

She pouted.

"I'll explain it to your dad," I said quickly and made a mental note to buy her some hair clips like mine. They were nothing fancy, but they did the job of keeping stray hairs in their place. "Now, why don't we all enjoy some pie?"

"Yes," Chad said, trapping me with his gaze and making me simmer. "Why don't we?"

Chapter Fourteen

Scarlett

On Saturday morning, I woke up with a grin. Yep, that's right. Not a smile but a grin. I was going to a *luncheon* with a sexy guy in the Garden District, and I was seeing Lafayette Cemetery.

I jumped out of bed, still grinning. I'd already laid my outfit out last night. Even though I'd been dead tired by the time I got back from the restaurant, I didn't want to waste any time in the morning choosing it. It hadn't been easy to pick an outfit that was okay for both a cemetery tour and a fancy brunch, but I was happy with my choice. It was a fluffy spring dress made entirely out of cotton, so even if it got warmer later on, I wouldn't perspire too much, I hoped.

While I went through my morning routine, I kept thinking about Chad. Were we going on a date? Was he just trying to show me around?

Oh, Scarlett, don't try to foresee what might happen. You've never really been good at that, so why even try?

Besides, the whole point of moving to New Orleans was to start over, and I was determined to do just that.

My pink dress was usually a killer with high heels, but I didn't want to wear out my feet so early in the morning, which was why I dressed in flats and took a huge tote bag with me, putting the high heels in it. My plan was to get off the cable car two stations earlier and walk to the cemetery so I could admire the Garden District. I needed good walking shoes for that.

I strolled to the cable car, soaking up the gorgeous sunny day. Then I broke into a run when I noticed it pulling up to the station.

It was such a different experience riding on Saturday morning rather than during the week. It was almost empty, and I easily took in my surroundings, daydreaming about the rest of the day. It was going to be amazing. I could feel it in my bones. And even though the trip to Lafayette from Loyola took a long time, for me it was almost like a tour in itself. I just sat back, enjoyed the ride, and wondered when my life had changed for the better.

Once I got out of the streetcar, I consulted Google Maps. I chose a specific route because there were several mansions that were definitely on my must-see list. I oohed and aahed at the gorgeous homes along the streets.

The architecture was absolutely gorgeous. I loved the Victorian style, but I also enjoyed the homes with the Greek-style columns. The gardens were living up to their name too. The manicured lawns and lush trees turned this place into a paradise. The humidity might not be fabulous for my hair, but it truly was magic for the plants.

One particular home stole my heart. It had a pink facade with green balconies and a wrought iron fence with some sort of exotic shrub all along it. It was high enough that I couldn't really see inside in the garden.

According to Google Maps, my walk to Lafayette Cemetery should've taken twenty-five minutes, but since I stopped every few feet, it took almost forty.

There was a small group in front of the cemetery when I arrived. The place was eerily quiet. A plethora of magnolia trees offered shade along the entrance.

I felt like I'd stepped right into an episode of *The Originals*. The place had a haunting energy even in broad daylight. I could only imagine what it felt like at night.

"Welcome, welcome," our tour guide said. "I'm Esther! We're a small group today, which I prefer. It's why I always take the morning tours. Many people prefer to come late in the evening to get the full haunted experience, but let me tell you, we're going to have the full experience this morning too. The cemetery is fascinating at any time of the day."

We all huddled around our guide as we walked inside. She started by explaining why the graves were built aboveground in the first place—to avoid them being flooded.

I was fascinated with the mausoleums and the tombstones. Some had intricate motifs or even sculptures.

"It's a mix of Gothic Revival and Greek Revival," the guide continued. "I'll point out what's what as we walk through the cemetery."

A particularly captivating tomb had a big statue in the shape of an angel in the center. Other tombs had columns around them or even iron rod fences. Esther regaled us with stories about the families who built them.

My feet were aching a bit. Maybe walking for so long before the tour wasn't the best idea; my feet weren't going to be happy when I changed into heels. But there was nothing I could do about that now.

As we approached the end of the tour, a movement outside the front gate caught my attention. I snapped my head in that direction, and sure enough, Chad was there, pacing. I sucked in a breath. How could I feel his presence from ten feet away?

"All right, unless you have any questions, this is the end of the tour," Esther said.

Usually, I was the most obnoxious person with a hundred questions and asking for a lot of recommendations too. But right now, I simply tipped Esther generously, then darted toward the entrance.

Chad stopped pacing when he saw me coming toward him and just stood with his legs wide apart, one hand in his pocket and the other one at his shoulder, holding his suit jacket with two fingers. He watched me intently, and I felt my body temperature rise with every step.

"You didn't have to leave early on my behalf," he said.

"Oh no, the tour is over. Everyone else is just asking questions."

He glanced down at my dress. "You look fucking stunning."

His words simply took my breath away. *We're starting the day by already using* fucking, *huh?* I had a hunch that things were going to come to a head today, one way or another.

"I wasn't expecting to see you in a suit," I said. "Maybe jeans and a shirt..."

"This is New Orleans. When in doubt, wear a suit. Although, I won't put on the jacket. It's too hot." He swallowed hard and looked at me so intently that I suspected he was fighting the impulse to check me out again. Then again, I didn't look half bad with my dress and my—

Oh my God, I'd forgotten to put on my heels.

I looked down at my feet and then back up at him and laughed nervously. "Would you mind turning around?"

He frowned. "Why?"

"I forgot to change into my heels. I planned to do that before meeting you."

He stared at me. "I don't get it."

"I walked a lot today and needed to wear flats, but in order for the outfit to be complete, it requires heels."

"Why do I have to turn around?" His frown deepened. He even tilted slightly toward me.

"I don't know. It feels weird for you to watch me change my shoes. I feel like I'm changing my clothes in front of you."

"Scarlett."

Belatedly I realized just how inappropriate that was. His eyes darkened while my entire body tightened up.

"Let me get one thing out of the way. If I ever had the privilege of you taking off your clothes in front of me, I'd like to watch and worship your body."

I couldn't even breathe. His words, the way he looked at me... God, he was intense. I'd never had a guy act this way around me. No one had ever wanted me so deeply, making me feel so needed. It made me wonder why I was holding myself back from enjoying Chad. Just because my last relationship was so crappy didn't mean that's what this could turn out to be.

Oh my, what am I thinking?

He broke eye contact, glancing at my feet. "I'll help you change. What do you need me to do?"

"Just hold my hand, I guess, while I put on the shoes."

There was a magnolia tree a few feet away that I could lean up against. But between a tree and a hot man, I preferred the support of a hot man, since he'd offered and all. It still felt a bit weird taking off my flats and putting on my heels in front of him, but what the heck?

I stretched out my left hand and he grabbed it, interlacing our fingers. The gesture felt very intimate. I quickly put on my heels, and when I straightened up, he squeezed my fingers even tighter and then drew his thumb over my palm. Sparks of heat shot throughout my entire body. I was so surprised that I wobbled a bit. Only slightly at first, but then my heel got stuck in something, and the next thing I knew, I was falling backward.

Chad disappeared from my field of vision, but then I felt his strong hands around me, and my back hit his chest.

"I've got you," he murmured in my ear.

I looked down at my feet. My heel had gotten caught in some tree roots poking through the asphalt of the sidewalk. I straightened up immediately.

"Are you okay?" he asked.

"Yeah. Thanks for catching me."

"No problem."

He stood behind me, keeping a hand on my waist for a few seconds longer. There was absolutely no need for him to linger, but I loved that he did. When he finally stepped to one side, I felt very cold and empty of his touch.

"Ready to go?" Chad asked.

"Definitely."

He held out his arm. I laughed, as he obviously wanted to make sure I didn't take another tumble on our way. "I didn't realize there were so many potholes."

I took his arm gladly, and we walked leisurely down the street.

"So, want to spill the beans now?" I asked.

"Yes. We're going to the 35th Annual Jazz & Jambalaya Garden Party."

"It's a private event, isn't it? I don't remember reading about it online."

"You're right. It's an invitation-only event."

"Oh, and you got one? You're important around here, huh?" I teased.

He bestowed one of those dazzling panty-melting smiles upon me before saying, "The Broussard part of the family actually started it. I don't think I've been for almost six years. Usually, I don't go to these types of events at all."

"So how come you're attending this year?"

"I wasn't going to, but I thought you would enjoy it."

"Chad," I whispered, "we don't have to go if you don't enjoy this type of thing."

"I like spending time with you."

I wasn't sure what to say. His words touched me deeply. "Oh, I can't wait. Who else is going to be there? Will I know anyone?"

"I don't think so. No one from the family attends, or at least I don't think they will." He frowned. "I should've checked."

"So there's a lot of jambalaya and a lot of jazz, right?"

"There's other food as well, but I'm sure there will be at least ten different types of jambalaya."

"That's a chef's heaven. I can't wait to taste them. I do want to sharpen my skills at local cuisine anyway. How far is the house?"

"Just a few minutes," he said.

As we continued walking, I kept wondering which mansion it was. Five minutes later, we stopped in front of one of the most beautiful ones I'd seen to this point. It was huge—white facade, grandiose columns, and dark blue shutters.

"Is this...? Does your family own this?"

"No, this is a museum. They rent out the garden for parties."

We walked through the front gate, which was wide open. The gravel path snaked through the perfectly manicured greenery, and we passed magnificent dark red roses in full bloom. As we walked around the house, the voices started growing louder.

"How many people are attending?"

"Probably a hundred," he said.

A young man came up to us, holding an iPad. I realized he was in charge of welcoming the guests.

"Hello. May I have your names, please?" he asked.

"Yes. Chad LeBlanc, for two."

"Oh, Mr. LeBlanc, the rest of your family is already here."

I whipped my head toward him.

"Who exactly is here?" Chad inquired.

The man looked down. "I have Julian, Xander, Zachary, Anthony, Beckett, Adele, Remy, Isabeau, Felix, Celine, and David."

Chad started to laugh and then frowned, looking at me. "My mistake. Should've checked in with my family. Apparently, the entire clan is here."

"All right. So what now?" I wasn't certain where we stood. Sure, I'd met his family, but this was a bit different.

He winked at me. "Let's give them something to gossip about."

I grinned and nodded. If he was up for it, then so was I.

He put a hand at the small of my back as he guided me farther inside the garden. It was very crowded, and I was certain it would take us a while to even find his family.

I was wrong. Two seconds later, Julian stepped up to us, staring at his brother incredulously.

"How did Mom even rope you into this?" he asked, then turned to me. "Hello, Scarlett."

"She didn't," Chad replied.

Anthony and Beckett came up then too. Or was it Xander and Zachary? No, I was certain I had them right.

All the LeBlanc brothers were tall and handsome, but there were subtle differences between them. Both Julian and Chad had the same dark brown hair and iridescent blue eyes. Anthony and Beckett had similar hair but vivid green eyes. Beckett looked really young. Xander's and Zachary's hair was even darker, and their eyes were dark brown as well.

"I guess now my entire family is complete," Anthony said. "And Scarlett, it's good to see you again. You know, we were so certain that Chad wasn't coming back to the bar that night. Imagine our surprise."

"Here's to you for kicking him out," Beckett said, holding up a drink.

Chad grinned. "Beckett, behave."

"That's not possible, man."

Holy shit. I'd been with the LeBlanc brothers for all of two minutes, and I was already blushing.

"What's the holdup?" Xander's voice came from behind. "Thought you were getting drinks."

He actually stumbled when he noticed me and then Chad. He immediately pointed at Beckett. "Behave."

I laughed. "Too late."

Xander sighed. "Really? You already gave her a hard time?"

"Not at all, man. I just praised her," Beckett continued.

"All right, I need to find out how this happened," Chad said. "How is the entire family here, and why didn't I even know about it?"

Xander shrugged. "Mom actually called us one by one and asked us to attend this year since it was a special anniversary. She might have mixed up the weekends and figured you were out of town."

Chad nodded. "My New York meeting got postponed."

Xander looked between the two of us with a frown. "So you came here on purpose?"

"He figured I might enjoy it," I chipped in, trying to help.

But now Xander was flashing Beckett a grin—he looked a lot like Julian at the moment. "I take it back. You do your thing. This is getting more entertaining by the day."

Huh? What just happened?

"Come on, let's go find the rest of the family," Chad said. He looked at me with a playful glint in his eyes. "Are you ready?"

I chuckled. "I'm not really sure how to answer that."

"That's for the best." That came from Anthony. "When it comes to meeting the entire gang, it's better if you keep an open mind and lower your expectations. You just never know what will happen."

Chapter Fifteen

Scarlett

We walked farther into the garden. There were many people milling around, holding drinks. I was proud of my outfit, and it perfectly fit the garden party vibe. I spotted Zachary first and then Celine and Isabeau. The latter two were sitting down next to elderly gentlemen, who I assumed were their husbands. Remy was there, too, with an arm around Adele's waist.

When we reached the group, Zachary noticed us first. He didn't even say hi to his brother, just gave me a wide smile and said, "Well, well! What an interesting turn of events."

"Chad, darling! What a surprise to see you here. Oh, and you brought our dear Scarlett," Adele said.

My heart fluttered. I was their *dear Scarlett*? How? Why? Though I had to admit, I liked the sound of it so very, very much.

She came over to me, kissing my cheek. "Mom, Isabeau, and I decided you're our good luck charm. Not just because you convinced Genaro to sell the restaurant his shrimp, but you've also made Bella very, very happy this week."

"Oh, it was my pleasure," I replied. "She's a very fast learner."

"Now, who here don't you know?"

The two elderly gentlemen rose to their feet with ease and each shook my hand.

"I'm David Broussard, Adele's dad. Very happy to meet you," the first one said.

"And I'm Felix LeBlanc," the other gentleman said. "Already heard a lot about you from my wife."

At that precise moment, I realized that both Celine and Isabeau were looking at me with far less reluctance than when I'd first met them. Celine actually rose to her feet and grabbed my hand, coming closer and kissing my cheek. How was no one shell-shocked that I'd shown up at all? Both she and Isabeau had their hair in very elegant updos and were wearing black dresses. They were both very classy and didn't look their ages at all—on the contrary, they looked very sophisticated.

"Did Chad tell you all about the event?" Celine asked.

I nodded. "Yes. He said there's a lot of jambalaya to taste."

"I figured she'd enjoy a slice of New Orleans culture," Chad said.

Isabeau laughed, and Adele gave her what I thought might be a warning look. "Oh, darling, don't think you can fool us. First you go to Julian's bar and now here." Isabeau winked at me. "Just so you know, that's not our grandson's usual behavior."

"I'm not even sure how to react," I said honestly, and the entire group started to laugh. I couldn't believe they were so laid-back. For some reason, I'd imagined them different. Probably because everyone I'd met seemed to cower away when they heard Isabeau's name.

"Isabeau," Adele chastised.

"What? Oh, darling, you know me. I say what I mean."

"Yes, dear, we're all very aware of your honesty policy," Felix said, clearly fighting laughter.

"Want to check out the jambalaya?" Chad asked me.

I nodded. "Oh, yeah. I'm definitely ready. Luckily I didn't have a big breakfast."

When I wobbled a bit on my feet as we walked through the gravel, Chad offered me his arm, and I gladly took it.

"Sorry about that. I genuinely didn't think we'd run into anyone here," he apologized.

"Your grandmothers gave a totally different vibe today."

Chad started to laugh. "Don't tell me you were actually afraid of them. You handled them perfectly that first day."

"Not afraid... but they did seem a bit intimidating."

"Yeah, they do have that intimidation tactic down pat."

"Your grandmothers are quite young, aren't they? I didn't realize that until now."

"Yes, very. They had kids early. I think Celine was nineteen and Isabeau twenty. And my parents also had kids at a young age. Mom was nineteen."

"Ah, now I understand why your grandparents weren't thrilled about your parents getting married."

"Exactly. So, this is the jambalaya table," he said, pointing at a long table with several bowls on it. There was a stack of cutlery on one end. I liked the simple yet elegant setup.

"Chad," I said as I grabbed a plate, "what did Isabeau mean when she said this isn't your usual behavior?"

He didn't reply right away, and I looked up, wondering if he'd heard me. His gaze was fixed on me.

"After my divorce, I sort of... stopped enjoying things. And they noticed. But ever since I met you, something's changed. I'm enjoying every second when I'm with you."

My heart soared. "So am I," I confessed.

His gaze turned, if possible, even more intense, and his lips curled up in a smile. This was more than just a panty-melting smile. It was panty exploding.

"Do you need a plate, or...?" an elderly man interrupted, and I realized we were in everyone's way.

Chad held a hand in front of me and said, "After you."

We moved forward, and I selected six different types of jambalaya. I frowned at Chad's plate. He only had one. "You're not tasting more?"

He shrugged. "I already know my favorite."

Once we'd finished, I looked into the distance at his family.

"Did you always know that you wanted to be part of The Orleans Conglomerate?" I blurted.

"Yeah. I don't think any of us ever thought we'd be doing anything else," he answered without hesitation. "As kids we all worked at the restaurants since we were twelve or something."

"That's young," I remarked as I tasted the fourth jambalaya. I was going to try Chad's favorite last.

"It was our parents' way of making sure we grew up with a good head on our shoulders. To get pocket money, we had to do chores or work at the restaurants. Or the bakeries. Then when we were of age, we worked in the bars too. It's all I ever wanted to do. Same goes for my brothers. We were happy carrying on with the Broussard and LeBlanc companies."

"Speaking of the devils," I said. Xander and Zachary were coming our way.

They looked at our plates. "Don't tell me you only got your favorite, Chad," Xander teased his brother.

"Why not?"

"You haven't been here in years. It never occurred to you that they might have changed some of the other recipes?" Xander asked. "Why don't you try to be more relaxed about things?"

Chad zeroed in on him. "*You* are telling me to be more relaxed? You're the one who always wants to control every detail."

"I accept that as a fault of mine. Or a quality, depending on how you look at it." He glanced at me. "Between the two of us, I think I'd rather consider it a quality."

I nodded and answered as seriously as I could. "I'm a chef, so I'm all about being precise and exacting."

Xander smiled triumphantly, then turned to Chad. "But when it comes to tasting jambalaya, there are no rules."

Zachary cleared his throat, looking between me and Chad. "Do you need me to come up with an excuse for the two of you to leave?"

And just like that, we went from making chitchat to me blushing again. What was it with me around LeBlanc men?

"Wh-What?" I stuttered.

Chad pointed at Zachary. "I thought I had to warn Beckett, not you."

He held up his hands. "Hey, I'm only trying to help. You know I'm very good at managing situations."

"We don't need your help, but thanks."

"Suit yourself. Anyway, we came to get you. Dad wants to talk about that deal with the drinks supplier."

"Sure. I'll be right there," Chad replied, then focused on me. "Want to come too?"

"Oh no, you go do your thing. I'll just explore."

"I won't be long," he said.

After the guys left, I finally tried the jambalaya he'd suggested. Damn—there was a reason why the man was running the restaurant part of the business. This one was far superior to the others. The flavors were more balanced, making it more complete. My chef's taste buds told me that they'd added some unusual spices as well, such as cinnamon and star anise. That was a very interesting and bold choice. I was going to keep that in mind for when I experimented with my own recipes.

"I see Chad has talked you into trying his favorite," Isabeau said.

I startled slightly.

"Oh, I'm so sorry," she said. "I didn't mean to scare you."

"I didn't see you come up." Pointing at the jambalaya, I said, "This is definitely the best."

She winked. "It's my recipe."

I started to laugh. "Chad didn't tell me that. It truly is amazing. Could I have the recipe?"

She looked at me for a beat before asking, "What do you know about great chefs?"

"Ah, you never give away your recipes. Then I'll just have to experiment on my own."

"That's my girl." She looked back at the group and said, "You know, I had a good feeling about you ever since I saw you that first day. I thought you lit something up in Chad."

I nearly choked on a mouthful of jambalaya. I didn't expect the conversation to go this way. The LeBlancs didn't pull punches.

"Whatever it is you're doing," she continued, "you have the family's support."

I blinked several times as I swallowed the food. "I'm not doing anything."

"Well, then keep doing just that. It's going very well," Isabeau said. "And during breaks, you're welcome to stop by my store."

"You have a store?" I was stunned.

"Yes. Once age caught up with me and I couldn't be on my feet all day, every day in the kitchen, I realized I needed to find something else to do. The idea of retiring is preposterous, so Celine and I opened a perfume shop in the Quarter."

"I'll definitely stop by. What's the name?"

"Fragrant Delights, on Dumaine. We can make you a custom fragrance if you want."

"Yes! I've always wanted one. I thought it was too difficult."

"It's not. From one chef to the other, we have a way with fragrances."

"I'm excited," I admitted.

"Lovely."

"Are your husbands also working with you at the shop?"

She chuckled. "Oh, no. Those boys couldn't wait to retire. They spend a lot of time out on the bayou, fishing. Let me tell you, I had to learn more recipes for cooking fish after I retired than in my entire career as a chef. But it makes them happy."

"I can share some of my fish recipes with you," I offered even though it was a cardinal mistake. Offering a chef recipes they didn't ask for was akin to telling them they didn't have an imagination.

To my astonishment, Isabeau said, "I'll consider it. And thank you."

"What for?"

"Getting Chad here today." She nodded toward the group. Celine was coming toward us.

"I really didn't do anything."

"Be that as it may, it's a nice surprise. Also, thank you for being so kind to Bella."

"She's adorable," I gushed. "So eager to learn."

"I know," Isabeau replied just as Celine joined us. Julian was also heading our way.

I narrowed my eyes. "I hope you weren't upset when Bella asked that I show her how to bake a pie."

"I was a little jealous when I first heard about it. But then I realized it was a fantastic way for you and Chad to spend time together."

"Isabeau," Celine said, "don't scare the poor girl away."

Isabeau turned to face Celine. "I'm not doing any such thing."

"She really isn't," I said. "Isabeau was just telling me that you have a store in the Quarter."

Celine roped her arm through Isabeau's and said, "Well, I wouldn't want to spend my retirement any other way other than making custom fragrances with this one all day long. Who'd have thought we would become such great friends, huh?"

"Not our parents," Julian said, joining us. The two women turned to their grandson, who was looking at me. "Did Chad tell you that there was a whole Romeo and Juliet situation in the family with our parents?"

"Julian!" Celine said.

"He didn't give too many details," I said, eager to know more.

"Yeah, the two of them were competitors, the bakeries, the restaurants, the bars. They weren't sold on their union for a long time. I always say that Mom called me Julian in loving memory of her favorite Shakespeare play, *Romeo and Juliet*. Mom can hold a grudge."

Celine started to laugh, but Isabeau didn't contradict Julian, which made me suspect that he might be onto something.

"Julian, darling, stop sharing family secrets," Isabeau said.

I couldn't believe it. He was *totally* onto something.

"One of these days, I'll learn how to keep my mouth shut," Julian said, "but today is not the day." He glanced at me. "Don't worry. Chad's coming to rescue you from us."

Chad was actually heading our way. He frowned when he noticed his grandmothers and picked up his pace. God, how could he be so attractive? His brothers were, too, but something about him made my knees go weak and my panties—

No, I wouldn't think about my panties right now.

"What's this about, Julian? You're letting these two corner Scarlett?" Chad asked.

"No, I came to rescue her. I was only half successful, but that just earns you a point as her white knight."

"Oh, Julian! Really!" Celine chastised.

"Come on, both of you. I'll walk back to the table with you so can pounce on me some more." Then he looked at Chad. "See? This is me sacrificing for your sake."

After the three of them left, Chad smiled at me. "All good?"

I nodded. "I like your grandmothers."

He looked down at my plate. "I see that you agree with me."

I glanced at the plate and laughed. The only heap of jambalaya I had finished was Isabeau's. "Your grandmother is an excellent chef."

"I'd say so. Listen, the jazz band is going to start playing soon. Do you want to stick around for them?"

"What's the alternative?" I asked, suddenly feeling breathless. When had he stepped closer to me?

"The alternative is you and me somewhere that we're not surrounded by every single LeBlanc and Broussard and their friends."

I bit the inside of my cheek. "Can we first listen to jazz and then do that?"

"Sure. Whatever you want."

I felt good about my decision... for about half an hour. Even though the jazz music was absolutely superb and in a league of its own, I couldn't help but think about whatever was going to come next. What did Chad want to do?

By the time he suggested we go say our goodbyes to the family, I didn't even hesitate. I liked jazz music, but I liked the thought of being alone with Chad a lot more. We didn't even get to speak to everyone because they were all engaged in conversations. And Anthony and Beckett had already left, so clearly a formal goodbye wasn't necessary.

Afterward, we walked back around the gravel path to the entrance. After spending a few hours on my heels, I was already getting blisters, so putting one foot in front of the other was painful, not to mention that it was affecting my balance. I was trying very hard not to let Chad notice, but it was clear that he did because he put an arm around my waist, shepherding me without saying a word.

And I thought I couldn't like this man even more.

Once we stepped outside the gate, he let go of my waist and said, "Scarlett, you look fucking sexy in those heels." I nearly dropped my bag from shock. Holy shit, I hadn't expected him to be so forward. "But I think you're in pain. Don't you want to change into your flats?"

"N-No," I stammered. "Really, this outfit goes best with heels."

"I was going to suggest we walk for a while so I can show you some of my favorite homes around the neighborhood."

"Okay, okay, I'll change," I said immediately because helloooo, having a local walk with me through the Garden District would be so damn amazing.

As gracefully as possible, I changed my shoes. After I'd secured my heels in the bag, I asked, "Which way? Do you actually live here in the Garden District?"

"No. My parents and grandparents live here, though. I have a house in the Marigny. I didn't want to be *in* the French Quarter but needed to be close by."

We walked around the Garden District for about two hours, and Chad was a great guide. He even knew the history behind some of the more famous homes. At around five o'clock, he suggested we head to the French Quarter, but my feet were too sore.

"I really don't think I can walk anymore," I admitted.

"No problem. What do you say about me cooking dinner for you at my house?"

Ooooh, danger, danger, danger. Alarm bells rang in my mind. Chad and me alone at his place? This had... *sexy potential.*

You're crossing a line, Scarlett. Remember the last time.

But I didn't want to remember last time. Chad was nothing like Simon.

So instead of coming up with an excuse to go home, I said, "I'd love that."

Chad smiled triumphantly. "I'll order us an Uber. Let's see what you think of my cooking skills. My ex—" He fell silent for a moment, then shook his head. "Sorry, I don't know why I even brought that up."

"I don't mind. Do you want to talk about Bella's mom?" I asked, feeling shy for some reason. I wanted to know more about him, his past, his life.

"There isn't a lot to say. We got married on a whim. We'd been dating for a while, so it wasn't hurried or anything, but looking back, we'd always been far too different to actually be able to last. We were already heading down the divorce lane during our first year of marriage, and then we found out she was pregnant with Bella."

I gasped. "Oh."

"We both decided to try our best, and well, it wasn't enough." He sounded frustrated.

"I'm sorry."

"I was determined to give it my all. I grew up in a huge family, and we've always been loyal to each other, and that was very important to me."

"Of course."

"Not to her."

I stilled, folding my hands in my lap. "I'm sorry." I didn't ask for more details, not wanting to rub salt in a wound.

"She thought our life would be attending one party after another. She's a socialite and somehow expected me to drop work and do the same. When we realized that we truly couldn't save our relationship, I suggested that we simply try our best to be Bella's parents and see if therapy could help. During the first therapy session, she nonchalantly mentioned that she'd been sleeping with someone else. That she'd taken our agreement to mean that we could lead separate private lives. I was shocked. Even the therapist told us there was no point in trying to save our marriage and that it would be in Bella's best interest if we went our separate ways. I filed for divorce the next day. I started by thinking it would be amicable, but it still took a long time. We're in a much better place now. We don't actually interact much, just when I pick up and drop off Bella. We're civil, but we'll never be friends."

"Civil is good, Chad."

He nodded, taking out his phone. "Now, let me order that Uber."

During the ride, we spoke about the Marigny and several other neighborhoods in New Orleans. Chad's home was a few blocks away from Frenchmen Street. His house had three stories, and there were no balcony railings, at least on the side facing the street, but I suspected there was something facing the inner courtyard.

"Welcome to my lair," he said, opening the door. He gestured for me to walk in first. I knew this was a defining moment for both of us.

"Thank you for the invitation" was all I said, putting a little extra sway in my hips as I walked in front of Chad. I felt his eyes on me the entire time.

And I liked it.

CHAPTER SIXTEEN

CHAD

"Your house is gorgeous," she said as we stepped into the living room. Three out of the four walls had huge sliding floor-to-ceiling glass doors that looked into the garden. "And the yard... I can't believe it. Are those twinkle lights?"

I laughed. "Yes. Bella insists on having them all the way from Thanksgiving until Mardi Gras. Actually, last year, she talked me into leaving them on for even longer. That's why I decided not to go through the trouble of taking them down."

She sighed, looking at them lovingly.

"You want me to turn them on, don't you?" I asked.

"How could you tell?"

"You lit up—pun intended."

She smiled. "They look cute. I've never seen a magnolia tree lit up."

"Say no more." I took out my phone. Two clicks later, the lights were on.

"A smart home—love it."

"The first thing I told my architect when I bought this place was that I wanted it to be a smart home."

She smiled dreamily at the tree.

"Do you want a drink?" I asked.

"Can you make a Sazerac?"

"Of course. I was born and bred in New Orleans."

"Well, I got a taste of it. Let's see if yours is as good as Julian's."

I tilted a bit closer. "It's better."

"I'll be the judge of that."

She'd gotten more and more relaxed today, and progressively sassier, which I thoroughly enjoyed.

"When did you move in here?" she asked as I led her to the bar area. It was small compared to the rest of the living room. The couch took up most of the space, but I liked it this way.

"Once divorce proceedings began, I started searching for homes."

Scarlett sat on a bar stool, and I realized her dress had a slit on the left side. It went very high up on the apex of her thigh.

Fuck me. You're not going to maul her, Chad. Not yet. Where the hell are your manners?

Instinct overpowered me, and I immediately moved to the other side of the bar. It was useless. How would it feel to have those long legs wrapped around me? I took out everything I needed for the Sazerac. Scarlett looked at me intently while I mixed the ingredients.

When I handed her the cocktail, she gave me a small smile before raising the glass to her lips. After the first sip, she closed her eyes and dropped her head back.

I wasn't going to be able to keep myself in check. I walked back around the bar, standing next to her. "So, what's the verdict?"

When she looked at me, she startled slightly. "This just sent me to heaven and back." She lowered her voice to a whisper. "And yeah, it is much better than your brother's. I won't tell him that, though. I don't want to hurt his feelings."

"Don't worry. I will. Competition is second nature in the LeBlanc family."

"Noted. " She moved, and her dress's slit fell open even farther. "Oh!" She quickly glanced from her lap up to me.

I was so hungry for her that I could barely control myself. So instead of fighting my instincts, I gave in to them. I captured her mouth, savoring the taste of Sazerac on her lips. She moaned the second I stroke my tongue along hers. I spread her legs wide and stepped between them. She instantly pressed her thighs against mine.

"I want you," I said.

She whimpered against my lips, opening her eyes.

"Yes," she whispered.

I touched her face with my thumb, moving it to the corner of her mouth and then her cheek.

"I want you so damn badly."

I kissed her again, but I didn't like this position. She was far too low. I wanted to be able to explore her neck, her chest, all of her. I slid my hands under her ass and lifted her from the bar stool to the counter. Fuck yes, this was much better. Now I could kiss her neck all I wanted, and that's exactly where I went next. I moved my mouth down the front of her neck and onto her chest, tracing a line on her skin.

"This has been teasing me all day. Are you wearing a bra?" I asked.

"No." Her voice was breathy. She was already shaking a bit. "The dress has padding—"

I didn't wait to hear the rest of the sentence. I pushed the fabric of her neckline to one side, and her left breast peeked out.

She'd been walking around like this all day? I teased her nipple with the flat of my tongue a few times before taking it into my mouth. She arched her back at the contact, and my erection grew so hard, it was nearly painful. I immediately undid the buckle of my belt and then the zipper, pushed down my pants and briefs, and gave myself a good squeeze.

It helped me relieve some of the tension, but not enough. Not nearly enough. I knew that only sinking inside her would satisfy me.

I uncovered her other breast and cupped it in my hand, feeling the weight of it in my palm before moving my mouth to that nipple. The second I sucked it into my mouth, she moaned, grabbing my hair. This nipple seemed more sensitive than the other one. I took my mouth off her only enough so I could speak.

"Are you wet for me, Scarlett?"

"Yes. Yes, I am," she panted.

"How wet?"

She laughed nervously and said, "Very."

"I'd better check."

I felt her entire body spasm. I was going to fuck her right here on this counter if she kept reacting so beautifully.

She lifted her ass as I pushed her dress up to her waist, and I yanked her closer to the edge of the counter. When I brushed my thumb over her panties, my vision turned completely black. She hadn't been exaggerating—the fabric was almost soaked through. She groaned, and I thought she was even more on edge than me. It wouldn't take much to make her come. I slid my hand inside her panties, grazing her clit first before dipping my finger inside her. Her shoulders arched backward.

"You're so damn wet."

"Yes. Yes!" Scarlett cried out when I pressed my thumb on her clit.

I straightened up a bit so I could take her in.

"You're so on edge," I said, moving my finger slowly. "After I left that night, did you pleasure yourself?"

"No," she whispered while sucking in a breath.

"You've been on edge like this ever since?"

She nodded.

"That's not good. I'll make sure to give you enough orgasms tonight to make up for that."

Her eyes flew open, and she looked straight into my eyes.

I drew her lower lip between mine before letting it go and confessed, "When I went home that night, I did take care of myself while thinking about you." She whimpered, closing her eyes and frowning as I increased the pressure of my strokes. "I thought about you, about how it would feel to sink inside you. It took the edge off, but it was nowhere close to what I wanted. I wanted your pussy."

"Oh my God, Chad." Her face was red. She let go of the edge of the counter and then grabbed it again even tighter.

"I'm going to fuck you so good tonight, Scarlett. I promise you, babe. We'll start with an orgasm here."

She went off the next second, dropping her head back. Her cry was guttural, animalistic. A wave of tension coursed through her body. I could practically see her muscles contract and then turn completely soft. Her fingers gripped the counter fiercely, and then she let it go.

I put a hand around her waist, splaying my palm wide on her back so she wouldn't hurt herself. Her eyes flew open, and she blinked, sitting confused for a few seconds. Then she grabbed at the collar of my shirt, pulling me closer. I kissed her so damn hard that I could barely breathe. She was different now after the orgasm, even wilder. I only paused because I needed to get my bearings; otherwise, I was liable to turn her around and sink inside her right here, right now.

First things first: I wanted her completely naked. "Let's get that sexy dress off you," I said.

She nodded, and I pulled it over her head. Her wrists got tangled in it, which gave me an idea. Instead of freeing her, I said, "How do you feel about me tying up your hands?"

She swallowed hard, licking her lips, then nodded wordlessly. My cock twitched as I used her dress to bind them behind her. Then I got another idea. "I'm in the mood for some Sazerac. Lean back."

I got rid of her panties as she followed my instructions. Then I grabbed the glass and poured a few drops of the drink between her breasts. She gasped as soon as it hit her skin. The ice had melted, so the liquid was cold. I licked the trail with the flat of my tongue, then poured more just above her navel. I let it almost reach her pussy before licking it up. I swiped her clit with the tip of my tongue in the process, and her thighs shook. She was ready to come again. Instead of putting my mouth on her pussy, I straightened up, claiming her mouth instead. I kissed her slowly, almost lazily.

The front of my body pressed against hers, and I felt every vibration that coursed through her. I pulled her ass all the way to the edge of the counter and pushed my pelvis forward, rubbing the length of my cock against her entrance.

Fuuuuuck!

I buried my face in her neck as I moved my pelvis back and forth again with slow, controlled moves. How could this already feel insanely good?

Belatedly, I realized why. I didn't have a condom on.

I pulled back, drawing a deep breath, and said, "Damn it, I need to get a condom." Then I remembered. "Shit, I don't have any." Why did I lose my mind like this?

"We don't need one, if that's okay with you?"

If that's okay? It sounds like heaven to me.

I looked her straight in the eyes. "I'm healthy. I got tested."

"So did I. I've been on birth control since forever. So please, Chad, don't stop."

I looked down between us and rubbed my cock up and down her entrance again. She was high on the counter, so I couldn't give her the full length, but I did brush her clit with the crown. Her legs shook again, and I knew just how I was going to make her come a second time.

I leaned over her, kissing her hard while I grinded up and down her pussy. Moving my hips in slow, deliberate movements, pressing all of my dick against her clit, I felt her coming closer with every stroke. When she finally gave in to the pleasure, it reverberated through my entire body.

She thrust her chest forward and moaned against my mouth. I'd loved hearing her scream the house down before, but there was something intimate about kissing her in this moment when she was so completely vulnerable.

It took her longer to recover this time. Her breath was completely erratic. I kissed down her neck, feeling her pulse against my lips.

"Chad," she whispered.

"We're going to the bedroom, sweetheart. Or I'm going to fuck you right here."

"Oh," she gasped. The way she looked up at me through hooded eyelids told me she wouldn't object to that.

As she sat up, I freed her hands. She immediately put them on my arms and looked between us, giggling before grabbing my cock and squeezing it.

"You like this?"

"Seeing you dressed up with your cock poking out? Yes, I do."

Putting one arm around her back and the other under her knees, I lifted her off the counter, then carried her through the house and up the stairs. They creaked with every step.

The master bedroom was on the second floor. The door was wide open, and Scarlett looked around as I stepped inside.

"This is exquisite," she murmured.

The bed was huge, with a metal railing as a headboard. I had very exact ideas about that headboard and her dress and wrists, but not right now. Her hands were busy working my shirt, and it was already on the floor by the time we reached the bed.

I laid her on the bed, and she quickly took off my pants and boxers. Kicking them away, I stumbled onto the bed. I scooted her toward the center of it and rested on my knees, just watching her. Her hair was in complete disarray. A few strands even fell into her eyes. Her knees were bent to one side, which gave me an idea.

"Turn onto your side."

"Okay." Her eyes widened, but she immediately moved onto her right side, looking at me over her shoulder. "Like this?"

"Yes."

I kissed the side of her body, starting from her ankle and moving up to the knee. I heard her suck in a breath as I went farther up her thigh. I was only touching her with my lips, my hands flat on the mattress. When I went up her rib cage, she sucked in a breath. I made a small detour to her breast, licking her nipple. Then I laid down on one side as well, positioning my cock behind her.

I lifted the leg she had on top and thrust inside her. I intended to only give her the head, but I couldn't hold back, not anymore. She was just so wet that she took me in all the way.

"Fuck, Chad." Her voice shook, and there was a light tremor in her body already.

She squeezed me good with her inner muscles. I could hardly breathe. My entire body felt on fire, especially my cock. I moved my hips, thrusting in and out of her, watching her gorgeous face.

I liked this angle because I could reach her clit easily. I pressed my fingers against it lightly at first but then started to circle her clit quickly at the same pace that I was pushing in and out of her.

She grabbed a pillow, putting it under her head. Her face was completely red, her breath ragged. "Chad, please, please, please," she begged. "I need... I need..."

I brought my mouth to her ear. "I want to hear you say it."

"I need to come," she said.

My body wasn't just on fire now, it was a live wire. My woman wanted to climax, and I was going to oblige.

I stopped moving my hand on her clit and just pressed three fingers against it while I thrust inside her deep and fast. She tried to bury her face in the pillow when I said, "Let me hear you. I need it."

She cried out my name the next second. Her previous orgasm had been strong, but this one was on a completely different level.

Scarlett cried out my name again and again. Her leg shot up in the air and then went completely soft. Her pussy was so damn tight and delicious that I gave in to my own needs. I finished right then with her, and it was completely glorious and intense. It took over my entire body.

Every cell was burning for this gorgeous woman who had barreled into my life when I least expected it.

Chapter Seventeen

Scarlett

I felt completely boneless, but so happy. Oh so happy. Astonishingly, though, I wasn't sleepy. Lying on my back, I turned my head to look at Chad, and he surprised me by wiggling his eyebrows.

"Why do you look so full of yourself?" I teased.

"Let's see. Why do you think?" He leaned forward, planting a small kiss on my shoulder. I laughed, and he moved farther down to my boob. "It's already beckoning to me."

"Of course it is," I said. I arched my back when he sucked my nipple into his mouth, sighing contentedly as he went farther down. And then, to my dismay, my stomach rumbled.

He smiled against my belly and patted my leg, straightening up. "I need to feed you."

"I'm not even sure why I'm hungry. I've eaten a lot today."

"Let's take a shower." He took my hand, kissing the back of it. "And then I'll make you dinner."

"I can make something delicious," I offered, getting out of the bed.

"No. You're on your feet the whole day at the restaurant. When you're with me, I'll take care of you."

I didn't even know how to react. He was completely sincere, and the idea was so foreign to me. My whole life, I'd been the one who took care of everyone, even my parents. I'd been on kitchen duty for as long as I could remember.

He held me from behind, his arm around my waist as he guided me to the bathroom. The walk was a bit weird, but I wouldn't have it any other way. I didn't want him to let go.

"Oh wow," I exclaimed when we entered the bathroom. It was huge. There was a freestanding tub in one corner of the room with an actual overhead lamp above it. I could imagine lying there in the hot water with a good book. He also had a huge walk-in shower and a single sink.

"I call dibs on the tub!" *I could spend every evening in here.*

I shook myself to erase the thought. I was here for the night, that was it. No way was it appropriate to daydream about doing anything in this bathroom past tonight.

"Sure. I can fill it with water for you. You can relax while I cook."

I turned around, eyeing him intently. "Are you serious? I can help and chop stuff at least."

He covered my lips with one finger. "No."

"I didn't work today."

"Scarlett, why are you so determined to not relax?"

"I don't really know how," I confessed.

He walked to the tub, turning on the hot water. "What's that mean?"

I folded my arms over my chest, feeling oddly uncomfortable having a conversation while naked.

"When I was a kid, my parents worked a lot, and I think I started to cook when I was around eight. Then I took over all of the cooking duties."

He frowned. "All the time?"

"Not all the time, but often." I tilted my head and said sternly, "Hey, don't judge my parents."

"I'm not. I'm just... I can't really imagine how that was."

"I was having fun, mostly. And when I was with *him*, if we wanted to eat, I had to cook. He always said that, as a chef, he was carrying the weight of the kitchen on his shoulders."

"So, what, you somehow worked less?" His nostrils flared.

"No, but he just implied that my work wasn't as important. We never really suited each other." Why I was telling Chad this now, I didn't know. "We started dating soon after he was hired as a sous-chef at the restaurant. By the time he was promoted, I'd been with him for two years. He'd always been standoffish, but then he became unbearable. To make matters worse, we were living together, so I had to put up with it both at work and at home." I swallowed hard, adding in a whisper, "It got really bad. Some coworkers actually straight up told him that the way he treated me was making *them* uncomfortable. It was my wake-up call, honestly. I moved in with my parents the following week and quit my job even though I didn't have another one lined up."

Oh my. Saying it out loud now really made me feel stupid.

"The guy better hope I never lay eyes on him."

"I don't see how you two could ever cross paths. Although I'd love for him to see you all handsome and perfect and having the hots for me."

He walked closer. "Why are you saying that like it's hard to believe?"

Why was I suddenly spilling all my deepest secrets and fears to this man? I couldn't shut up. "It doesn't matter," I said.

He stepped even closer, touching my face with one hand. "I want to know."

"When we broke up, he used to say that I'd never find someone. That he was the very best I could do because I looked like something the cat dragged in most of the time, with my kitchen uniform and the toque—"

"Okay, let me stop you right there." Chad pinned me with his steely eyes. "You're fucking amazing. I actually think you're very sexy in your chef's attire."

"Oh, now you're laying it on thick."

"I mean it. You have no idea how hard it is to keep my hands to myself when I see you in uniform."

I opened my mouth to further tease him, but his eyes turned dark. I sucked in my breath. "Oh my God. You really mean it."

"Fuck yes, I do. Don't doubt yourself, especially not because of that moron."

"Oh, I'm a work in progress. Most times I'm doing okay."

He brought his mouth to my ear. "Any other time, I'm right here to remind you that you're amazing."

"Right. First you make me come, then you make me swoon. Why not tell me what else I can expect?"

He straightened up. "A delicious dinner. I'm going to take a quick shower and then let you relax."

I watched him step into the walk-in shower. And let's just say, his backside was as good as his front. I decided to go in after him, following him under the spray of water.

He still had his back to me, not realizing I was there with him—or so I thought.

"I heard you."

"I wasn't going to startle you. Just figured you might need some help soaping up that gorgeous back and ass."

"I won't say no to that."

I liked this easiness between us. I hadn't expected it because nothing ever came easy to me. It was wonderful.

"This is nice. I didn't get the chance to do this before," I murmured, lightly running my hands up and down his back. Then I decided to be naughty and soaped up his front, too, especially his cock. I gasped when I realized he was sporting a hard-on already.

He grinned, turning around.

"How did that happen?" I was genuinely confused.

"Sugar, I'm hard most of the time when I'm around you."

"Well, at least now I can do something about it." I meant to wrap my palm around him, but he caught my wrist.

"No."

"Why not?"

He grabbed my hair, tilted my head slightly forward, and kissed down my cheek. "Go take your bath, Scarlett. Your body needs a break."

He moved his lips down to my jaw and then stepped back under the spray of the shower.

How was he so considerate?

I didn't tempt him further, though. Instead, I went to the tub, which had filled up somewhat, and lowered myself into it. I had the perfect view of him in the shower, and I liked it.

He got out a few minutes later and wrapped a towel around himself.

"When do you need me downstairs?" I asked.

"I'll call you." After securing the towel, he walked to me and leaned down, kissing my shoulder. "Just relax. I'll take care of everything."

My entire body loosened at his words.

"Thank you." I was the type who always felt the need to do something. But as I laid in the tub, looking at the ceiling, I realized I actually enjoyed relaxing.

I stayed in the water until it was lukewarm and then decided to join Chad in the kitchen. No matter what he said, he could always use some help.

I toweled off and considered wrapping a dry towel around me, but I decided to put my dress back on. I didn't bother with the panties, though.

The house smelled wonderful. As I left the bedroom, Bella's room caught my attention, and I grinned. It was full of *Harry Potter* stuff, and it made my heart happy that Chad indulged her.

I knew he'd made a gumbo before I even stepped in the kitchen. At the foot of the staircase, I stared at him without announcing myself, wanting to observe him for a bit. He looked absolutely delicious. Those abs were so damn impressive. I remembered how wonderful they felt against my body.

"Did you get your fill?" he asked.

"You knew I was here?"

"The stairs creak like crazy. I heard you come down."

I joined him the next second. "It was a good moment to just admire all these muscles at work."

I glanced in the simmering pot, then took off the lid and sniffed the aroma.

"I smell celery." My stomach rumbled even louder.

Chad kissed the back of my neck, and I shuddered. "It's ready. Sit down and I'll pour each of us a bowl."

"No rice?" I asked.

He cocked a brow. "You think I'm an amateur?" Then he pointed to the right.

"A rice cooker. Smart."

"I always cheat with rice."

"It's not a bad idea because then you don't have to keep an eye on two things at once."

He filled two bowls and got a huge portion of rice out of the cooker before joining me at the dining table.

I took a mouthful and nodded in surprise. "Chad, this is amazing."

"You expected me to feed you crap?" he asked with a smile.

"Of course not. But this is chef-level good."

"I told you I worked in the kitchen."

"Thank you for cooking and taking care of me."

He put a hand on my knee. "Any time. Why did you put on your dress?"

"I didn't know what else to wear. It seems a bit silly to run around in a towel. And your bath sheets aren't big enough to hide everything." I ran a hand through my hair, but it got stuck. "Crap, I should've washed my hair. I'll do it when I get home."

"Here's an idea." Smiling, he brought his mouth to my ear. "How about you stay the night and I'll spoil you with breakfast too?"

My stomach somersaulted. I hadn't counted on this at all. Everything since I'd met this man had been completely unexpected.

"On one condition," I said.

"What?"

"You take advantage of me thoroughly tonight."

I loved feeling his breath on my ear as he murmured, "I was planning on seducing you after dinner anyway."

"Good to know."

"What are you doing tomorrow?"

"No plans. You?"

"Going fishing with my dad and grandfathers."

"Out on the bayou?"

He nodded. "I haven't gone in a long while, and I want to make sure they're all doing fine."

That was so cute. "How often do you go?"

"Whenever I have time. My brothers do the same. My dad goes with the grandfathers most of the time. But lately I'm starting to think Dad needs some adult supervision too."

My goodness. It was adorable that he cared about his family like this. It made me wonder if that was just Chad. Simon was all about Simon—I'd just figured that out a bit too late.

I always stayed on top of what my parents were doing because I cared about them. I figured that was an only-child thing. Except Chad was proving it wasn't.

After we finished dinner, I reached for our plates to clear the table, but he stopped me. "No, I'll do this."

I stood with my hands on my hips. *This man.* "Chad, really! What am I supposed to do?"

"Prepare yourself for the rest of the evening." He fondled my ass for good measure.

I locked my lips. "Are you sure you want me to spend the night?"

In response, he simply pulled me close to him. "Yes. Why not?"

"We both have our... reasons and rules."

He smiled, touching my lower lip with his thumb. "'They're already broken, sugar. So why don't we just keep breaking them?"

Chapter Eighteen

Scarlett

"I didn't even know you could look sexy in fishing gear. But it's your superpower to just look sexy in anything, isn't it?" I asked. He was wearing khakis, but somehow he made them work.

He laughed and kissed my forehead. "Are you ready to go?"

I nodded. "You don't have to drive me."

"Sugar, indulge me."

"Don't people usually go fishing very early in the morning?"

"They've been there since five o'clock, but I couldn't leave you in my bed all on your own. In fact," he said, stepping closer, "I'm having second thoughts about going at all."

"You can't bail on them."

"A commitment is a commitment." That's what my dad used to tell me when I was younger. It built character. He was right.

He nodded, taking a deep breath. "You're right."

"Okay, then. Let's go," I prodded because Chad was starting to get a sexy glint in his eyes. I knew that meant he was planning to undress me.

I had pep in my step as I walked to the car. Once inside, I realized I hadn't checked if I had everything I needed in my bag. Then again, I didn't even take a lot of stuff out last night, but you never knew. Locating my phone, I noticed a missed call.

"Funny. I have a missed call from a number I didn't save. It doesn't look like spam, though." I handed it to him. "Do you know if it's the restaurant or something?"

He glanced at the screen. "That's Isabeau."

I startled. "How would she even have my number?"

Chad laughed as the car moved forward. "You're joking, right? My grandmother is a force of nature. She gets whatever she wants. Your number wouldn't even be that difficult to find. It's in our HR files."

"What do you think she wants?"

"No idea. Call and check."

I felt slightly uncomfortable with the idea of having a conversation with Chad's grandmother, but it would be rude to ignore her, so I called her back.

"Good morning, Scarlett. This is Isabeau."

"Hi, Isabeau."

"I hope you don't mind that I asked around for your number."

"Not at all. How can I help you?"

"Celine and I are at the store. We were wondering if you have any free time today. We'd love for you to stop by."

I glanced at Chad, who'd clearly overheard what his grandmother said. I mouthed, "Would that be okay?"

He nodded.

"Sure," I said into the phone.

"Excellent," she replied.

"Not sure when I'll be there."

"Oh, take your time, child. Sundays aren't for hurrying. We can't wait to see you."

"I'm excited too," I confessed.

After I hung up, Chad asked, "Want me to drop you directly there?"

"Um, no. I have to change first or your grandmothers will put two and two together."

He smiled. "I'd be surprised if they haven't already."

Heat creeped up my face. "How would that even be possible?"

"Well, for one, I texted my grandfathers this morning to tell them I was going to be late, which I never am."

"So I'm the bad influence here, huh?"

Chad started to laugh. "I'm not saying that they know. But they might suspect."

"And how do you feel about that?" I asked, then chastised myself. I didn't want to put the man on the spot.

"I don't mind the family knowing. I just don't want them to corner you." He frowned. "You do want to go to the store, right?"

"Yes. I think it's super exciting that they decided to open a business once they retired."

"We were all surprised, especially the grandfathers. But they're very happy with it."

"What gave them the idea?"

We continued speaking about the store until we reached my building. Damn, why couldn't I live farther away? I wasn't ready to say goodbye to Chad.

When I got out of the car, he did as well and walked with me to my building. Once inside, we climbed the stairs side by side.

"You really didn't have to walk me to my door," I murmured when we arrived at my unit.

"Manners before everything else," he said.

"I do like this Southern gentlemen thing."

"Gentleman, singular. Me. Only me."

I swallowed hard as I unlocked the front door. "Of course only you." As I looked him in the eyes, I had to confess, "And I wasn't even counting on you."

"Hmmm." He twirled a strand of my hair between his fingers. "I could say the same."

"Have fun with your dad and grandfathers," I replied. We held each other's gaze, and then I poked him in the chest. "You're getting that glint again. Just so I know, it's wired to dirty thoughts, isn't it?"

"Yes, it is. I can't believe you can tell." He smiled, straightening up.

"It was an educated guess based on very intense observation."

"All right, then no goodbye. It'll just fuel those thoughts. Have fun today, Scarlett. Let me know if you need saving."

"I'm sure I won't," I said and went inside my apartment.

Heading toward my dresser, I changed quickly into pants and a tank top. I wanted to wear a dress again just because I loved being all girly in my free time, but I absolutely needed to wear sneakers. My feet were still protesting after yesterday.

I arrived in the Quarter almost an hour later and followed the directions on my phone to get to Fragrant Delights.

I've been on Dumaine Street quite a few times since moving here. How did I miss their store?

A few minutes later, it became clear why. It was very small, the front only as wide as one window. The sign with the name was rusty and hard to read.

From the window, I could see that there were quite a few shoppers inside. And sure enough, Celine and Isabeau were milling around, helping their customers. The store seemed very long and narrow, extending all the way to the back of the building.

A bell rang as I opened the door, and Isabeau snapped her head in my direction. "Welcome, child."

"We'll finish up with these customers," Celine said, "and then we'll be right with you."

"Take your time. I'll look around."

Both women were wearing their hair up again. Isabeau also wore black eyeliner, and it fit her perfectly. Celine seemed to prefer a natural look.

The place was fascinating. The air was full of fragrances, but it was hard for me to distinguish one from another. My chef's nose was excellent when it came to spices but not perfumes. The walls on both sides were filled from floor to ceiling with shelves containing glass jars in all shapes and sizes. Most were small, but there were quite a few larger ones with lids. I wondered what they contained.

There were dried flowers in between and, to my fascination, crystals in all colors. The labels on the jars were gorgeous. At first I thought they'd used a cursive font, but each label was different. The place simply exuded calmness and tranquility.

There were also lotions at the back of the store. They, too, were in small glass jars. I immediately noticed Bella's favorite jasmine hand cream. There were many others, such as rose body butter and lilac oil. On the back of each jar was a list of ingredients as well as its alleged properties. There was a tester for everything, so I shamelessly opened a bunch of them, sticking my nose in to smell the fragrances. I wanted to spend my first paycheck on the entire contents of this store.

Since I spent so much time surrounded by kitchen smells, I typically chose creams that didn't have any fragrance at all, but these were different. They didn't send my senses into overdrive. Instead, they had a calming effect.

Their store sold scented candles too. I could spend hours here and start from the beginning and smell everything I hadn't tried yet.

The bell jingled again, and all of the customers filtered out.

"Oh, they were a group," I observed.

Celine and Isabeau both came to me. "Yes, we have lots of those. Some tourist info stands spread the word about us. But today we're extra busy because we're going to be closed next week. We're taking Bella to Disney." They both brimmed with pride, as they should.

"We're so glad you came," Isabeau said as she arranged my hair on my shoulders.

It was such a motherly gesture, and it completely caught me off guard. I wasn't used to this. Not because my mom wasn't loving. She was one of the most loving people I knew, but her life had always been hectic, rushing from one job to the other. She never had time to stop and do those small things mothers did.

"Did you have fun yesterday?" This came from Celine, who had followed my gaze and was now looking at the candles.

"Yes. I was out and about in the city, and it was amazing." I clamped my mouth shut before I gave them too many details.

They exchanged a glance. Isabeau kept looking at my smile. Oh man, it was taking over my face. Could they tell that Chad and I had been up to no good?

"Would you like a custom fragrance?" Isabeau asked.

"I'd love that."

"It's what most people come in for."

"This place is completely incredible. The smells, the jars, and the crystals. What do the crystals do exactly?"

"They balance the energies," Isabeau explained. "Come with us behind the counter."

"Truly," Celine said in a slight voice, "I think it might be easier if she's in front of it. We can take a better look at her."

Isabeau nodded. "You're right. Scarlett, you can sit on one of the small chairs here."

The counter was cleverly built so you could slide your legs under it.

"What kind of perfume do you usually wear?" Isabeau asked me.

"None," I admitted. "I'm afraid it'll mess up my sense of smell in the kitchen."

She sighed. "The bane of a chef's existence. But if you trust us, we'll make you one that won't get in the way of your cooking."

"I trust you," I said easily. These two women had a calming effect on me.

"All right, then. Give me your palm," Celine said. "I want to check your lifelines."

I started to laugh because I was certain she was pulling my leg, but she didn't laugh back.

"Wait, you're serious?" I asked.

Isabeau tsked. "Celine, you have to go easy on the girl. She'll think we're cray-cray."

Celine scoffed. "Everyone already thinks that. I was under the impression that you didn't give two craps."

"I don't when it comes to strangers, but I do want Scarlett to like us."

"I do like you," I said. Then to prove it, I held my palm out to Celine.

"Mm-hmm," she said, staring at the lines and then frowning some more, as if she didn't quite like what she was seeing. But then she looked up triumphantly and said, "Isabeau, come take a look here."

Isabeau walked up right behind me and leaned in to look at my palm.

"That's what I thought," Celine said.

"Can someone fill me?"

"Oh, no, no," Isabeau said. "That's just for us to know so we can pick a good fragrance."

"You needed to read my palm for that?" I challenged. It was obvious that these two ladies had far more on their mind than they were sharing.

Celine winked at me. "I used to think this was all bull crap until about thirty years ago. A lady who was old as dirt—even older than the two of us—told me that Isabeau was going to become my best friend. I thought she was barking mad. That was during the time when neither of us was thrilled about our kids getting together. We thought they were too young. And what do you know? Now she's my best friend. So I'm a firm believer that these lines aren't completely random."

"And yet you're still not telling me what you're seeing. What awaits me?"

"We're not fortune tellers, darling," Celine said quietly.

"Oh." I was a bit disappointed because I'd gotten hyped up about knowing what my future held. Then again, I was always one for anticipating what life had in store.

"But certain lines are linked to certain traits, much like a horoscope. And it helps us pair you up with fragrances you might like. Let's see if we're correct," Celine added.

As the two moved about, mixing their concoctions, I thought about my move to New Orleans and how fortunate I'd been—both with my job and with Chad. I was terrified of things going wrong, but at the same time, I couldn't deny how much I wanted him to be part of my life.

They exchanged a glance. "We can give her our secret ingredient too."

Isabeau waved her hand. "She might not even like it."

"What's the secret ingredient?" I asked eagerly.

"Let's see if she likes it first," Isabeau told Celine as if I hadn't said anything at all.

"It works even if she doesn't like it," Celine replied.

"Celine," Isabeau chastised.

What was going on?

Celine bent down and disappeared under the counter for a split second. Then she straightened up, holding a tiny violet bottle. Taking off the cap, she held it for me.

I took a sniff. "Oh my God, this is amazing. So fresh but also deep. What is it?"

"Lilac. We're convinced it's actually a love potion," Celine said. "At least, I've always been convinced of it. My grandmother and my mother used to make their own perfume. At the age of eighteen, they gave me one that had a few drops of lilac. I was married within the year."

My heart stuttered. "That's interesting. I mean, I'm not even sure I want to get married," I said honestly.

Isabeau laughed. "Oh, darling, you might change your mind. And we'd love to throw a wedding."

It took a few seconds for her words to sink in, and then I felt my eyes widen. I tried to keep a poker face, though, because both of them were watching me intently.

"And then I gave this to my dear Adele when she was young," Celine said. "She was desperate because no one asked her to prom. I wanted to give her a nudge. She met Remy the next month."

"And the rest is history, as you know," Isabeau replied, looking at me with a smile on her lips. "So, what do you think? Want it in your perfume?"

That was a trick question. If I said no, it would probably shut the conversation down, but... I really liked it.

"I'd love it."

CHAPTER NINETEEN

SCARLETT

I stayed at the shop for another half hour. Isabeau and Celine packed my perfume in a super elegant bottle, tiny and dark green with a gold cap. They assured me that they could make more any time because they had the formula written down.

I would've lingered in the shop for the rest of the day, too, but a group of customers came in, and I didn't want to be in the way. Once I left with my small bag, I ventured down the streets without any goal. They became more alive as the day went on. I crisscrossed the French Quarter without bothering to check my map, taking in all the small boutiques. I preferred exploring like this versus simply speed-walking past everything to reach a certain destination. I only headed home around five o'clock in the afternoon.

I was full of giddy energy when I stepped inside my studio. I looked around, biting my lower lip, then sat down on the pullout couch, closing my eyes for a bit. How could I be so exhausted? Then again, I hadn't slept that much last night, and today had been full of adventures.

I took my phone out of my back pocket, intending to order something for dinner. No way was I going to cook. My heart somersaulted when I noticed I had some messages. Oh, whoops. They were all from Chad. Ha, guess who was grinning. Yep, me—from ear to ear.

He'd sent the first one after I arrived at the shop.

Chad: I hope the grans aren't driving you crazy. Let me know if you need rescuing.

And then a second one, one hour later.

Chad: All good? We're having quite a productive day.

He sent me another one just half an hour ago.

Chad: Through the family grapevine, I found out that you survived the day. Call when you can.

I felt bad, but I wasn't used to checking my phone during the day. The pace in the kitchen was too intense. I immediately called Chad, and he answered before the first ring was even over.

"I was starting to get worried."

I winced. "I'm sorry. I don't really look at the phone during the day. It's a work habit."

"Are you still in the Quarter?"

"I'm home. They made me a custom perfume," I said, bursting with pride. That meant I had their seal of approval, right?

Oh, Scarlett, what on earth would you need their approval for? You and Chad spent a delicious night together, nothing more.

"So I've heard. They're both thrilled."

"We had a lot of fun," I agreed. "The shop has an amazing vibe. I can see myself doing something similar when I retire."

He chuckled. "Really?"

"Yeah. I mean, part of being a chef is playing with aromas and making sure everything fits. Making perfumes isn't that far off. It's just way less intensive."

"I'm glad you had a good time together." His voice suddenly had an edge to it.

"Why did you doubt it?"

"Some people find them too much."

I laughed. "That's impossible. Who would say that?"

"My ex," he replied instantly.

"Oh." My stomach dropped.

"She made it a point to avoid the family, especially my grandmothers."

"That's sad," I whispered. I couldn't imagine anyone not liking Celine and Isabeau. "How was the bayou? See any alligators?" I asked in jest.

"About half a dozen."

"You're joking, right?"

"No. We can do a tour on the bayou whenever you want. You'll see gators galore." He laughed.

"Ummm... thank you for the generous offer, but I think I'll pass."

"I thought you were all about exploring."

"I draw the line at alligators."

He chuckled. "Duly noted."

My stomach rumbled. "Ugh, I need to order something to eat. I should've stayed longer in the Quarter and grabbed a bite. But I was a bit tired, considering I spent the night doing anything *but* sleeping."

"Do you regret not sleeping, sugar?" His tone was teasing, but I could tell he also really wanted to know the answer.

"Not at all," I whispered. Swallowing hard, I added in a small voice, "You?"

Please don't let him say yes.

"No fucking way." And yep, I was grinning again. "You know what? I have an idea. Don't order anything for dinner. I'll send you something."

"What do you mean?"

"I'll send you something. You're going to enjoy it."

"You want to surprise a chef with food?" I asked incredulously.

"That king cake worked well in my favor," he said.

I had to laugh. "True. You getting me king cake in April is a big part of you getting in my pants so quickly." I pressed my lips together, a bit embarrassed for blurting it out like that, because I'd actually wanted him in my pants long before that. *Scarlett!*

"Then I can't wait to see what tonight's surprise will do."

After we hung up, I called my parents, happy to get a chance to catch up with them. Dad answered the phone, immediately turning on the camera.

"Hey, sweetie pie!" I loved that he still called me that. He used to read me bedtime stories every evening when I was a kid, and he'd kiss my forehead right before I fell asleep, whispering, "Sweet dreams, sweetie pie."

Even though they worked long hours, they both gave me a lot of love growing up.

"Listen, that good-for-nothing Simon messaged your mom on Facebook the other day. He asked if you had a new number."

My throat closed up. I hadn't told my parents the extent of Simon's mistreatment because I didn't want to upset them, but they had good instincts, and I was sure they knew.

"I'm so sorry, Dad."

"I flipped him off. Via message, too, with that emoji thing. Told him to leave you alone."

"Oh, you! Why did you tell her that?" Mom asked, appearing in the frame. "Don't worry about anything, dear. Tell us about your weekend."

I swallowed hard, resisting the urge to ask more about Simon. "Umm... I had a great weekend. Actually, I spent some time with Chad and his family, outside of work."

Dad frowned. "He's got his eyes on you? Hope he treats you right."

That was Dad to a T. I smiled. "He does."

Mom beamed from ear to ear. "That's wonderful, dear. We're very happy for you."

My parents' enthusiasm filled me with joy. I *refused* to worry about Simon. I'd wasted enough time on him.

Besides, I had a surprise from Chad to look forward to.

Chapter Twenty

Chad

"Do you need anything else?" I asked my grandfathers once I dropped all the fish off in their kitchen. They drove with Dad, but my trunk was full of fish, and I had no use for it. Bella hated it.

"No, son, we're good," Grandfather David said.

Grandfather Felix checked his clock. "The girls are still at the shop, huh? They're going to be very tired tonight."

It always made me laugh that my grandfathers referred to the grandmothers as their "girls."

"I'll make po' boys for them so it's fresh when they return," David said.

The house was eerily quiet without the grandmothers and Mom.

"All right. Well, I'm going to pick up Bella," I said. "Let me know when you want to go out on the bayou next time."

"You know," David said, "you don't need to come watch us."

I stared at him. "I'm not watching you. I'm fishing with you."

"Right," Felix said. "Son, you're smart, but so are we. Think we can't tell that you and your brothers are volunteering to come out fishing more 'cause you think these two old farts will somehow end up sinking the boat? What are you afraid of? That we'll end up as an alligator snack?"

The thought had crossed my mind. Repeatedly. As usual, he picked up on it.

"You could take that worry away by investing in a better boat," I countered.

David scoffed. "That boat's done us well for thirty years. No need to splurge on anything else."

Fuck my life. The LeBlanc and Broussard family was one of the richest families in Louisiana, yet my grandfathers didn't want to even buy a boat. I'd have to bring this up to my brothers. We usually respected their decisions and left them to their own devices, but that crappy old thing was going to flip over soon. If we gifted them one, they'd use it. They'd throw a tantrum, but they wouldn't turn it down.

"By the way, we heard from your grandmothers that they've made one of their custom perfumes for Scarlett," Felix said.

I eyed them intently. "When did you even talk to the grandmothers?"

"On the car ride, obviously," David said.

"They even mentioned it was something with lilac." Felix laughed.

I drew a blank. "Is that supposed to mean something to me?"

"I'll tell you one thing—you should be scared," David said.

I laughed. "Why?"

"Because whenever they bring out the lilac, some serious shit is about to go down," he concluded.

It was bizarre to hear him use that expression. But he insisted that he wanted to "keep up with the times." That included keeping up with slang.

I waved my hand. "I've heard some stories involving lilac, but I don't remember any of them."

David looked at Felix and said, "Then don't tell the boy anything more. It never helps to know too much."

My family was truly something else.

"Okay, gotta go. I don't want to be late picking up Bella."

I headed straight to the car and wondered why they thought I came along just to keep an eye on them.

Though I couldn't deny that I enjoyed the day, too, as I always relaxed best when I was with my family. I didn't have to pretend or be on guard. Being a CEO meant spending a lot of my time putting up my professional facade so people knew not to mess with us. But I could be myself around family.

However, I would've much rather spent it with Scarlett. Last night had been far too short, and this morning too. Every interaction we had was hurried, or it had an expiration date on it, and I didn't like it. I wanted to take my time with her. I had half a mind to surprise her with an afternoon espresso and spend time with her even if it was just a few minutes, but I was already late picking up Bella. I was addicted to Scarlett. And I knew my idea for dinner would make her evening.

I called The Sister Club. It was a mom-and-pop shop that had once been run by two sisters. Now it was run by two cousins, and they made hands down the best meat pies in the city. Bella and I always had them on Sundays after I picked her up. It was our tradition.

"Good evening."

"Hey, this is Chad LeBlanc."

"Hi, Chad," Giselle, the owner, said.

"Listen, can you send an extra delivery tonight?"

"Sure. To your house? Same thing as usual?"

"No, not my house. I'll text you the address."

"How much should I send?"

"One portion."

"Is this for one of your brothers? Because I've got to tell you, I've got a beef with Julian."

I laughed. "Who doesn't? But no, it's for...," I began, but then said, "for the chef who just started at my restaurant."

"Scarlett."

I nearly dropped my phone. "How do you know?" I asked. New Orleans was by no means a small town.

"Think we wouldn't find out that LeBlanc & Broussard's has a new chef? The whole Quarter knows, darling."

"Right."

"Okay. We'll make a portion for her too. Anything else?"

"Just make sure you send it with another guy so we get delivery at the same time." They had their own drivers, which allowed them to be fast and efficient.

"Sure."

"Thank you."

I arrived at my ex's house five minutes too late. She was already outside with Bella, who was jumping up and down with joy. She liked spending time with her mother, but she was so eager to return home on Sunday evening.

"Daddy, you're late."

"Yeah. I'm sorry, cricket. Had to drop the fish off with the grandfathers." I looked up at Sarah. "Weekend all right?"

"We had fun. We went shopping." She narrowed her eyes. "I heard your chef went to your grandmothers' shop."

I leveled her with my gaze. "Yes, she did. They like Scarlett."

"I like Scarlett, too, Mommy," Bella said.

"Yes, you've told me that." That would probably explain why she was aware of Scarlett at all. "But it's different. Your grandmothers don't like anyone."

My grandmothers liked plenty of people, but they'd never hit it off with Sarah. They'd tried, but Sarah always felt superior somehow. She'd been shell-shocked that, despite our fortune, we weren't interested in attending "high society events," as she called them. Sarah had been into all this stuff ever since she was a debutante at twenty-one. Prior to dating her, I hadn't even realized debutante balls were still a thing. She did charity work for the exposure—basically, anything to benefit the image of Sarah.

"See you in two weeks, okay, butterfly?" she said, hugging Bella.

"Yes, Mommy." Bella was on vacation next week, and both sets of grandparents were taking her to Disney World.

"Have a lot of fun at Disney, and don't tire your grans out. Remember, they can't keep up with you for hours a day."

"I'll try to remember, Mommy."

After she gave her mother a hug, Bella darted toward the car.

I turned to leave, but Sarah said, "You and the chef... Is something going on there?"

I looked straight at her. "It's none of your business."

"You're right. It's not. But I was curious."

"You can always drop by the restaurant and meet the whole staff." I deliberately didn't single out Scarlett. I felt 100 percent overprotective of her, and I knew how Sarah could get.

She rolled her eyes. "Right, because I've got nothing better to do."

"I'll drop Bella off two Fridays from now."

"Sure." She walked back to the house without another word.

She may not care for me anymore, but at least she loved her daughter. That was one thing that concerned me when we first found out about the pregnancy, but Sarah never wavered in wanting our child. Once Bella was here, though, she confessed that motherhood wasn't at all what she'd imagined.

Bella had gotten in the car, but she couldn't secure herself in the child booster. I did that for her, kissing her forehead before getting into the driver's seat.

"Dad, are we having pie tonight?"

I barely stifled a laugh. She asked that every time I picked her up, almost as if afraid I would say no.

"Of course. They'll be delivered soon after we get home."

"I'm so excited."

We arrived at the same time as the delivery guy. I tipped him generously before heading inside.

I took the meat pies out and put them on the kitchen island.

"Dad, can you put me up?"

I scooped her with one arm, putting her next to the pies. This was another tradition. We never set the table Sunday evening. We literally ate from the carton.

Taking out my phone, I texted Scarlett.

Chad: You got the delivery?

I received a message a few minutes later—a picture. Scarlett was biting into a pie, holding her thumb up.

Look at that grin. She was happy, completely and utterly happy. She'd had the same expression when she'd tasted the king cake.

Scarlett: This is delicious. I need the address.

I replied right away.

Chad: I'll give it to you in exchange for a kiss.

She sent a blushing emoji back.

Scarlett: Such a shameless negotiation.

Chad: It's my style.

Scarlett: In that case, I'll make things harder for you and I'll get the name another way.

I started to laugh. Damn, I wanted this woman right here with me and Bella. That was a thought I'd never imagined having with anyone. At least not when Bella was this young.

When I received custody, I'd promised myself that I would be an exemplary father. That I wouldn't subject her to the uncertainty of me dating. But everything was becoming a blur.

I texted back quickly in between throwing away the empty cartons.

Chad: I need to start Bella's evening routine. Are you free to talk in about two hours?

Scarlett: Free as a bird. Unless I fall asleep. I have to catch up on sleep after someone corrupted me last evening.

I wanted to corrupt her into doing even more, but I couldn't right now.

As I went upstairs with Bella, I asked, "Where did you go shopping this weekend?"

"Ohhh, everywhere. Even a voodoo shop. It wasn't scary at all."

That made me chuckle. "You're a brave girl."

"Of course I'm brave. I'm in school now. I'm not a kid anymore." That felt like a punch to my chest. She'd always be my baby girl... my cricket. But it also alerted me to something I didn't like.

"Cricket, you don't need to be brave just because you're at school. It's okay to be scared."

She narrowed her eyes. "You never get scared."

I laughed. "You know that's not true."

"That's right. You're afraid of clowns."

"And many more things, like the dark," I said as I started to comb her hair.

I wasn't afraid of the dark, but I knew she disliked it, and I wanted her to feel like she could share her fears with me.

Bella looked up at me. "Daddy, can I ask you something?"

"Sure."

She put her hands together in a pleading gesture. "Can you ask Scarlett if I can learn to make more pies with her?"

"What pie would you like to bake?" I focused on combing her hair. It was semi-curly and had a lot of knots, but I'd found a detangler that worked well.

"Any pie. I just want Scarlett to be the one showing me how."

And there was the gist of it. I figured this couldn't really be about pies.

"I like her, Daddy," she continued. "For one, she likes *Harry Potter*. And she's funny, and she's so pretty. Don't you think she's pretty?"

I thought she was fucking gorgeous, but having this conversation with my daughter was bizarre.

"I'll talk to Scarlett," I promised, "and we'll see what we can do."

My daughter's plea only further fueled that dangerous line of thought that started earlier.

After I brushed her hair, she went into the bathroom. Bella was old enough now to do her evening routine alone. She simply disliked brushing her hair.

While she was in the bathroom, I started packing her bag for tomorrow. My grandparents were picking her up in the morning. New Orleans was a long drive from Orlando, but they insisted on making this a road trip. Bella was a good traveler. She never got carsick or anything like that.

I checked the weather quickly and made sure she had two changes of clothes every day, then added a few extras in case things got wild at Disney World.

While I packed her bags, my mind was still processing her request. Could I make this work for her but not give her further expectations?

By the time she came out of the bathroom, I was done packing, and she settled into bed as I started to read her favorite story, *Aladdin and the Magic Lamp*. She fell asleep before I reached the end, as usual.

I kissed her forehead and turned off the light before leaving her room. She didn't need a night-light; the lampposts outside cast enough of a glow that it wasn't pitch-dark.

I carefully closed her door and went downstairs to the kitchen to call Scarlett. I needed to hear her voice. I couldn't explain this insatiable craving I had for her. And it wasn't just about sex.

It rang over and over. I checked the time. It was only nine o'clock. Then again, she did say she might go to bed early.

I was about to hang up when she answered.

"Hey." Her voice was sleepy.

"Fuck. Did you fall asleep?"

"Erm, yeah. In front of the TV."

"I'll let you go back to sleep and—"

"No, no, I need to get up or I'll wake tomorrow morning with a completely stiff neck."

"I can preemptively put a meeting on both our schedules and give you a morning massage," I offered.

"Oh my God, Chad! Give a girl a warning. I'm half asleep. How am I supposed to react to that?"

"Just say yes."

She started to laugh. "I wasn't expecting this."

"What exactly?" I asked even though I had an inkling that I knew what she meant.

"Um, I'm not sure how to put it in words. So, how is Bella?"

"She's excited that she's going to Disney World tomorrow."

"Yes, they told me. The grans. They're very excited too."

"And actually, she misses you."

"Oh, that's so cute. You know, I was hoping she'd ask to come around the kitchen again." I could hear the smile in her voice.

Did she know how much that meant to me?

"She likes you," I said. "And so do I."

That dangerous thought pushed all the others to the side, and I threw caution to the wind. I needed Scarlett on a level I couldn't understand. But maybe I shouldn't try. All my life, I'd tried to be rational. That had served me well in business, but not so much in my personal life. Right now, I didn't want to overthink this. I was letting my feelings do the talking, which was new to me.

"I want to spend more time with you, Scarlett."

"Well, um, that's going to be a bit tricky, I think, considering that someone's making me work very long hours." Her voice was teasing, but I knew she was right. The chef's job was no joke.

"But see, I'm actually free this week, considering Bella is gone."

"What did you have in mind?"

"Stay with me this week," I said, and she gasped.

Why did I just blurt it out like that? I should've laid more groundwork.

"As in... stay at the house?"

Since I'd gone ahead and run my mouth, I might as well continue. "That way I can take care of you every evening after all of those long hours of work."

"Hmm, you *are* great at taking care of me."

"You're hesitating. Why?"

"I don't know," she whispered. "This is a bit sudden and more than I expected. I..."

"You don't have to give me an answer now." It was unfair to put her on the spot when the idea had been percolating in my mind for hours.

"That's good. I'll think about it and let you know tomorrow, okay?"

"Sure. And Scarlett, if you'd rather not, it's completely okay. I understand. I don't want you to feel pressured into anything."

Just because I was ready for more and craved her presence at all times didn't mean we were on the same page. That thought didn't sit well with me, but I wanted her to be happy. And I was going to do my very best to convince her that she belonged right here with me.

Chapter Twenty-One
Chad

Mayhem ruled in the LeBlanc-Broussard household when I brought Bella the next morning. No one was ready, so the two of us spent an hour making po' boys for the road while the grans finished packing. Mom had made coffee for the trip and her signature scones. My family didn't believe in stopping to eat.

Finally, at about nine o'clock, they managed to get out the door.

I headed straight to the Quarter, but instead of going up to the office—even though I was late already—I went by Maria's Coffee Shop and bought two espressos. I knew the staff would arrive in about an hour, but I also knew Scarlett always came earlier on Mondays.

I used the employee entrance and smiled the second I stepped inside. Scarlett was singing, her voice filling the empty kitchen. I watched her for a few seconds, and then she turned around, gasping when she saw me.

"Chad, when did you come in?"

"Just now."

She glanced at the cups in my hands. "That for me?"

"Obviously," I said, walking right up to her. I leaned in, attempting to kiss her neck, and said, "Fuck. You smell incredible."

"It's my new perfume. The lilac stands out, doesn't it?"

The word jogged my memory, but I couldn't place it at all. I just moved my mouth down the side of her neck and then back up. She shuddered in my arms.

"Chad," she whispered, "you're not even going to behave while I have my morning coffee, huh?"

"Not until after this," I said, putting the cups on the counter before covering her mouth with mine.

I needed this even more than I'd realized. I wanted to do this the whole day. Just spend time with this woman, kissing her, making her laugh, finding out more and more things that pleased her.

She moaned lightly, putting her arms around my neck. And then I lost control of myself and moved both hands to her ass.

She stepped back, immediately grinning. "No, no, no. Someone could come in at any time."

"You're right." I cleared my throat and grabbed my cup of espresso.

She did the same. Closing her eyes, she smelled the drink before taking a sip. Then she opened her eyes and said, "I've thought about your question."

I put my cup back down and looked at her intently. If she said she wasn't ready, I wasn't sure how I'd react. I needed her, plain and simple. And I was beginning to think I wanted more than just a week.

"And I'd be more than happy to spend a week with you."

"Yes! Fuck yes!" I exclaimed, and then I kissed her again.

She gasped, and I realized she was still holding the cup. It had tilted to one side, but I caught it just in time so it didn't spill, setting it on the counter.

This time, I kissed her because I simply needed to. Relief flooded every cell in my body. I hadn't even been aware that I'd been so tense while awaiting her answer. But now that she'd given it to me, instead of calming down and patiently waiting for tonight to devour her, all I wanted to do was throw her over my shoulder and carry her down Royal Street to my home. I didn't care if the whole Quarter saw us.

Scarlett gave in to me beautifully. Her mouth was soft, as was her body. I kept my hands firmly in place on her waist, though. I didn't want to risk losing my head again.

When we finally paused to breathe, she leaned slightly forward, eyes still closed. Then she opened them slowly, glancing up at me, and gave me a shy smile.

"Right... We need a firm rule. No kissing at work."

I frowned. "I don't like it."

The corners of her mouth twitched. "Neither do I, but things have a way of... spiraling out of control."

I nodded.

"So, how are we going to do things... logistically?"

"I'll pick you up after your shift. We can go to your house so you can grab whatever you need for the week at my place."

She grinned. "Great!"

"All right, then. I'll see you this evening."

"Now shoo, get out. I know for a fact that Joel is going to arrive in a few minutes."

I chuckled. "You're kicking me out of my own restaurant?"

"No, I'm just making sure that Joel doesn't catch us in a compromising position."

"We're just drinking coffee," I said.

"Yes, but see, you just gave me two delicious kisses. You sort of kick-started my appetite."

I threw my head back, laughing.

"What? It's true. I don't think I'm explaining it too well."

I cleared my throat, straightening up. "You're not, but I still understand what you're saying." Taking my cup, I walked backward, pointing at her with my other hand. "I'll see you tonight, sugar."

She nodded. "I can't wait."

I felt on top of the world. Once I went out to my office, I checked my phone and realized I had a missed call from Zachary. I'd called him yesterday, but he didn't pick up. I returned the call as I stepped inside the office.

"Good morning," he said. "We need to be quick because I'm about to go into a meeting."

"Sure. Listen, I want us to buy a boat for our grandparents and—"

"Get rid of that old shit boat?" Zachary finished for me.

"Yes, exactly."

"Good call."

"They'll kick our asses for basically overriding them, but it's time," I said.

"So what exactly did you want from me?"

"I'll take the hit and actually buy the boat, but I need you to smooth things over when the time comes."

"Dude," he said, "I can manage situations, but I can't perform miracles."

"If there's one LeBlanc who can do it, it's you."

"Fair enough. When are you planning this?"

"I'm thinking this week, since they're gone anyway."

There was a pause, and then Zachary said, "You know there are waiting lists for boats, right?"

"I know how to pull strings to get what I want," I reminded him. "I'll put Anthony on it."

Anthony had a thing for boats. He owned several, which made it all the more frustrating that my grandfathers insisted on going out on the bayou in a piece of rusty metal.

"Keep me posted on the when and where, and I'll do my best."

"That's all I ask for," I assured him.

After I hung up, I debated diving into work. But since the day was already getting away from me, I figured I might as well start the boat project, so I called Anthony next. He wasn't an early riser, but it was already somewhat late in the day, so he might be up. He answered a few seconds later.

"Chad?" he said.

"Hey, I know Monday is busy for everyone, so I'll be quick. I need your help with something."

"Finally decided to forget that stupid idea of celibacy and need someone to be your wingman? Because I'm your man."

I jerked my head back. "What the hell? How do you even know?"

"Sazeracs. Julian. You can put two and two together." He laughed. "Sorry, that's not what you need help with. I apologize. First of all, your idea had merits. But just because an idea has merits doesn't mean it doesn't suck. The two things aren't mutually exclusive," Anthony pointed out.

"I'm not even going to dignify that with a response. But in any case, I wouldn't need a wingman."

"Are you sure? You've been out of the dating world for a while. Although, judging by how you behaved with Scarlett at the bar, you do have some game left."

"Thanks for the vote of confidence," I said dryly. "It's not about any of that. I want to buy a boat for the grandfathers."

"For the bayou? Fuck yes. I was of two minds to sink that boat myself. Beckett actually had a good plan for it, but we just never got around to carrying it through. When do you want to give it to them?"

"As soon as possible. When they come back from Disney on Sunday."

"That's gonna be hard. What are the specs?"

"Boats aren't my thing. You're the pro, so you choose one, and I'll pay for it."

"I'll pull all the strings."

"Thank you. I appreciate it."

"Anything for the grandads," he said.

That was our motto. Anything for the family. There was nothing I wouldn't do to make sure everyone was safe.

Both our granddads wanted to retire years ago, and I'd been a vocal advocate. They'd worked hard their entire lives and deserved to rest. Some of our business partners and investors had been vehemently against it—like they got a fucking vote. More than one threatened to stop cooperating with us if both of them left at the same time.

Xander and I met with each of them one-on-one and, simply said, put the fear of God into them. And it worked. None of them jumped ship, and our grandfathers could retire in peace. One of those business partners even confessed, much later, that he appreciated us stepping in like that for our grandfathers.

Anthony and I discussed some more details about the boat before hanging up.

After that, I managed to finally start my workday. My focus was off for the rest of the day, though. I was restless, and I knew it had to do with Scarlett. I was dying to have her to myself for an entire week, and I already knew it wouldn't be anywhere near enough.

Chapter Twenty-Two

Scarlett

I was dead on my feet at nine o'clock that evening. The day had been incredibly difficult. I'd been calling it Unlucky Monday because we had mishap after mishap. First, we had a small fire. Nothing was damaged, but it threw us off schedule. Then we had an alarmingly high number of guests with special requests—some even wanted to see me personally. That slowed me down. I always wanted to make sure my guests felt looked after, but if I spent too much time out there reassuring them that I wasn't going to use any of the allergens they indicated, then I couldn't be back here overseeing the kitchen.

So, at 9:00 p.m., I stepped out of the employee entrance and took in a deep breath. I closed my eyes and leaned against a brick wall.

"Good evening, gorgeous."

I nearly jumped out of my skin before I opened my eyes. Chad was half hidden in the shadows, but I could still see the smile on his face. The light from the nearest lamppost illuminated his upper body.

"Oh my God," I said, putting a hand on my chest. "I completely forgot you were waiting for me. The kitchen was crazy."

He closed the distance to me and tilted my chin up. Suddenly, my entire body was like a live wire. Adrenaline kicked in, and I felt like I'd just drunk five of Maria's espressos.

"I'm sorry to hear that. Are you ready to leave?"

I nodded and almost leaned in for a kiss when he pulled back, giving me a cheeky grin. "Remember the no-kissing rule."

My heart pattered. "Yeah, I put that in place. That was a stupid idea."

He growled. "Just say the word, and I'll kiss you right here against this wall. I've been fantasizing about your lips the whole day."

I licked my lower lip and said, "No, no, no." I did have good reasons for the rule. Though I couldn't remember them right now.

He touched my neck with his fingertips but didn't attempt to kiss me again. Good thing, too, because I would've given in.

"Let's go. Don't think about anything else tonight. I'm going to take care of everything."

And I truly believed he would.

He took my hand, leading me to the back of the building. There was a small lot a few streets away where all the employees parked.

I looked around, smiling to myself. God, was this really happening? I was living in NOLA, and this gorgeous man had asked me to spend a whole week with him at his house. This was incredible.

Once we got in the car, I realized there was a real risk that I might simply doze off, but I didn't. "It's a good thing I managed to pack everything last night. I'd be too exhausted to do it today."

"Scarlett, if you're too tired, we can just relax at your place. We don't have to move things in tonight."

"Oh, no, no. I do want to do it tonight. I mean, I'll be tired every evening, although today was particularly weird. I'm not sure whether all the customers were more demanding or if I just kept making more mistakes."

Chad made a sound that sounded a lot like a chuckle. I turned my head to face him. "Are you laughing at me?"

"No, but I've had a similar problem today. I couldn't entirely focus on my work. It pleases me to know I'm not the only one."

"Feisty, huh? I don't think you'll be so pleased with me if bad reviews start coming in."

He leaned closer to me once he'd stopped the car for a red light and whispered, "Nothing you do could displease me. Never."

I felt completely warm, as if the seat heating had suddenly started. He didn't know how much those words meant to me. I was enough just the way I was. I didn't have to behave or perform a certain way to earn his approval.

"If you need help in the kitchen, let me know," he added. "We can always hire more staff."

"No! I'm up for the job," I said, proudly sticking my jaw forward and rolling my shoulders back.

"Scarlett, I know. I wasn't implying that. I'm just saying that some periods are far busier than others. We've had temporary staff additions before. That doesn't mean you can't do the job." I relaxed a bit in my seat. "I think it was just a weird day. But if it keeps happening, let me know, all right? I guess some others from the staff will also eventually come forward if they feel like the kitchen is in need of more personnel."

"It's a bit weird to talk about work," I confessed.

"Then we'll talk about anything else except that. Or... we don't have to talk at all."

I laughed. "I knew it. You're luring me to your place for a week of nonstop sex."

He growled, and I covered my mouth. "Oh, I must be exhausted for my filter to be shut off like this."

"Don't say that again," he warned. "You have no idea how many times I fantasized today about coming down to the kitchen and taking you away."

"Huh," I teased. "Really? That would've been something." I was secretly relishing the thought because I wouldn't have minded at all.

When we pulled in front of my apartment building only a few minutes later, there was obviously a party somewhere nearby, because we could hear groups cheering.

Once inside, Chad looked around. "Have you done anything with the place since I was last here?"

"No. Honestly, I don't have time. I'm going to order some things online. By the time I finally make it to Home Depot, I'll have lived out of my suitcase for, like, two months. I just need to find something that I can easily build myself to store some of this stuff away."

He cocked a brow. "Or you could call me. I can help with anything you might need."

I wiggled my eyebrows. "Okay, on one condition. You do it without your T-shirt on."

Chad looked at me incredulously, then burst into laughter.

"Deal," he exclaimed through guffaws. Clearly my filter was completely off today. "All right, so what are you taking with you?"

I pointed at my packed suitcase by the door. "I'd love to take a quick shower, though. I really need to refresh."

"Sure, I'll wait."

"Thanks."

I usually spent a long time in the shower after work. The hot water relaxed me. But now, I washed quickly, then changed into fresh clothes. I also applied my amazing perfume right under my ears.

"Ready to goooo," I exclaimed as I darted out of the bathroom.

"Love your enthusiasm," Chad said with a grin.

He took my luggage easily in one hand, but we still used the elevator. On the way to his home, we spoke a bit about the upcoming week and what Bella was planning. It was endearing that the entire family was driving with her to Disney World.

When we stepped inside his house, I felt a little bit on edge. *God, is this really a good idea?* I'd been so excited that I hadn't considered the pros and cons too carefully.

I glanced out the huge window into the courtyard and sighed. "The tree lights are already on."

"I knew you'd enjoy them. Let's go straight outside. I have a surprise for you."

I narrowed my eyes at him. "Really? More surprises than this?"

This man is determined to make me fall for him, isn't he?

We moved outside, and as I approached the tree, I immediately noticed a blanket underneath it along with some comfy pillows. There were also a few trays covered with glass lids.

"I'll bring something to drink too," he said nonchalantly as if he didn't just knock my socks off.

"You prepared this for us. When did you have time to do it?"

"I left the office at around six. That gave me plenty of time to think about how to pamper you tonight. Go lie down on the blanket. I'll bring everything."

"No, I can—"

"Scarlett," he said in a warning tone.

"Got it. I'm just going to lie down there and do nothing—except look at you."

He smirked. "Precisely."

As he disappeared inside the house, I took off my shoes. I loved the feeling of thick grass under my feet. He must have laid several blankets on top of one another, because it was super soft and comfy. I wanted to stay here forever.

I laid down on my back, hands bundled under my head, and looked up at the gorgeous tree. I felt like I was in a dream or something. This was so romantic.

Chad joined me a few minutes later with a bottle of wine. As he pulled out the cork, I pushed myself up into a sitting position. I watched him pour a bit and then hand it to me.

"Let me know if you like it," he said.

Like I was going to criticize it after all the trouble he went to. But I didn't have to because the wine smelled absolutely delicious. I took a sip and then another one.

"I love it," I confessed.

"Perfect!" He poured more for both of us before putting the bottle in the ice bucket and taking the lids off the trays. It was an assortment of cheese and grapes. I wasn't hungry at all, but I loved having a snack with the alcohol.

He positioned himself somehow behind me, and I protested, turning around. "No, not there. Stay here where I can see you."

"Relax. You're tired, sugar," he said. The affection in his tone reached deep inside me. Chad was very affectionate and charming, and I loved it.

I leaned back, comfortably resting on his chest. But far from relaxing, I was starting to get sexy ideas inspired by all those hard pecs I was lying against.

I dropped my head back slightly, resting it on his shoulder. Seconds later, the tip of his nose moved down my neck. I felt that touch intimately, as if he had run his fingers between my thighs. Moaning, I pressed my legs together.

"What do you need to relax tonight, Scarlett? Tell me and I'll make it happen."

"You. I just want you."

He put his hands on my shoulders, then pressed up and down along my spine.

"This is good," I said. I could feel myself relaxing, but it wasn't nearly enough. I had no idea why I was so insatiable. This was completely new to me.

"Chad," I murmured, and then I put my glass down and snuggled my hand between my back and his chest.

I felt him suck in a breath when I reached his belt buckle. He put a hand around my wrist.

"Scarlett," he said on a groan.

And I knew right then and there that he needed me desperately.

Chapter Twenty-Three

Chad

Fucking hell. I'd wanted to pace everything tonight to perfection, but her hand was already testing my self-control. She wiggled it out of my grasp and then turned around slightly, moving it up and down my chest.

"Scarlett," I said. "Your wine."

She smiled, moving once more until she was on her knees, then placed her forearms on my shoulders. Her breasts were practically in my face. It was all I could do not to tear off her dress and suck a nipple into my mouth.

"The wine can wait until later." She grinned.

I was crazy for Scarlett. There was no other way to put it.

I pulled her into my lap, parting her thighs wide so she could sit on me. Then I kissed her the way I'd wanted to the whole fucking day. This morning had been nothing compared to this. I gave her my tongue, kissing her deeply, tilting her pelvis so she could feel my growing erection between her legs. She whimpered when the zipper of my pants pressed against her clit. When I ran my fingers up her arms, there were goose bumps on them.

I moved my mouth from her lips down to her neck. This position wasn't my best idea—I couldn't explore her the way I wanted—so I shifted us, opening an eye to make sure I didn't accidentally knock over our wineglasses.

"What are you doing?" she murmured. "Oh, you're laying me down."

I put her on her back so she'd be comfortable. I paused for a second, just watching her. She was like a vision, here in my yard under the lights of the trees, smiling like I was the best damn thing that ever happened to her.

I put a hand on her thigh, moving it farther up until it disappeared under her dress. She closed her eyes and sucked in a breath as I covered her panties. I skimmed my thumb up and down her pussy over the fabric, and at the same time, I captured her mouth. I repeated the motion with my thumb and felt her get wet, then wetter still, until her panties were completely drenched. She pressed her thighs together, trapping my hand. Her hips bucked off the blanket, and I deepened the kiss even more. I couldn't get enough of this woman.

She pushed me away slightly and said, "Chad, the neighbors."

I set my jaw. *Fuck.* "I forgot that we're outside."

"What if people saw?"

"I was simply kissing the most beautiful woman in the world."

"And your hand was up my—"

"No one saw that," I said through gritted teeth. It was more than just reassuring her. I couldn't bear the idea of anyone seeing her so vulnerable, so open. That was just for me.

I got on my feet and then helped her up. Taking her hand, I led her inside.

"Much better," she murmured.

I'd come to terms with the fact that Scarlett had an effect on me unlike anyone I'd ever met. When I focused on her, the rest of the world simply faded away. I forgot where we were, what we were doing, or what my intentions were.

The second I closed the door, I pressed the button to lower the blinds. Then I pulled her toward me before kissing her even harder than before. Her lips were so damn amazing. Everything about her was amazing.

I walked with her deeper inside the house, but instead of going up the stairs, I ended up leading her in the direction of the living room.

I didn't stop kissing her even as she worked at the buttons of my shirt. I bunched her dress to her waist and then ran my fingers up and down her ass cheeks, giving each buttock a good squeeze. Her muscles tightened against my palms.

I paused the kiss long enough to throw her dress over her head. She got rid of her bra the next second, without me even having to ask. I looked down at her gorgeous breasts. She was so turned on that I was seconds from pulling my pants down and just taking her like this, standing in the middle of my living room. I lowered my head slightly to wrap my lips around one nipple and pull it into my mouth. She gasped, and I reached between her thighs and into her panties, pressing two fingers against her clit. She jerked her hips back and then forward, right into my fingers, riding them.

I moved to her other breast and spoke against her skin. "Have you been fantasizing about me the whole day, Scarlett?"

"Yes," she confessed. "I didn't mean to, but it kept happening."

"It happened to me too."

Her breasts were exquisite, but I wanted to taste her pussy now.

Glancing around, I zeroed in on the couch. That would do.

I moved her toward it, clasping her shoulders and indicating for her to sit. She immediately did, looking up at me with anticipation in her eyes.

"Put your ass on the very edge of the couch," I instructed.

Licking her lips, she positioned herself as I told her, which left her even more exposed.

I kneeled before her, pulling her lower body toward me until her ass was almost hanging off the couch. That was exactly how I wanted her. I put both of her legs over my shoulders. Since I hadn't taken her panties off, I pushed the fabric to one side. Her pussy was red from where I'd pressed my fingers before. I blew warm breath across it.

"Ohhhh, Chad!" she exclaimed, her voice shaking.

I lazily drew the tip of my tongue up and down. It was a slight and torturous movement, and the effect it had on her was fucking delicious. The pleasure was simply consuming her; I could tell by the way she pressed her eyes tightly together and then her lips. The corners of her mouth tilted up and down. Her hands were wild on the couch, tugging and scratching, then tugging some more at the pillows.

I could make her come just like this, but it would take too long. She couldn't stand so much torture—at least not for now. So I gave her the flat of my tongue too. I pressed it on her clit before drawing it farther down until I reached her entrance. Then I pushed my tongue in and out of her the way I'd do with my cock. I couldn't see her face anymore, but I felt her body transforming for me.

Her inner muscles pulsed. Her thighs became rigid. Her cries were so delicious that I had to undo my belt and free my cock or I was going to be in pain soon.

By the time I pushed my pants down, I was completely hard for her. I needed her, but I wanted her to climax first. Her body was so wired up that I knew she needed this release more than her next breath. So I gave it to her. I moved my mouth up to her clit and pushed one finger inside her. She came even before I had time to slip in the second one. Watching her succumb so quickly and so fiercely was damn exquisite.

"Oh my God, Chad. Oh my God." She blinked her eyes open, looking down at me, taking in huge, deep breaths. "I'm not even sure how that happened."

I pulled her down from the couch onto her knees so her pussy was level with my cock. "Because you trust me with your body and your needs. You're so fucking open and raw with me, and I love it."

She licked her lips, looking down between us. "I don't know how to be any other way with you."

"And I'll reward you for it."

I grabbed my cock at the base and nudged her clit with the head. She jerked her hips back. Point taken—her clit was still too sensitive. But I could pleasure her in other ways. We weren't going to make it upstairs, though. I needed to sink into this woman right now.

"Turn around, Scarlett. "

She nodded and twirled to face the couch, still on her knees. I pressed down on her shoulders, and she leaned forward, folding her arms at an angle that allowed her to put her hands under her head. Her ass was up in the air, fucking beautiful and perfect and waiting for me. I didn't even take my pants off properly, but it didn't matter. I could fuck her like this too.

She was too glorious and too ready for me to waste any more time taking off my clothes. I couldn't understand my desperation. So I did the only thing I could: I gave in to it.

I tilted her pelvis slightly so her ass was even farther up in the air before I pushed in. I intended to give her only the tip of my cock, but she was so wet that I slid in all the way without even trying.

She panted, "Oh my God, Chad. I'm going to..."

"Come?" I asked her.

"Yes." She lifted her head, then pressed her forehead against her hands again. "I don't know if I can, but I need to so damn badly."

"You can. Trust me. I'll take good care of you, I promise."

I leaned over her, kissing the back of her neck. I knew what she needed, and it was cruel to make her wait, so instead of thrusting inside her, I simply stilled and brought a hand to her clit. When I pressed my fingers against it this time, she didn't jerk or pull away. She simply cried out my name.

I circled her clit and tried to keep myself from bursting by drawing in deep breaths. Her perfume filled my senses. It only made me want her even more.

I was desperate to move, but I wanted her to climax fast. She tightened around my cock. "Fuck. Fuck."

I could come just from feeling her pussy pulse around me. I increased the pace of my fingers, circling her clit, only slowing when she was close. This time when she exploded, her sounds were completely muffled. She was biting into a pillow.

No! I didn't want her to hold back. But instinct pushed away any thoughts plus my ability to form words.

While she was still coming, I started to move my hips back and forth as if through a haze. Her orgasm took over her body, intensifying with every thrust.

When her cries finally subsided and her breathing slowed down, I paced my thrusts until she took her hands from under the pillow, splaying them on the couch. I put my hands on her shoulders, tracing a straight line with my middle fingers from her shoulders to her elbows, then to her forearms. I interlaced our fingers, squeezing them tightly while I moved back and forth at a slower pace.

"How are you feeling?" I murmured in her ear.

"Happy. And overwhelmed."

I was fucking proud of myself. I didn't just satisfy her—I made her happy.

When her muscles started to contract again, I knew she was ready for yet another orgasm. She might not realize it yet, but I was certain of it.

I increased the pace of my thrusts once more, sliding in and out of her like a madman. The sound of my pelvis slapping against her ass filled the living room along with her moans. Her entire body shuddered just as mine started to burn. I was damn close.

I brought our interlaced right hands to her pussy. She sucked in an audible breath, and then we both touched her pussy at the same time. She pushed her ass backward, taking me even deeper.

Her body changed once again, going from soft to completely taut. Pleasure was building inside her. I could practically feel every time she reached a new high.

"Chad, I'm going to—"

"I know. Let it happen. Let it happen for me. I want to feel you come around me once again."

I stroked her clit. Her own fingers trembled. She couldn't do it anymore, but I was more than happy to push her over the edge.

And then it happened. One stroke later, her cries filled the room once again. I only had the privilege to listen to it for a few seconds before my own grunts resounded in my ears. My muscles were taut and relaxed at the same time. The blood rush gripped my entire body in a vise. I was moving and breathing on instinct because my mind was a blank slate. I was only aware of how incredible this woman was.

Our cries mingled, and we both rode out our climaxes until there was nothing left, and we were completely boneless and spent but utterly satisfied.

I wanted the pleasure of making this woman happy every single night.

But I had her for one week only, and I was going to make it count.

Chapter Twenty-Four

Scarlett

"You know, I'm jealous," Ariana said. "Is that wrong of me to say? How did you find the perfect guy?"

I'd called her first thing Monday morning, right before my shift, and totally spilled the beans.

"I have no idea how I got so lucky," I admitted.

"Balancing the scale, maybe? You had the shittiest luck with Simon, and now it's just the opposite."

I bit my lip. "Do you have any more news on him? He contacted my mom through Facebook Messenger, asking if I changed my number."

"That fucking idiot," she sneered. "I haven't heard from him, but he knows better than to do that. Though he did ask around the staff, too, whether they were in contact with you. I take it you blocked him everywhere?"

"Hell yes. All social media. And put him on the spam list in my email."

"Good for you."

"Thanks."

"Listen, he'll self-sabotage, as usual. Don't you waste time thinking about him, okay? Just enjoy that fantastic man you've got."

I grinned. "I plan to do just that."

The next week was hands down the best one of my life. Chad was... Well, he was absolutely perfect. I thought it might be weird to live with him and also work in the same place, but nothing could be further from the truth. Since I typically started later than him, I lingered in the house longer in the morning. In the evening, I arrived after him. And I came home to his pampering every day. The man truly knew how to spoil me.

On Tuesday evening, he prepared a bath in that amazing tub of his. On Wednesday, he cooked for me. Bizarrely, even though I was spending more time with him than before, I missed him more and more during the day. How was that even possible? It didn't help that I knew he was only a few floors up.

I was looking forward to seeing him again tonight. I wanted a chance to spoil him too.

I was always pretty beat after I finished the workday, but I was determined to take care of him just like he was taking care of me. He was actually picking me up today, so at the end of my shift, after I'd changed out of my chef's attire, I was ready to dart out the door.

Just as I was finishing up, Jade said, "A customer is asking for you. Table 14." She was one of our newest servers, and I quite liked her.

I pressed my lips together, cleaning my hands under the spray of water. "What's the complaint about?"

"Honestly, I don't think it's a complaint. The guy was kind of looking forward to seeing you. Maybe it's someone you know."

How could it be? But it didn't matter. I'd just go see what it was about.

Of course, it wasn't a secret that I was working here—I'd posted it all over social media and my LinkedIn. But I couldn't imagine any of my friends showing up unannounced. Grabbing my bag and the rest of my things, I left the kitchen.

The restaurant was chock-full, but I zeroed in on table 14, which was in the corner by the window. It was my former boss, Mark. I couldn't believe that he'd just dropped by out of the blue—Seattle wasn't exactly around the corner.

I hurried over to him, and he smiled big when he saw me. I gave him a reserved one back, as we didn't part on bad terms, but I didn't expect to ever see him here.

"How's my favorite sous-chef?" he asked.

"I'm happy. What are you doing here?"

"I was in the neighborhood," he said with a wink.

"Really? All the way from Seattle."

"NOLA is a popular tourist destination, and LeBlanc & Broussard's is an attraction in itself. I couldn't pass up the opportunity to taste the food, especially if one of my own was running it."

"How's the family?" I asked.

"Exploring the city. They're on a bike tour. Not my thing. I initially wanted to come here with them, but no way could I get a table for four people. I barely managed to convince your reservations manager to even take me."

I gave him a heartfelt smile now. It was good to see him, but I still didn't really think he'd come here just for a meal.

"So, the dinner was to your liking?" I asked and looked back toward the kitchen.

"Am I keeping you from something? I specifically waited until the end of your shift so you'd have some time."

I focused on him again. "No, sorry. That was a force of habit. I'm all yours."

"You know, I always liked you better than Simon."

I jerked my head back. "I really don't want to talk about Simon."

"You're right. That's not why I came here." It was on the tip of my tongue to ask why he *was* here, but I had an inkling that he wasn't going to get to the point tonight. "I'm extremely proud of you."

That took me by complete surprise.

"Thank you!"

"I regret that we lost you. You were an asset to us. You're doing well here? Are you happy?"

"Well, I'm still on probation," I joked. "So the better question would be, are they happy with me? But they're treating me right. I'm enjoying working with the staff. And I love the city."

He narrowed his eyes. "How's the situation in the kitchen? I got the impression that you're a bit short-staffed."

I bristled. "Was anything late? Or not to your liking?"

"No, but you know, after seventeen years in the business, it's just a feeling."

"Someone at the salad station called in sick tonight," I admitted.

"As long as they're not overworking you."

"I'm honestly pretty damn happy."

"Do you want to head out, maybe grab a drink? Then we could chat more."

What would we even have to chat about? He promoted Simon, who then started to behave like an ass, to me in particular. End of story.

"Sorry, I have plans," I said.

"Tomorrow night, then."

I bit the inside of my cheek. I didn't want to be rude, but I needed to make my point clear. "Listen, I appreciate you stopping by and complimenting my skills, but I really don't think we'd have anything to talk about over drinks."

He nodded once. "All right, I know when to give up. Then come on, let's walk out. I already paid the tab."

"Okay."

He immediately rose from his chair. I waved at the staff, who waved right back as Mark and I walked side by side.

Once we were outside the restaurant, he asked, "Are you sure about those drinks? I saw a really nice-looking bar."

"No, thanks. Really, I have plans tonight."

"All right."

"What's going on? Is he bothering you?" Chad's voice boomed from behind me. I startled as he stepped up next to us. He must have been tired of waiting for me in our alley.

"No," I said. "Hi, Chad."

He looked strangely tense. His shoulders seemed rigid.

"This is my previous boss from Seattle. Mark, meet Chad LeBlanc."

Mark held out his hand, and Chad shook it rather strongly.

Okay, so it wasn't my imagination. He really was tense.

"He was visiting from Seattle and decided to stop by the restaurant," I explained.

"A LeBlanc himself, huh? You've got a great place. Ambience is perfect. Fits the city. Food is delicious, but of course it is. You've got Scarlett. You've got a good one." Mark turned to me. "I'm still in town until Sunday. If you change your mind about those drinks, just call me. I'm flexible and look forward to catching up with you."

"I'll keep that in mind," I said curtly.

I really didn't want to shut him down a third time. It felt impolite. I couldn't understand why he was insisting, though. We'd never been friends or anything more than employee and boss.

He turned around and walked away, probably toward Bourbon Street to grab that drink.

"Right," I said, turning to Chad, smiling from ear to ear. "I'm ready to go."

I was more than ready to spoil my man, who was still frowning.

"What was he doing here?" he asked me. His voice was unusually tight.

"Honestly, I don't know. It was a bit bizarre. He said he wanted to check out the food."

"And take you out for a drink."

I looked at him intently, but it wasn't easy to read his expression. The lamppost cast the light right behind him, and his face was hidden in shadows.

"You knew your ex was coming to visit and you didn't say anything?"

I blinked. "What are you talking about? My ex?" And then it dawned on me. "Oh my God, you're jealous." I grinned.

Chad stepped forward, wearing a full-on frown. "This is not funny."

"I'm sorry, but it is." He was jumping to conclusions, but I loved that he cared about me so much.

I wanted to kiss him right here in the middle of Royal Street. But nope, I kept my impulses in check and even grabbed my hands behind my back to resist the urge to touch this delicious man.

"I can see how you got confused. My ex was the chef, Simon, and I was the sous-chef. That's why I referred to him as my boss. But that was actually the *owner* of the restaurant. I guess he's the Seattle version of you."

He growled. "There is no other version of me."

"I *so* like this."

"What, torturing me?" he asked.

My smile fell. I stepped to the side, grabbing one of his arms with both hands and pulling him into our alley. "No, of course I don't like torturing you. I just think that it... I don't know. It was cute to see you jealous, I guess. It made me feel special."

"So he's not your ex?" Chad continued.

I could see the tension still hadn't left his body.

My, my. I have a lot of work ahead of me tonight.

"No."

"Then what was he doing here?"

"Beats me," I admitted. "I saw the man every day at work. He was always in the restaurant, but we didn't have a friendly relationship or any kind of relationship."

"He wanted you to go out for drinks."

I swallowed hard. "I know, Chad. I heard him, and I still don't know what he wanted, but I turned him down. Anyway, I'm sure he can make plenty of other plans with his family."

For the first time since I saw Chad, he visibly relaxed. All the muscles in his face somehow became loosened, and his shoulders dropped. "He's here with his family?"

Holy shit. He really thought my old boss had come here to hit on me and take me out for a drink. No, this simply wouldn't do. I had to show him that he was the only man for me. The absolute only one.

But I needed to get home for that, or we might make spectacles of ourselves.

"Chad," I said slowly, "I think you've got the wrong impression here. Why would you jump to such conclusions?"

He ran his fingers through his hair, shaking his head and looking at his feet before finally focusing on me. "I honestly don't know."

"Hmm," I said.

"I just... I've been out here, watching you talk with him for some time. First I thought he was just a client complaining, but then I realized you knew him. And when he walked out with you and asked about the drinks... I don't know."

"Well, well. I had plans tonight to spoil you anyway, but now I'll have to double down."

"Wait," he said. He took one of my hands in his, pulling me flat against him, and brought the other hand to the low of my back. "You're not even mad?"

"I think we all have our fears and insecurities. I'm not judging. Who knows what this triggered?"

"I'm trying to think about that, but I don't really know."

He touched my lower lip with his tongue, tilting his head forward.

"No, no, no," I said and took a step back. "Oh, I knew I shouldn't have let you pull me that close. Let's go home, and then you can maul me all you want."

"Fuck yes!" he exclaimed.

Less than twenty minutes later, we were already at the house. I'd made a solid plan during the drive. First I was going to lure him into the sexy bathroom and get him in the bathtub. While we were in there, I was going to give him a thorough massage, and then he was getting the best sex of his life. I was super determined.

The second we arrived, I said, "I'm going upstairs to run some water in the tub."

He grinned. "Not so fast. Kissing first."

"No. I said you could kiss me. I didn't specify when."

He groaned, and before I knew it, he came forward, pressing his chest against mine, and walked me backward until my back was against the wall.

Well, when you put it that way, maybe kissing first is a good idea.

CHAPTER TWENTY-FIVE

SCARLETT

"What are you going to do now?"

"Since you've got me trapped like this, I guess I'll have to endure the hardship," I teased.

When he tilted toward me, I closed my eyes. I felt his lips on my eyelids... then my mouth. I'd never get used to this man's attention. It was slow at first, teasing. He only brushed his lips against mine. But then the kiss turned ferocious. God, the things he was doing to my mouth with his tongue. His hands, too, were going low on my waist, and then one slid between my legs, two fingers pressed straight across my clit over the dress.

I moaned without any restraints. I had no inhibitions around Chad, and it felt glorious. I'd never felt so free or happy with anyone.

I was already dreading Sunday when I'd go back to my studio. I didn't want to lose this closeness. Sharing living quarters had brought an intimacy between us that I'd never imagined, and I wasn't done exploring it.

"Anyone home?" resounded throughout the house.

Chad instantly pulled back. I was rooted to my spot. The voice belonged to one of his brothers, but I couldn't tell which one.

"His car was in the driveway," another one said.

"Maybe he's upstairs," came a third.

One was Zachary for sure. The other was maybe Xander? I thought the third one might be Beckett.

Chad looked straight at me and then gave me a half smile. Then he shrugged as if to say, *"What can you do?"*

"Come in," he said loudly.

What was I supposed to say or do? I wanted to quickly look in a mirror. The man had kissed me so thoroughly that I wouldn't put it past my mouth to be completely red and swollen. But there was no time for that because three men came into view. Xander stood a foot away from Zachary and Beckett. He was the one who noticed us first and narrowed his eyes. Zachary's face exploded into the biggest grin I'd ever seen on anyone.

"What the hell, man? You're making her work after hours too?" Beckett asked.

Zachary actually burst out laughing. "Dude, that is not what's happening here."

Aaand my face was on fire. I was certain that he'd picked up on the fact that I'd been very thoroughly kissed just now.

"You move fast, brother," Xander said.

Understanding dawned on Beckett's face. "I see. Bella's out for the week, so you two are having some fun."

To my astonishment, Chad said, "Scarlett is staying with me this week," and then put an arm around my shoulders.

The way he uttered the statement made it sound official somehow.

Beckett's eyes bulged, and Xander pointed at him. "No comment."

"I didn't have one," Beckett said. "I'm actually too stunned to say anything."

Zachary shook his head, zeroing in on me. "Forgive Beckett. He's never actually lived with a girlfriend, so for him, that's outlandish."

My stomach dropped a bit, but I smiled anyway. I wasn't exactly Chad's girlfriend. I was... Well, I wasn't exactly sure. Yes, I was staying with him this week, but it was nowhere near the same thing as a girlfriend living with her boyfriend. That was permanent. This was... What was it?

"So, what are you three doing here, and why did you come up unannounced?" Chad asked.

"You know what's funny?" Xander said. "You think you can ask us to come hang out with Bella at the drop of a hat, but we can't just drop by when we want to?"

"Not unannounced," Chad pointed out. "And you know I appreciate that you're always here for me and Bella."

"Right. How about a do-over?" Beckett said. "We go out, we pretend to call him, he finishes... well, whatever it is he was starting."

"Jesus, Beckett," Xander and Zachary exclaimed at the same time.

"I'm just going to leave you guys to chat," I announced because I felt like I was going to seriously combust.

"You're not going anywhere," Chad replied sternly.

"Forgive Beckett," Zachary said.

"Actually, don't forgive him," Xander chimed in. "Just accept that he's a bit different."

Xander glared at Beckett, who just shrugged and then said, "We're here to talk about the boat."

Chad didn't hesitate. "Where's Anthony?"

"He's got some stuff to deal with tonight. But I'm his representative," Beckett said.

"What boat?" I asked.

Chad smiled, gesturing for his brothers to go to the living room. Then he grabbed my hand and said, "Let's go sit down."

"Okay, I just want to drink a glass of water first," I said.

"Sure."

As they went to the seating area, I quickly downed a glass. My throat was parched. Then I hesitated. Maybe I should stay back so they had privacy. To give myself something to do, I took out my phone and checked my emails. To my surprise, Mark had emailed.

Hey Scarlett,

It was great seeing you. I'm happy you're doing well. Your food is top-notch as usual.

I glanced at the email again, wondering if it had been cut off short. But no, he had finished it with best wishes. What was the point of him writing to me? But I didn't want to be impolite, and I definitely didn't want to burn any bridges. I never knew when I'd need another recommendation.

I sent him a neutral reply.

Hey, thanks a lot. It was good to see you. If you're ever in New Orleans again, feel free to stop by.

"Scarlett?" Chad asked, snapping me out of my thoughts. "Everything okay?"

"Yeah, sure." I hurried to the couch, sitting so I could still see my gorgeous lit-up tree out of the corner of my eye.

It's not your tree, Scarlett. You don't live here. Don't get overly attached to it, or to Chad.

"So, about the boat." Beckett pulled out his phone and showed it to Chad. "These are the options."

"That's good. I like all of them." Looking at me, he explained, "My grandfathers both refuse to spend the money on a boat when, and I quote, 'we have a perfectly good one out on the bayou.'"

"It's nowhere near perfect," Xander pointed out.

"Yeah," Zachary agreed, "and that's not just because he's a perfectionist. That thing is one gator bite away from sinking to the bottom of the bayou."

"Because manners are important to the family," Beckett said, "Chad had a genius idea. He's going to give it to them as a present so they can't turn it down."

"That *is* genius," I stated. *And extremely thoughtful.*

"All three are good. Which one will be delivered faster?" Chad asked.

I glanced at the iPad, too, and nearly fell off the couch. *Holy shit, how could a boat cost as much as tiny studio?* Maybe I was imagining one more zero. I leaned in slowly without being overtly obvious. No, I was seeing correctly. I sat back on the couch, stunned.

"The third one."

"All right, then let's get that one," Chad said.

That was the most expensive one by about 30 percent, and he didn't even bat an eyelash.

"Perfect," Beckett said. "I'm sending this to Anthony right now. Now we need to work on a strategy to actually sell this to the grandparents."

"You said it's a gift," I countered.

"We need to find the perfect time," Xander said and then looked at Zachary. "Zachary, you're the expert at managing situations."

Chad was also looking at Zachary intently.

Zachary himself narrowed his eyes and then leaned back farther on the couch. "I think we shouldn't make that the main event. The focus should be something else."

"Sounds smart," Chad began. "But what should that be?"

"Not a birthday," Zachary went on. "We don't want to overshadow anyone."

"Besides, no one's got a birthday anytime soon. When will the boat be delivered?"

"Two days," Beckett replied.

Zachary and Chad exchanged a glance.

"Are you thinking the same thing as me?" Zachary asked.

Chad grinned. "Sunday is showtime."

"What's happening Sunday?" I asked.

"All the family is back from Disney. They'll spend an inordinate amount of time showing us pictures and bragging about who got to do what with Bella. And within all that, I'll slip in the news about the boat," he explained.

"Chad, you can't be serious. This is a monumental gift. There is no 'slipping it in' between vacation pictures and such," I replied.

"It actually could work," Zachary said.

Xander pointed at him. "Let's walk through that scenario."

"Dude, that's not how I work, and you know it," Zachary countered. "I do my best work in the field."

"We're not going to war," Beckett huffed.

God, these guys were so hilarious.

"That's debatable," Xander said, "because if all four grandparents full-on confront us about ambushing them with the boat, things could turn bloody."

Chad shook his head. "Both Isabeau and Celine have been nagging them for years to change it. They'll side with us."

"Well, I think we got everything we came for," Zachary concluded. "We chose the boat and the day to tell them. We can go."

"We could stay for a drink," Beckett suggested.

Xander narrowed his eyes at him. "We'll have the drink somewhere else. Let's go to Julian's."

When Beckett opened his mouth, clearly in protest, Xander said, "Beckett." He glanced at me and Chad out of the corner of his eye. I wanted to bury my face in my hands, but that would be too obvious.

"Right. Sure. Let's go, then," Beckett replied awkwardly as all of us rose from the couches.

We walked them to the entrance, and as soon as they were gone, Chad turned to me, smiling. "Sorry about that."

"No, it was fun. And unexpected."

"I'll tell them not to drop by unannounced for the rest of the week."

My stomach bottomed out once again. I didn't like the reminder that I wasn't going to be here anymore after Sunday.

"Xander and Zachary didn't seem at all surprised that I was here in the living room."

"They were. They just hid it way better than Beckett," Chad replied.

"And that's okay?"

"Sure. They were going to find out sooner rather than later."

"Good thing we weren't in the tub already. But we've wasted enough time. Let's go upstairs."

He made to lean in, but I stopped him. "That's a very firm no." He pinned me with his gaze. Well, maybe it wasn't that firm, but he didn't need to know that. "You start kissing me, and we'll never get in that tub."

"I don't mind at all."

"But you need it."

"Oh, really?" he asked skeptically.

I took his hand and walked in front of him up the staircase. I looked over my shoulder as we reached the upper level. "Would it sweeten the offer if I told you that I plan to jump in with you?"

His face instantly lit up. "You should've led with that."

Chad

While the water filled the tub, I undressed in the bedroom. Scarlett was out in the hallway.

She'd better not be joking about joining me in the tub. Sure, my muscles were tense, and the hot water would do me good, but I wanted her there with me so I could spend every minute with her.

"Scarlett?" I asked. "Where are you?"

"Oh, I'm in Bella's room," she said.

Wrapping a towel around my waist, I walked out of my bedroom and into Bella's. Scarlett was fiddling with the drapes, binding them at odd angles.

"What are you doing?"

She looked up at me sheepishly. "Uh, sorry. I bought these today and was curious to try something out, but I don't want to leave you waiting." She put the box of fabric on the bed and then dashed toward me, taking my hand again and walking with me to the bathroom. She was still fully clothed.

"What's with that fabric?"

"Bella mentioned that she wanted more *Harry Potter*-themed things in her bedroom, and I saw these curtains…"

I tilted her chin up. "You're fucking fantastic. You know that?"

"I'm super happy that I found some with Hedwig. She's all white, so it doesn't clash with the rest of the colors."

"I don't understand. What's a Hedwig?"

She giggled. "Oh, how can you be such a Muggle, really? You miss out a lot by not watching the movies."

"I can't believe you went out to buy fabric for Bella."

"Why not? Every morning, I looked around in the Quarter for a shop that might sell *Harry Potter* stuff. I didn't want to order online because I wanted to actually see the fabric, and one day, I got lucky."

"I'm the one who's lucky. So fucking lucky." I leaned in, pulling her lower lip between mine.

"What are you up to?" she murmured against my mouth. "You want to get me naked, huh?"

"Of course." I dropped my towel right before I grabbed her dress and yanked it over her head. She removed her bra in the next breath.

I'd never tire of watching her take off her clothes.

"Want to do the honors?" she teased, hooking her thumbs in the elastic band of her panties.

"No, I want to watch you do it. Turn around."

"I see. Want to have a view of my ass?"

"Always."

She turned around, moving her hips slowly, then bent at her waist and lowered the panties. Her ass was fucking exquisite. It was all I could do not to push her against the vanity and make her mine right now.

She straightened up, looking at me over her shoulder. I took a huge step until I was right behind her, her ass pressed against my cock. I groaned, burying my face in her neck.

Fuck, how is it already Thursday? That only gave me three more nights with her, and I hadn't had nearly enough yet.

"What are you thinking about?" she asked.

"That it's already Thursday."

Her entire body softened against mine.

"I know," she murmured.

I looked at her in the mirror, and she glanced right back at me. I wanted her here with me long after Bella returned, but that was a crazy idea. Bella didn't even know that Scarlett and I were seeing each other. She didn't even know what that meant. I couldn't possibly be selfish enough to do this. Even though all I wanted was to keep Scarlett here.

I pushed her hair to one side, kissing her neck. I could explore her back to my heart's desire.

"Come with me on Sunday," I said. "To lunch at my family's house."

She sucked in her belly. "But Bella will be there."

"I know." Then it occurred to me that maybe she didn't necessarily want Bella to know. *Fuck.* But if that was the case, I had to know. "We can use that event to let the whole family know that you and I are seeing each other, Bella included."

She turned around, blinking rapidly. "Are you serious?"

"Why wouldn't I be?" I still couldn't gauge what she really wanted. I could usually read her. Why not now?

"You said your promise of celibacy was so Bella wouldn't have women—"

"Just you. Only you."

She glanced up again. I cupped her face with both hands. "I don't have the power to make this week last longer."

"But you'd like to?" she whispered.

"Yes. It's all I've been thinking about since you got here. That I don't want you to leave again."

She swallowed hard. "Oh, Chad, that would be crazy," she murmured.

"I know."

It was on the tip of my tongue to ask her to stay, but I reined myself in for both of our sakes. And Bella's. Especially Bella's. She wouldn't understand this. I had to move slowly.

Scarlett hesitated. "Are you sure it's okay with the family if I come?"

"Babe, Isabeau and Celine made you a perfume. That's their seal of approval."

She gasped. "Why didn't anyone tell me that?"

"I thought that was obvious."

"Well, no, it wasn't. I just thought they wanted to be nice to me."

"If they wanted to be nice, they would've baked you a pie. Making a signature perfume for you is something else entirely."

She seemed stunned for a few seconds, but then her face transformed with a gorgeous smile. "Huh, I've got their approval." Then she took a small step back and started to move her hips. "I've got their approval. I've got their approval," she chanted, then burst out laughing.

This woman was something else.

When she faced me again, I flattened her against me, cupping her ass with both hands. Her breasts pressed against my chest. I could die a happy man right now with this woman naked in my arms. We'd lose all this by the end of the week: the playful evenings, the sexy nights, and everything in between.

But something had changed between us just now. She was going to come to our family brunch. After Sunday, my daughter would know Scarlett was mine. The entire family would.

"Let's get in the tub," she said. "It's almost full."

I wanted to take her straight to the bedroom, but the bathtub would do too.

I got in first and then took her hand, helping her get in as well. The water was pleasantly warm, not too hot. We both sat down, facing each other, and then she immediately shifted, getting up on her knees. "I didn't think this through. I need you to turn the other way around."

"Why?"

"So I can start on your back massage."

I wiggled my eyebrows. "You can give me a front massage too." I pointed at my cock.

She smirked. "That's going to be my last stop."

"You've been planning this bit by bit?"

"Not exactly," she said. "Just broad strokes. My goal is not to let you hijack my plan midway with hot kisses and such."

"Scarlett, I have news for you," I said, rising on my knees, too, and meeting her halfway. "I'm going to do that anyway."

CHAPTER TWENTY-SIX

CHAD

Sunday came around far too quickly. Right before heading to dinner with my family, we dropped off Scarlett's bags at her home.

"Fucking hell. I'd forgotten how small this place was," I said when we stepped inside.

"Hey, don't be so judgy. I like it here. It's cozy." Biting her lip, she glanced around. "Let's go so we're not late."

She was fiddling with her thumbs. I stepped in front of her, wanting to see what this was about.

"Scarlett, are you nervous?"

"It's that noticeable, huh?"

"Of course." I looked at her intently.

"Yeah, I am," she whispered.

"If you prefer not to come, that's okay. I don't want to pressure you into anything."

I sucked in a breath. What if she took me up on my offer? I wanted to make things official to the family, but what if she wasn't ready?

She tilted her head as if seriously considering it. "No, no. I'm not a chicken. I want to come."

I rolled my shoulders back, suddenly feeling lighter. "Perfect. Then we should get going. They shared their location earlier, and they'll be home in around five minutes."

"Oh my God!" She went ramrod straight. "So we're already going to be late."

I chuckled. "No, we're not. It's good to give them time to settle in before we arrive."

"I can't wait to hear what Bella was up to this week."

I kissed her forehead, inhaling deeply. Her perfume was addictive. I'd never get used to hearing her talk about my daughter with so much warmth. I couldn't believe I was so lucky.

"I miss my girl," I confessed. "It's always hard for me when she leaves with the grandparents, but I know she has a lot of fun."

"You're a great dad."

Hearing those words from her meant the world to me.

After depositing her suitcase next to the dresser, we headed down to the car.

"You said they live in the Garden District, right? Did we pass by the house when we went there the other day?" she asked once we were on the road.

"No, I would've pointed it out."

"It must be huge if they all live there."

"That's an understatement." I didn't give her any details, though. She'd see it soon enough.

We arrived twenty minutes later, and her reaction was priceless.

"Chad," she said slowly, "I think it's the biggest home I've seen in the Garden District." Her voice was hoarse.

"I can guarantee that it is," I said.

The van was already parked in front, and there was no one there, which meant they'd already unloaded all of the bags. I saw my brothers' cars scattered around the street.

All right, so everyone was here. We were going to make a grand entrance.

When we got out of the car, I looked at Scarlett closely. She beamed as she took in the house and then glanced at me.

"You know, when you said everyone lives together, I truly couldn't picture it, but I assume everyone has their own wing of sorts."

"That was the initial idea, but it didn't work out like that. The grand-parents use the ground floor so they don't have to deal with stairs, and my parents are on the upper levels. They make it work."

She grinned. "Funny, when I was a kid, I always thought that when my parents were old, I was going to buy them a cute house not far away from me just so I could look out for them."

Fucking hell, this woman. I didn't think I could like her even more, but the longer I knew her, the more she proved me wrong.

"Let's go inside," I said.

"Is anyone expecting me?"

"Only my brothers," I said.

"So you didn't tell anyone else?" She sounded panicked. It was so damn endearing.

"It's going to be fine, I promise."

"Okay. It's showtime," she said and wiggled her hips.

I wanted to pull her against me and kiss her senseless. How the hell was I supposed to drop her off at her home later tonight after I'd had her all to myself this week?

We walked together up the front steps. I didn't need to ring the bell because they always left the front door open when they were expecting us. We simply went inside.

Scarlett looked around with a warm smile. "This house has such a good vibe. It's so welcoming."

"I think so too," I replied. "And somehow they managed to agree on decorating it in a style that pleases everyone."

We only heard faint voices, which meant everyone was in the living room, farther away from the entrance. I guided Scarlett there.

As soon as we stepped inside the living room, Bella yelled, "Daddy, you're here," and then ran straight toward me.

I'd missed my little girl so damn much. Whenever she was away, it felt like a part of me was gone.

I lowered myself onto my haunches, opening my arms wide, and she jumped straight into them, the way she did when she was tiny. Then I rose to my feet with her in my arms, hugging her tighter and then tighter still.

She gave me a huge kiss on the cheek and then pulled back, smiling at me. Then she turned to Scarlett.

"Hi, Scarlett."

"Hey, Bella. I can't wait to hear about your week."

"Dad, can you put me down? I want to hug Scarlett too."

I felt a pang of jealousy. Actual jealousy. My girl usually liked to stay in my arms for at least ten minutes after a trip.

She hugged Scarlett just as tightly as she'd hugged me.

"I had so much fun," she said when she pulled back. "I got autographs from Cinderella and from all the princesses and from Snow White."

"You did, huh? You also have pictures?"

"Yes. The grans have everything on their phones."

I looked from Scarlett and Bella to the rest of the family. I'd been right. All of my brothers were already here. And by Julian's and Anthony's smiles, they were well aware of the fact that Scarlett had been living with me this week. In fact, the only ones who seemed surprised were my parents, though Mom had a hint of a smile on her face too. Both sets of grandparents simply looked smug—especially Celine and Isabeau.

"I missed you, Scarlett," Bella told her.

"I missed you too," she replied.

The three of us walked farther inside the living room, greeting everyone.

"This is a nice surprise, Scarlett. It's very good to see you again," Mom said.

Dad seemed too stunned for words, so he simply shook Scarlett's hand.

Celine was positively beaming. "Oh, darling. I knew that perfume would do the trick."

Isabeau sighed. "Celine, you're not supposed to say that out loud."

Then she glanced at Bella, who was already telling Scarlett and me about her favorite encounter—with Mickey Mouse. Grandfather David was looking at Julian with a suspicious glance, so I suspected that he was already in the know. But Felix was simply looking at Celine. He always claimed that her perfume theory was a lot of nonsense—so did I. But if it made Celine feel better, then who was I to disagree?

"All right, well, since we only just arrived and obviously didn't have time to cook, how about we order some jambalaya?" Isabeau suggested.

Scarlett straightened up. "I'd love to cook for you. I bet you have some rice and maybe frozen veggies and shrimp. If you show me the kitchen and your supplies, I can whip up a jambalaya."

"Scarlett," I said, putting an arm around her shoulders, "you will not cook."

"Darling!" Mom exclaimed, looking at Scarlett with a mix of surprise and warmth. "It's very nice of you to offer, and we really appreciate it.

But you spend enough time in kitchens as it is. In this house, you won't ever step foot in it."

"Don't disagree with Mom," I said, "especially when it's about the kitchen."

"All right," Scarlett said, but she sounded a bit uncertain. "If you're sure."

"Why don't we all sit down?" Dad suggested.

They had a huge living area with couches and chairs, so we all took a seat.

Keeping my hands to myself around Scarlett was becoming more and more difficult, but I didn't want to confuse Bella by being overtly affectionate. It was a great start that she was so happy to see Scarlett here, but I wanted to have a proper conversation with her and explain everything. That would have to wait until we were back at home, though.

Bella came over and sat right in my lap, holding a phone and flipping through pictures.

"Oh, Cinderella is gorgeous," Scarlett exclaimed.

"I know, right? But she was cheating. I looked at her shoes, and they were not made of glass. She was wearing sneakers!! No princess does that."

"Well, even princesses get tired," Scarlett said. "Especially if she's on her feet all day."

"Hmmm…," Bella said, still sounding unconvinced.

She showed us nearly three dozen photos. I was beyond grateful that my girl had had such a great time, but I was a bit out of my depths regarding the characters. I didn't remember most of them, but guess who did? Scarlett.

After Bella finished showing us all the pictures, she ran straight to Xander.

"Uncle Xander, you lied to me."

"I did no such thing," Xander said somewhat theatrically. "I never lie."

"You said Goofy was ugly."

"And I stand by that."

"But he's not ugly." Bella stomped her foot.

"That, Bella, is a difference of opinion," Xander said. "You believe one thing, and I believe the other. Doesn't mean either of us is lying."

"But there can be only one truth."

My brother had opened a can of worms, but he was always good at that. Then again, he treated Bella almost like an adult. His conversations with her were always challenging, but my girl enjoyed them.

As they debated the pros and cons of opinions versus the truth, Anthony, Beckett, and Zachary came over to me and Scarlett.

"So," Anthony said, "we've got the boat."

Scarlett chuckled. "You guys really are efficient."

"Hell yes!" Beckett said. "I'm very convincing. It's at the family dock out on the bayou."

That was true. Out of all of us, Beckett was the most skilled.

I grinned. "I'm impressed. I assumed we would just have the paperwork today. All that's left is to break the news."

We all turned to look at Zachary, including Scarlett.

"You know what? Everyone is relaxed and in a good mood. I don't think any prep work is necessary. We'll rip off the Band-Aid and see how it goes," he said.

Anthony groaned.

"Come on, man," Beckett said. "Let's discuss at least several strategies."

"What are you all talking about?" David asked from across the room.

"See? It's not good to get them suspicious," Zachary said. "That will just get their defenses up."

I nodded. "You're right. I'll tell them right away. By the time the jambalaya is delivered, you'll have smoothed everything over."

Zachary stared at me. "Chad, I'm good at smoothing things over, not making the unthinkable happen."

"Fair point."

"Besides," Zachary said, "Scarlett being here actually helps."

"Really?" she said, grinning. "What can I do?"

Once again, the impulse to pull her somewhere we would be alone and kiss her almost overwhelmed me. I liked how eager she was to be part of all this. Sarah always said our antics were below the LeBlanc name.

Fuck, Chad. Stop it. It's not fair to compare them.

"Your mere presence helps," Zachary explained. "The grandmothers will focus on you fairly quickly. They won't let David and Felix put up a fuss for too long."

I glanced around the room. This was as good a time as any.

"All right, everyone, I've got some news." I said loudly.

Xander and Bella didn't stop talking, just lowered their voices to whispers.

"Darling, you don't have to spell it out," Celine said. "We can read between the lines." She looked between Scarlett and me with a lot of hope.

I squeezed Scarlett's hand, then said, "Actually, this concerns our grandfathers. We've got a surprise for you out on the bayou."

Felix lit up. "You went fishing while we were gone?"

"No. I bought a new boat."

Zachary had a point. There was no way to tiptoe around this. Ripping off the Band-Aid was the smartest idea.

"For you two," I clarified.

David and Felix started talking at the same time.

"We don't need one," David exclaimed.

"Why waste the money?" Felix added.

Celine and Isabeau continued staring at Scarlett and me, obviously thinking we were going to announce something. Funny how that wouldn't bother me. What we had felt real, and I knew that when the time came, I wouldn't hesitate to celebrate with my family.

"Oh, well, that's nice, boys." Celine sounded disappointed. It was then that I realized I needed to find out Bella's stance, her thoughts on Scarlett being part of our lives.

Because I knew one thing for certain: I wasn't going to let Scarlett go.

Chapter Twenty-Seven

Chad

"When you're old as dirt, time loses meaning," Grandfather Felix countered. "Is it too late to cancel?"

I felt triumphant. My brothers snickered as well. It was a stroke of genius to have the boat delivered.

"Yes," I stated.

"As he said, it's out on the bayou already," Anthony said lazily.

Felix looked at my brother. "You're involved in this too?"

"Yes, he is, and since we're fessing up," Beckett said, "so are Zachary, Xander, and I."

Julian held up his hands in self-defense. "I had nothing to do with this, but I fully support it. If you turn down that boat, I swear to God, I'll personally sink that old metal rusty thing. I've thought about doing that a few times over the years anyway."

"You boys are stubborn," David said.

"I guess we're a lot like you, then," Zachary said. "Listen, the boat is already out there and paid for. There is no way to return it." He emphasized the word *return*. "You might as well enjoy it. It's big. Has plenty of areas for shade."

"Oh, shade would be good," Felix said. "We've been cooking on it lately. The sun's getting stronger, so I'll definitely like that."

David shook his head. "I don't want to learn how to drive a new boat."

Anthony didn't miss a beat. "I can show you. I tried it out. I specifically chose one that had an easy learning curve."

Felix and David still looked a tad unconvinced, although Felix had come around surprisingly quickly.

"I'm sure you can take it back. There's always a fourteen-day policy, or even a thirty-day policy of returning merchandise, isn't there?" David asked.

"Not for custom orders." Okay, so that was a lie, but he wouldn't find out. When something was for someone's own good, white lies were acceptable... Sort of.

He humphed in response.

Felix turned to him and said, "Let's at least look at this thing. If we hate it too much, they can always resell it."

Zachary and I exchanged a glance. We hadn't even thought about that, but they wouldn't.

"Perfect," Anthony said. "We'll find a day to go out and try it. Maybe next week."

I glanced at the grandmothers, who usually sided with their husbands, but Celine looked extremely relieved.

"It wouldn't be bad for you to have a more comfortable boat," Isabeau said. "You two spend a lot of time out there."

"We're fine in ours," David said.

Celine put a hand over his. "When Isabeau and I bought furniture for the store, you boys insisted on us only buying the most comfortable chairs. It's time you took your own advice."

Felix grunted but didn't fight anymore. He rarely fought with Grandmother.

"I suppose we can try it out next Saturday," he said.

Zachary and Anthony exchanged a triumphant glance. We'd actually done it.

Scarlett leaned in to me and whispered, "This is mesmerizing to watch. I'm so proud of you guys."

"But I'm telling you one thing," David said, determined to have the last word as usual. No one tried to contradict him. "If I don't like it, it goes back or we sell it, end of discussion."

"You can revisit that after you're on the boat," Zachary said.

His voice was completely neutral and even. I respected my brother for always being calm. He didn't often partake in negotiations, but if he did, he'd be better than Julian and me put together.

"All right," Celine said. "So what have you two been up to this week?"

I glanced at Bella. She was still at the far end of the room, talking to Xander, who hadn't said one word, but then again, my daughter demanded his full attention.

"Celine, don't be intrusive," Isabeau chastised, which made me laugh because I knew she wanted to ask the same question.

"I just have one question. I promise not to ask anything else," Celine said. Isabeau gave her a warning look, but I could see her shift a bit at the edge of her seat, staring at us intently. "Are you two in a relationship?"

I hadn't expected Celine to be so direct. By the gasp that went around us, I realized no one else had either. Even Zachary's eyes bulged.

I cleared my throat and put my hand on Scarlett's shoulders. "Scarlett and I are together."

"Yes," Celine exclaimed. "That's all I wanted to know. No more details required. Except maybe—"

"Mom." That came from my mother. "Let's give it a rest, okay?" She looked at us with a huge smile. "For what it's worth, we're very happy to have you here, Scarlett. I truly hope our shenanigans won't scare you away. I think we're all a bit extra excited tonight because we've been away for so long."

"Darling, don't try to sugarcoat the truth," Dad said. He kissed Mom's hand but kept his eyes on Scarlett and me. "We're always like this."

Scarlett beamed. "I'm happy to be here tonight. And don't worry, I'm not at all scared."

"Attagirl." Isabeau beamed. "Then again, we already knew you were fierce."

"How so?" Scarlett asked.

Isabeau shrugged. "The notes in your perfume reveal a lot."

"What notes were those exactly?" Mom asked, and then her eyes went wide. "You included lilac, didn't you?"

"Of course, dear. We're not amateurs," Celine said.

Mom and the grandmothers launched into a debate about the famous lilac right up until the doorbell rang.

"That will be the jambalaya," Mom said.

Dad got up too. "I'll help you bring it in."

Beckett trailed after them without even being asked. Anthony went too. The second he was out of earshot, David straightened up.

"You give it to me straight, boys. Can Anthony really not return the boat?"

Zachary pointed his thumb to me. "Chad bought it, and—"

"Give it a rest, David," Felix said. "The boys want to do something good for us. We'll go out and try it and see how it goes. We owe them at least that much."

"Hmm," David said, but he didn't argue further.

Once my parents and brothers brought the jambalaya in, we all moved to the dining area. The table was huge, although it was rarely used because no one ate at the same time. Everyone had their own schedule. But it did come in handy when all of us came together. Even Bella hurried to the table.

"I missed jambalaya." She looked at me. "And I missed our pies, Dad."

"We'll eat them this evening," I assured her, and she lit up immediately.

I was so happy she was back home. I intended to spoil her rotten this upcoming week.

After dinner, Bella came to sit on my lap.

"Dad, when are we going to Disney again?" She always liked to schedule the next adventure when she was done with the previous one.

"We'll see, cricket." I had to check with Sarah and see if she wanted to spend Bella's next vacation with her.

She frowned. "That's no fun."

I knew why she liked Xander so much. She was just as exacting as he was.

She looked at Scarlett. "When can we bake another pie? And don't say, 'We'll see.'"

Scarlett laughed, but she didn't say anything.

"I can come in the morning again," Bella went on.

"Cricket, Scarlett is on her feet all day. If she meets us in the morning, then she'll have to work even longer. I want to find a solution that's not too tiring for her either."

"Oh, okay," Bella said.

"Which pie do you want to learn how to make?" Scarlett asked her.

"What's your favorite?"

"Hmm," Scarlett said, tapping her chin. "It's a rhubarb one that my mom used to make when I was a kid."

Bella wrinkled her nose. "I don't like rhubarb."

"We'll find something you like," Scarlett assured her. "Now, you forgot to tell me something important. Which castle did you like most at Disney? Did you know that I've never been?"

"No way. Every child goes to Disney," Bella said as if she couldn't possibly imagine a reality in which that didn't happen.

Sometimes I forgot that we all lived in a bubble.

"Baby girl, not everyone can go. The United States is large. For some people, it's too far away and too expensive," I explained.

"Oh, okay," Bella said, then turned to Scarlett. "Why didn't you tell me that? I need to tell you *everything* I saw."

She got down from my lap and climbed onto Scarlett's, who immediately put her arms around my girl.

I couldn't get enough of seeing them together. I never thought I'd meet someone like Scarlett. She listened patiently while Bella described every castle in detail, asking questions of her own every so often.

By the time we left two hours later, Bella still hadn't finished talking about the castles. Once we were in the car, though, she immediately fell asleep. She'd done that as a baby too. In fact, when she couldn't sleep in the evening, I'd often take her for a night drive through the city. She always went out like a light.

"Are you okay?" I asked Scarlett, interlacing our fingers as I kept my left hand on the wheel.

"Yes. I have a bit of adrenaline. Being around your family is like drinking five espresso shots."

I laughed. "That's the most accurate description of the gang."

We arrived in front of her building far too quickly. Damn it, I wanted her to come with us, but I knew it wasn't possible. It was too much too soon for all three of us.

"No, you don't have to," she whispered as I opened my door.

I cocked a brow. "I won't say goodbye like this, Scarlett."

"Oh, okay."

Even in the dark of evening, I could see her blush.

I closed the door without making any sound, and Scarlett did the same. Then I rounded the car and was about to lean in, but Scarlett placed a hand firmly on my chest.

"I invoke the no-kissing rule."

"Why?"

She looked back at Bella.

"She's asleep," I said.

"What if she wakes up?"

"She won't, trust me."

"See, I don't trust you on that. What if the poor girl wakes up and sees us mauling each other? You do have a history of pinning me against whatever surface you can find."

"That's true," I conceded. There was a real risk that things would spiral out of control. And my girl could see us. *Fucking hell, how could I lose my head like this?* "Tonight was incredible."

She smiled. "I loved it too. And honestly, I didn't want to interfere earlier, but I really don't mind if she comes in the mornings before school at the restaurant."

"Sugar, you work too much as it is. I have half a mind to hire another chef."

She gasped. "Why would you do that? It's my job."

"I want more time with you," I said.

"Absolutely not. This is the typical schedule of a chef."

I opened my mouth but then closed it again. Fuck, what was I doing? I couldn't ask for her to work less just because I wanted to be with her for more hours in the day. Yet all my instincts told me to do just that.

"You're right. I take that back. I don't know what got into me." Swallowing hard, I added, "I'll talk to Bella. We could do weekends as well."

"Won't Sarah mind?" she asked.

"No, she won't. Sarah isn't... Well, let's just say she didn't put up a fight when I insisted that I wanted custody of Bella and for her to live with me during the week. She actually fussed at the idea of having her daughter every weekend. Because she needs free time too."

I tried not to sound bitter, but I couldn't hide how I felt about it.

"Oh," Scarlett said. "That's too bad. But it's amazing that your entire family dotes on her. It's lovely."

I instinctively knew that she hadn't had all this as a kid. Was it crazy that I wanted to fulfill every single desire she had?

I walked closer to her, but then she jumped to one side.

"Nope."

"I was just coming closer," I pointed out.

"That ends up in a smoking-hot kiss most of the time, so it's better to have a foot between us. Actually, it's best that I go upstairs. Good night, Chad."

"Good night."

I watched her as she went inside her building. I wanted to walk her up and kiss her against that door, just as she'd said, but that wasn't possible tonight.

Things would change soon, though. I was going to make sure of that.

Bella slept during the whole drive. Once we were home, I carried her upstairs to her bedroom. The second I put her on the bed, though, she opened her eyes.

"Daddy, where's Scarlett?"

"We dropped her off at home, remember? That's where we were heading first."

"Oh. I didn't get to say goodbye." She pouted. "Dad, is Scarlett your girlfriend?"

Figures. My daughter definitely took after my grandmothers.

I'd intended to ease her into this, to explain things in a language she could understand, which made me realize... "You know what a girlfriend is?"

"Of course. The fourth graders at my school already have girlfriends. My best friend, Delaney, also has a boy who likes her, but she doesn't know if she's his girlfriend."

Not overreacting took a monstrous effort. In fact, I chose not to react at all.

"Would you like for Scarlett to be my girlfriend?" I asked.

I needed to divert my focus to something else besides the possibility of my daughter—

Nope, not even going to go there.

"Yes, Daddy. We can bake anytime then, right? If she's your girl-friend. Aaaaand we can watch a *Harry Potter* marathon."

That reminded me of something. "Actually, Scarlett has a surprise for you. Look at your drapes."

She turned to them with sleepy eyes and then sat up. "Hedwig!"

"That's right. The white owl."

She raised a brow. "You know who Hedwig is? Did you watch *Harry Potter* without me?"

"No, I didn't. Scarlett explained some of the characters to me."

She bounced up and down and then smiled at me with her little face all lit up. "I really love Scarlett."

So do I.

After my girl fell asleep, I went to my bedroom. My mind was on Scarlett. I took a shower, turning it as cold as I could handle it, but it still didn't take the edge off. Once I stepped out, I got in bed. Usually, I'd read a newspaper article or two before falling asleep, but right now, I wanted something different. Picking up my phone, I texted Scarlett.

Chad: Bella is very happy about us. And she loves the drapes.

Scarlett: YES. YES. YES.

Chad: I miss you already.

Scarlett: And so do I.

Chad: What do you miss most?

Scarlett: Oh, that's hard to say. Hmm, let's see. That gorgeous tree and the twinkle lights, the view from your living room, or possibly that amazing hot tub. Oh, and you, of course. I miss you.

Chad: Sassy. You have no idea what I'd do to you if you were here.

Scarlett: Oh, do tell.

Chad: No. I'll show you next time we're together.

That was going to be very, very soon. I wanted her back. I needed her right here.

Chapter Twenty-Eight

Scarlett

"Is it just me, or is this a particularly crazy day?" I asked Joel on Monday morning.

We'd both arrived early, as we always did on Mondays, and it turned out that all of our deliveries were late for one reason or another. We'd been here for nearly two hours, and no one came. The crew would arrive in twenty minutes, and we had to start prepping lunch.

"Was there a storm or something?" I asked.

Joel rubbed his neck. "Not that I know of, boss, but some of our suppliers do come from outside the city."

"I'll have to get a bit creative. Please check what we have in the freezer to get things going for the day. And then we'll use the fresh produce for tomorrow or dinner. But if we want something for lunch, we can't wait any longer."

He nodded. "Yep, you're right, boss. I'll make an inventory right away and tell you what we have."

"Thanks, Joel," I said, then yawned.

I went to sleep late last night after a certain sexy restaurant owner kept me up with messages, but I had zero regrets. Besides, my bed felt so foreign and cold that I had trouble sleeping anyway. Maybe I shouldn't have spent the whole last week with Chad. Now I was struggling to get back to the way things were before. I had no idea when I was going to see him next or exactly how we were going to see each other at all. We couldn't meet up after work any longer.

My heart grew heavy. What if that week was all we had?

But that wasn't possible. He'd taken me to meet his family.

After Joel left, I did my morning email check and groaned. I had an email from Simon. He'd changed his email address, so of course the spam filters didn't block him.

I heard Mark was in New Orleans. I hope you didn't fill his head with more crap, or you'll regret it.

This guy was just unbelievable. I was tempted to write back that I never speak of him, but I didn't want to engage, so I deleted his email and put the new address in the spam filters as well.

"Scarlett?" Joel said, face a bit pale.

I looked up from my phone.

"Oh, what's wrong? Tell me our freezers aren't broken or something."

"No. There's someone in the front for you."

I swear to God, if it's Mark again... But I couldn't see that happening, since he said he was only here for the weekend.

"Who is it?" I asked.

"Sarah," he said, sounding a bit uncertain.

I nearly jerked my head back. "And you're sure she wants to talk to *me*?"

"She specifically asked for you."

"I'm going to see what she wants. You looked at the freezer?"

"No, not yet, but I'm on it."

"Good. I want a report when I return," I said.

I unconsciously moved my hand to my chef's hat, intending to take it off. Oh, what the hell. I could leave it on. Otherwise, I need to fasten it again afterward. So what if I didn't look great? I wasn't trying to impress her.

I quickly walked up to the front. Sarah was sitting at one of the tables. She was absolutely beautiful. Bella didn't look much like her, though; she resembled Chad and his family more. I wondered if Sarah had modeled or something.

"Good morning," I greeted.

She whipped her head in my direction. She had freckles on her nose, and they looked adorable with her blue eyes.

"Scarlett," she said, "thank you for coming out to meet me."

"I have to say, I'm surprised. How can I help you?"

She cocked a brow. "Really? I had to find out from my daughter that you and my ex are dating. I would've appreciated a heads-up."

"Oh."

"But then again, that's a bone I have to pick with Chad, not with you."

I frowned. "Then I'm still confused. Why are you here?"

"I wanted to meet you. If I leave it up to Chad, it'll probably be another million years before he introduces you to me. I figured something was off when my Bella was spending all that time with you."

Oh shit.

"I just showed her how to bake some pies."

"And yesterday you were at the LeBlanc-Broussard crazy house."

I winced. That's what she called it?

"Which tells me all I need to know," she continued. "The family is in on this."

Sarah was antagonizing me, which I didn't expect. Perhaps she was simply protective of her daughter.

"Bella called you Chad's girlfriend."

Oh my God. My heart warmed.

"I knew he was going to find a replacement eventually." She looked me up and down. "You're... surprising."

"Let's focus on your daughter," I said. "Are there any rules you want me to respect?"

"Chad knows all the rules. I want to know more about *you*. As far as I know, your contract here is limited, yes?"

I bristled. "Yes, but I've been getting good feedback."

She smirked. "Of course."

"I do my job very well. The reviews are great."

She nodded. "Yes, I've read them. Everyone enjoys your food. You're originally from..."

"Seattle."

"Right. And you plan to stay here for good?"

"Yes. I mean, that's what I hope."

"I see. Have you been around kids before?"

"No," I admit, "but I like Bella very much. She's an adorable girl."

Sarah softened somewhat. "She told me about the Hedwig curtains."

"Yes. I looked for them everywhere in town. I'm sorry if that crossed a line. Were you the one decorating her room?"

"No, that's Chad's house. He and Bella decorated it. It shows, if you ask me."

I didn't like the disdain in her voice.

"I appreciate that you're being kind to my daughter, but I would've liked Chad to wait a bit before making you a part of her life until he was sure that..."

She didn't finish her sentence, but I knew exactly what she meant. I couldn't entirely blame her, but she couldn't understand this connection Chad and I had.

I heard footsteps come from the back and wondered if Joel needed me. But it wasn't Joel who joined us. It was Chad.

"Sarah," he said, "what are you doing here?"

She scoffed. "Let me guess. That helpful Joel let you know I was here?"

"Yes," he said.

I didn't mind talking to Sarah, but I was glad that Chad was here.

"I'm going to leave the two of you alone," I said.

Sarah smiled at me.

"It was nice to meet you," I told her.

"Likewise," she replied, and she did seem to mean it. But her eyes went completely cold when she focused on Chad again.

"I'll come find you in the kitchen," he said to me as I was about to head out.

"No need. The staff will arrive soon, and things are already off to a crazy start."

He frowned. "What's wrong?"

"Don't you worry. I've got it all covered," I said.

I was going to figure it out. As a chef, I was used to crises in the kitchen.

Sarah showing up and asking me questions, on the other hand, threw me off completely.

<hr />

Chad

Once we were alone, I asked my ex, "What are you doing here, Sarah?"

"I came to meet your girlfriend."

I closed my eyes. "Bella told you."

"What did you expect? She was bursting at the seams with joy."

Fuck yes. I was glad my baby was happy.

"I don't really care who you're seeing, but I'd like to know before you introduce someone into my daughter's life, especially if she's been at your house."

I stilled. "Are you having me watched?"

She laughed. "Don't be ridiculous. You don't matter to me. But she got Bella Hedwig-themed curtains, and I'm guessing that wouldn't be possible unless she'd been in the house."

"I don't appreciate you coming here and ambushing Scarlett."

"So overprotective of her, aren't you? What exactly do you think you need to protect her from, me or your family?"

"She happens to like my family," I say.

"Or she's just faking it, you know, to get you to—"

"Stop right there."

"I just wish you'd waited longer before you told Bella."

"Why?" I asked.

She rolled her eyes, leaning back in the chair. "Come on, Chad. She's what, twentysomething?"

"She's thirty."

"Yes, and you're thirty-five. Doesn't seem like a huge age gap, but it kind of is. You think she's going to stick around New Orleans forever?"

"She likes the city, and she likes me and Bella."

"Be that as it may, she's been here for a very short time. You got Bella's hopes up. It's not fair. What if she lets her down?"

Even though Sarah and I didn't see eye to eye on many things, I couldn't deny that she was right. But Scarlett and I weren't having a fling. It was so much more.

"I have a good feeling about this," I said.

"Yes, well, we had a good feeling about each other, too, and that went to shit, didn't it?"

"Sarah."

She shook her head. "Look. It's your right to date. I always thought your idea to be single was batshit crazy."

I frowned. "You spoke to Julian?"

"No, I overheard your brothers talking. I don't think I've actually had a conversation with them in years, and that includes when we were married. They were all too... much." She rolled her eyes. "This is just like you, isn't it? You go from zero to full-on involved in no time. I sincerely hope you know what you're doing and that you won't break our little girl's heart."

"I'd never do that," I said.

"Let's hope so. What time are you dropping her off on Friday?"

"Three o'clock okay?"

"Sure. That sounds good," she said.

Remembering my conversation with Scarlett, I asked, "Would you mind if Bella spent some weekends at my house too?"

"Hell no. I've been in weekend-prison for way too long."

Fucking hell.

"You know I'm always happy to spend the weekend with her too" was all I said.

"Would Scarlett be there too?"

"Probably."

"Fantastic. That would free me up to travel. Best news I've gotten all day." Sarah got up from the table. "All right, I'll be going, then. Good luck with... everything."

"Thanks."

She waved before heading to the front door.

I could never understand how Sarah and I were ever together. We were so damn different.

I watched her go out of the restaurant and then went toward the kitchen. It was fucking insane. The staff were running around. I couldn't see Scarlett anywhere.

I caught Joel foraging the big storage rooms. "What's happening?"

"We have some delivery delays. Chef is on top of it, though," he said proudly.

"She's a good one."

"Yes, she is, boss. She's the best chef we've had."

I liked that he was protective of her.

"Thanks for finding me earlier." Joel had told me about Sarah wanting to see Scarlett. I really appreciated that.

"Sure," he said.

As a general rule, Scarlett and I weren't hiding, but neither of us had come out and informed the kitchen staff that we were dating. But Joel was a smart guy. He'd put two and two together.

"Although Chef does look a bit tired today," he said.

Yeah, well, that was my fault entirely. But I knew exactly how to fix it. I was going to take a detour by Maria's Coffee Shop and buy an espresso.

Even though finding time for each other was going to be challenging from now on, I was still determined to spoil her every chance I got.

There was a line at Maria's shop when I got there a few minutes later, but she was efficient, so it moved quite quickly. She looked at me with a triumphant smile.

"Coffee date's back?" she teased, which made me laugh.

"Two espressos, and mind your own business."

"How about I give you one for free if you spill the beans?"

"No can do, Maria," I said.

"Well, fine." She grudgingly made the drinks without asking me anything else.

Sarah's words still resounded in my ears on the way back. I hated to admit it, but she did have a point. I was determined to push it to the back of my mind, though, as there was no point dwelling on it. One of my mantras had always been not to search for problems and simply deal with them as they came. In my experience, 99 percent of the stuff you tried to foresee simply didn't happen. Other shit happened, just not what you expected.

I went straight to our courtyard, put the coffees down on the small table, and texted Scarlett.

Chad: I'm waiting in the courtyard. Can you spare two minutes?

She didn't reply at all.

I looked at the phone for a minute before realizing she probably wasn't going to check it at all. I didn't want to wait for too long, risking the espressos getting cold, so I headed into the kitchen.

I took a few seconds to just look at her. Scarlett was a force of nature. She always talked respectfully and in a calm manner, but she was also firm. She was currently instructing Joel, talking with her hands, the way I loved.

Joel pointed at me, and Scarlett looked over her shoulder, her mouth slightly open. I motioned for her to join me outside.

She hesitated for a split second but then hurried to me, and we walked side by side in the courtyard. "Coffee?" she asked unnecessarily.

"Obviously. Just the way you like it."

"Oh, I would chastise you for distracting me from work, but I really, really needed this."

I sipped my espresso, watching her do the same.

"Are you okay? I'm sorry about Sarah showing up here," I said.

She looked up from her cup. "Um, I didn't expect it, but it's fine. She does have a point about meeting me."

"True, but that's my responsibility to handle—and to shield you from."

She gave me a cheeky smile. "You don't need to protect me all the time. I'm a big girl."

"I know that, but I want to do it anyway. Now, we didn't get to talk about how we're going to do this now that Bella is back. So first thing's first, I want to reinstate our coffee dates."

"Is that so?" she teased. "*Reinstate*. Are you even going to consult me?" Her voice was full of sass.

"I'm doing that right now."

"That sounded a lot like a demand. A deliciously sexy demand, but a demand nonetheless."

"I need to see you," I confessed. "Scarlett, I don't know how to go an entire day without seeing you early in the morning."

"You know just what to say to convince me."

"So that's a yes?" I asked.

She nodded. "But we still have the no-kissing rule."

I smirked. "Deal."

She narrowed her eyes at me. "You agreed to that very fast."

"I'm not saying I won't renegotiate it, but for now, we have a deal."

Chapter Twenty-Nine

Scarlett

Chad was right. Starting every day knowing I'd see him for our coffee date was amazing. And yet, after we'd spent an entire week together, it wasn't enough. Not nearly enough. That's why I was beyond ecstatic when he texted me on Friday morning to make plans for the evening.

Chad: Morning, beautiful. I'm dropping off Bella at Sarah's this afternoon, and I'll wait for you in our usual spot after your shift.

I texted back the next second.

Scarlett: Yes, yes, yes.

Chad: I can't fucking wait.

I sent back a selfie with a huge smile. It was a tad theatrical. I was also batting my lashes, which I wasn't sure he could actually tell from the picture. But I was certain that he got the gist of the message.

After I sent it to him, I decided to check my emails before putting the phone away for the rest of the day. To my surprise, I had another email from Mark.

Hey Scarlett,

I wanted to discuss something with you while I was in NOLA, but it didn't quite work out. How is your contract at the restaurant? When does your trial period end? Would you be willing to return to us?

I frowned. He really thought I'd give up my position as chef here to be a sous-chef again? Unbelievable.

I was tempted not to reply at all, but I didn't want to be rude.

Hey, thanks for thinking about me, but I'm perfectly happy here. That was neutral, I hoped.

I slipped the phone into my locker and decided to forget all about it. It wasn't difficult. Working in the kitchen was the best way to stop an overthinking mind.

Chad and I weren't having our coffee date today because he had a meeting at that time. At eleven thirty, I already had withdrawals, though I wasn't sure if it was from the coffee or Chad himself. I kept busy looking over our supplies. I was so lost in trying to calculate whether we had enough scallops that I didn't hear Joel until he was right in front of me.

"Boss, you got a delivery," he said.

I looked up and grinned. "Coffee? But how?"

He held a hand up in self-defense. "I don't know any details. The delivery boy said it's for you."

Oh, Chad. How is this man even real?

I downed the coffee in no time and then hurried to my locker. To my astonishment, I didn't have a message from him. *Oh, that's right. He's in that meeting.* But yet he'd coordinated for me to get my coffee.

I texted him anyway. He'd see it whenever he was free.

Scarlett: Thanks a lot for the coffee. Can't wait for tonight.

The rest of the day was slightly insane. We had a last-minute cancellation, but then we had a large group unexpectedly pop by. Since we had an opening, we took them too. They had all sorts of dietary requirements as well as allergies and intolerances, which slowed the kitchen down somewhat, but we managed.

By the time I was done at nine o'clock, I felt like I'd run a marathon. I was so proud, though. We'd gotten some fabulous feedback today.

My legs felt like rubber as I left the restaurant. The street seemed even darker than usual, but I could still spot Chad.

"I've missed this," I confessed as soon as I was close to him.

He unhitched himself from the wall and came to me.

"I miss you," he growled before kissing me right there against the restaurant wall.

I responded with just as much desperation, rising on my toes. I almost jumped him before remembering that this was my place of work, and someone could come out at any time.

"Chad, I just... I..."

"I know, I know. Fuck. I hate to admit it, but that rule of yours is good."

"What are we doing tonight?" I asked.

He wiggled his eyebrows, making me laugh. "How about strolling the night market on Frenchmen Street?"

"I'd love that." Just like that, I didn't feel exhausted anymore.

"I actually intended to take you there last week, but..."

I giggled. "Yeah."

We couldn't really keep our hands off each other long enough to make plans outside the house, and that was more than fine by me. But I was looking forward to tonight.

The night market was amazing. Street vendors were selling an array of things—mostly art. I especially loved a huge painting of Jackson Square at sunset. The sky colors were amazing. I wondered how it would look in my studio. There were twinkle lights hanging above us all the way. I wasn't an art connoisseur, but some of the paintings truly spoke to my soul. I also had my eye on a leather purse at a stand that sold handcrafted items, but it was too expensive. I simply liked soaking up everything, especially the jazz music surrounding us.

"Anything you want, let me know, okay?"

"I love walking around."

We also passed by a stand that sold tarot cards and crystals, plus all sorts of weird items that I didn't recognize, but mostly we were surrounded by paintings and sculptures.

After we went through the market once, Chad asked, "Want to go back and buy anything?"

"No. I like for things to marinate in my head."

"But you seemed to really like that painting of Jackson Square."

I smiled. "It's my favorite spot in the city. But I don't like to buy things on instinct. I'm assuming I'll find it again if I come to the night market."

"Probably," he admitted.

His phone beeped. He took it out and grunted.

"What's wrong?"

"Sarah says that Bella asked to sleep at home tomorrow evening because she misses her Hedwig curtains."

"Oh my God!" I put a hand to my chest. *I just melted.* "I can't believe she loves them that much."

"She'd sleep wrapped up in them if she could."

"That just gave me an idea. I could buy her *Harry Potter*-themed sheets. The store in the Quarter didn't have any that I could see, but I could stop by again. Or I'll buy them online."

He smiled at me. "Want to go home?"

"Sure."

"We can walk, and I'll get the car tomorrow."

"Yes, let's do that."

We weren't far from his house, so it made sense. Besides, it was a fantastic evening for a stroll. The days were getting hotter, but the humidity was bearable in the evening.

"So, this means we'll be spending tomorrow together, right?"

Chad tilted his head. "You don't mind?"

"Look at this smile," I said, pointing at my face. "Does it look like I mind? I'm ecstatic about it."

"I bet Bella will be too."

I bit the inside of my cheek. "But you're telling Sarah, right?"

He nodded. "Don't you worry about it. I didn't handle that well before, but now I'm on top of it."

"Okay," I said.

He texted back and forth with Sarah on the way home. While he did that, I googled Harry Potter-themed sheets. Several websites popped up.

Oh yeah. Bella will love these.

Once we were inside, he tucked the phone away. "All right. So tomorrow the three of us are spending the day together. But tonight, you're all mine." He stopped and looked at me, raising a brow. "What are you thinking about? You're smiling from ear to ear."

"Depending on when Bella comes tomorrow, we could start that *Harry Potter* marathon we've been threatening you with for a while."

Chad's expression turned stony. "You're not joking, are you?"

"No, but let's see first if she wants that."

"Scarlett, if you even bring up the words, she'll say yes."

"Ah, a girl after my own heart," I said. Chad started to laugh. "Don't mock us, okay? Also, if you watch it, you'll understand the passion. And by the way, while you texted Sarah, I found these." I pulled out my phone and showed him the themed bedsheets I'd found. "Think I could order them for Bella?"

"Fucking hell, woman," he exclaimed, and instead of answering my question, he simply kissed me.

Chad

Every time I thought she couldn't surprise me, she proved me wrong. I was starved for her. This week had been pure torture, but now I could explore her all I wanted. She consumed my thoughts every day and every damn night. Now she was finally mine again.

"Chad..." Her voice was soft, throaty.

"I need you, Scarlett."

"I need you too." Her voice was even weaker than a few seconds ago, almost pleading.

My cock was already twitching, but I pulled back and said, "Let's go to the living room."

"Oh," she teased, "I figured you'd maul me right away."

"No. For now, I just want to kiss you."

I laid down on the couch and pulled her on top of me. She toppled down even though I helped her up the best as I could. I brought a hand to the back of her head and kissed her again so damn slowly, just the way I'd imagined every night when I sat right here, texting with her.

"I fucking missed you this week," I said, running a hand down her back to her ass.

She wiggled it on top of me, and I groaned against her mouth. "Woman, don't."

"Please," she whispered in reply.

She was going to be the death of me.

I want to keep her here.

Most of the time, I managed to push that thought to the back of my head, but not when I was with her. I was too open and raw and vulnerable to deny it.

Despite her plea, I didn't quicken my exploration of her. I still kissed her slowly, savoring her. Feeling her get more and more turned on was a privilege all on its own.

She started breathing more rapidly. Before long, almost every exhale was a light moan. Her entire body tensed under my touch. When she started to move her hips, rubbing herself against the zipper of my pants, I nearly lost my mind. My woman was taking what she needed, but this wouldn't do. *I* wanted to give her pleasure, so I pushed my pants past my ass, groaning when I freed my cock. And thank fuck I did, because the pressure was already too much to bear.

I pulled her dress up to her middle and felt her entire body relax. She knew she was going to get relief. Pushing her panties to one side, just enough to uncover her pussy, I nearly lost my damn mind. She was already wet just from my kiss. This woman was exquisite and all mine. I grabbed her ass, positioning her so her pussy was right over my cock, and rubbed up and down her opening without sliding inside her.

"Chad," she murmured and reached between us.

"No. Not yet."

I rubbed her even slower. I was completely hard now, and feeling her bare skin against mine was fucking delicious. She was soft and wet and so damn ready.

When I knew she needed more than this, I tilted her pelvis forward, changing the angle so I could nudge her clit every time.

"Chad. Oh God!" Her voice was strained.

I grabbed her buttocks with both hands, holding her at a specific distance. Then I moved my hips under her, rubbing up and down, up and down.

"Fuck!" I exclaimed. How could this feel so damn good?

She started to whimper, and then a groan escaped her lips. I knew she was close, but even so, her climax took me by surprise. She went completely tense above me, head buried in my neck, mouth muffled against my chest as she called out my name.

I'd promised myself that I'd wait for her to ride out her orgasm before sliding inside her, but I was only human, and I couldn't resist any longer. I craved this closeness more than anything else in my life. So even though she was still moaning, I positioned my cock right at her entrance and pulled her down on me. Her cry intensified.

"Fuuuuuuuuuck, you feel so good," I groaned in her ear.

She simply moaned in reply. She was still coming, and being inside her while she rode out her wave of pleasure was insanely good. I wasn't moving slowly any longer. I drove inside her, hard and relentless. Her body was made for me. *She* was made for me. This connection I felt with her was surreal. I couldn't understand how it had formed, let alone how it seemed to deepen every time we were together.

When her body started to soften, I knew she was coming down from the cusp, and I forced myself to slow down. After all, I wanted to work her up again, not rush this. I pulled my cock in and out slowly, feeling her clamp down on every inch. My left foot nearly went off the couch.

Fuck, I need a better position than this.

While I was still inside her, I pushed myself up into a sitting position. She pressed her knees to my sides. I'd intended to get up from the couch and walk upstairs with her, but instead, all I managed was to kick off my pants and boxers entirely, then place her on the rug. She smiled, letting go of my neck and instead putting her arms around herself, feeling the fabric beneath her.

"Oh, this is soft," she murmured.

"You make me lose myself, Scarlett."

I leaned over and circled her clit with my thumb. I wanted to kiss her breasts, but I needed to take off her dress first.

"Where's the zipper?" I asked.

"Oh, here."

She reached sideways, lowering it. Then we pushed the dress out of the way. She was wearing a bra, too, but I was too impatient to get rid of it, so I simply moved it up, freeing her breasts. It bunched up around her neck as I lowered my head, sucking one nipple into my mouth. I lightly pressed two fingers against her clit, and then I slipped one finger inside her, curling it, rubbing her G-spot.

She reacted beautifully, her hips bucking off the floor. She pressed herself up on her heels, and then my cock was trapped between her pelvis and mine. My vision faded for a split second. How could the pleasure be so intense? I pulled my finger out of her, then thrust my cock deep inside, but she had no problem taking me in.

She licked her lips, touching her breasts with her eyes shut firmly. Was she already bracing herself for another climax? She was always gorgeous, but she was exquisitely beautiful right before she came, when her entire body was at my mercy, waiting for relief.

It wasn't fair to her for me to prolong this—besides, we had the whole night to ourselves—so I positioned myself on my knees in a way that allowed me to both thrust at the pace I wanted and touch her clit with one hand. She gave herself to me with abandon. There was no way for her to muffle her sounds. Even better.

She cried out, jerking her head forward and lifting her shoulders from the floor a few inches. I doubled down my efforts, thrusting even faster. Then I grabbed both her legs, placing her feet on my chest. I pressed her thighs together because I knew it would make the sensations even more intense for both of us.

My orgasm rolled through me slowly, but even so, I didn't have time to brace against it. When I felt Scarlett go over the edge, I completely lost myself to her. I moved out of instinct, nothing more. My senses, my thoughts, and my entire body were engulfed in pleasure.

"Scarlett, sugar, fuck," I exclaimed. "You're exquisite."

She didn't reply at all, just simply hummed, a small smile playing on her lips even though her eyes were still closed. She was still lost in the wave of her orgasm.

I was going to wait for her to calm down before starting to work her up all over again.

CHAPTER THIRTY

SCARLETT

I blew a strand of hair from my eyes as I glanced into the oven. The pie was almost ready. Chad had left half an hour ago to pick up Bella, and I'd stayed behind to preside over the baking process. I'd made pecan pie, and the timing was perfect. I couldn't wait to see Bella's face when she noticed it.

While I waited on the pie, I checked my email. *Oh, for fuck's sake.* Simon had sent yet another one.

Stop your communication with Mark. Completely. Remember the car lease? It's in both our names. If you continue talking shit about me, I'll just stop paying it. See how you deal with that. You can't handle jack shit.

I reread it a few times, growing angrier by the second. How petty could he be? I didn't give two shits about the car lease. If he stopped making the payments, he'd just lose the car. I moved across the country and started my life with nothing, and he thought he could intimidate me with a freaking car lease?

Clearly I couldn't hide my head in the sand. He would just continue to berate me and put me down.

I needed to confront him. But it wasn't going to happen today because the front door opened just then.

"Scarlett!" Bella exclaimed, running up to me.

My heart instantly filled with joy. I lowered myself onto my knees and hugged her tightly.

"It smells good," she told me.

"I made pecan pie for you."

"Can I eat some?"

"It's going to be ready to eat in about half an hour."

Bella looked at me with narrowed eyes. "Twenty minutes."

I jerked my head back, looking over at Chad in surprise. He was a couple steps behind Bella.

He shrugged. "She knows how to negotiate, and I don't even think she learned it from me."

"No, Uncle Xander taught me," she explained. "He said it's a good skill to survive in the family."

Chad's eyes bulged. "I'm going to have a word with Xander."

"So, Bella," I said, "your dad said you were missing your Hedwig curtains."

"Yes." She nodded. "Mom doesn't want to put any in her house. Says it ruins the aesthe-something."

"Aesthetic," I finished.

"Exactly."

I frowned. That was interesting but none of my business. I was going to spoil this girl rotten when we were together.

I looked at Chad, who nodded lightly, and then turned to Bella. "So, Bella, since it's only lunchtime, I was wondering what you think about watching a *Harry Potter* movie with your dad as well."

"Oh my God, yes!" she exclaimed, smiling from ear to ear.

"Why don't you pick your favorite, and we'll watch it?"

"He has to start with the first one," she said in a voice that clearly indicated she wanted to add a *duh*. "Otherwise, he won't understand anything."

Chad tried to hold back laughter but couldn't. He managed to pass it off as a cough, though. The man had skills. I had to learn that from him.

"All right, then. We'll watch the first one," I said.

Bella turned, looking at the oven. "And do you think we could bake another pie after?"

"Sure," I replied. "I've got ingredients for another pecan pie and even for an apple one."

I had spotted some gorgeous apples in Chad's pantry when I looked in it this morning.

"Which one is easier?" Bella asked.

That was an interesting question.

"Honestly, that's not easy to answer. The answer will always be whichever one is easiest for you."

"That's a bit confusing."

"Bella?" Chad asked. "What's going on?" He came on my other side but remained standing.

"Remember we have that baking competition at school?" she asked.

"Yes, of course," he replied.

"I don't want to make a fool of myself!" She put both her feet together, looking down at the floor.

I had to come up with a good plan, because some pies truly were easier than others in the sense that they required fewer steps.

"When is it? What are the requirements?" I asked.

"It's coming up in three weeks," she whispered, "and I'm afraid I'll mess it all up."

"You won't." I glanced at Chad, then back at her. "We'll find a way for the two of us to bake every morning, okay?"

She looked up with a smile. "Really?"

"Yes. Don't you worry. I promise that you'll be the best baker in the competition."

She looked at me suspiciously. "How can you promise that?"

"Because," I said slowly, "baking is easy. You simply have to follow the instructions and it'll work out. And if we meet every morning at seven and bake a pie, then you'll have practiced a lot by the time the competition comes around, and I'm sure you'll do great."

"Will you come watch me?" she asked with hope in her eyes.

Oh, I wanted to say yes, I really did, but I didn't want to overstep. I didn't know if it was appropriate or if Sarah would even want me there. I looked at Chad, deferring to him.

"I'd love to have you there too," he said.

Oh, be still my beating heart. How is this happening?

"Then I'll come watch you, of course."

"Yes, yes, yes!" Bella exclaimed, then threw her little arms around my neck.

She almost strangled me with the force of her hug, but I didn't protest at all because I loved it.

"Do you want us to start baking right away?" Chad asked, and I couldn't help but laugh because by the hopeful tone in his voice, I knew where he was going with this.

Bella pulled back, frowning at him. "No, Daddy. First we're watching *Harry Potter and the Philosopher's Stone*. Not *Sorcerer's Stone*. They only said that for the American market, like we're stupid or something."

I opened my mouth and closed it again. Holy shit, Bella had some strong views. And I totally agreed with them.

"Bella," Chad said, "we don't use those words."

"Not even when it's true?"

I pursed my lips together, on the verge of laughing.

"Bella," he replied sternly. "That isn't right."

"I know, Daddy, but I'm not perfect. And you always say that no one's perfect, right? We just have to try our best."

"Our very best," Chad said.

I loved how gentle he was with her even when he was correcting her. Finally, I rose to my feet as Bella turned around and pointed at the TV.

"Okay, can we start the movie now?"

"What's the rush?" he asked.

She looked at him over her shoulder and said, "We don't want you to change your mind."

That time, I *did* burst out laughing. I couldn't fight it anymore.

"Your daughter goes toe-to-toe with you, doesn't she?" I asked.

Chad nodded. "Apparently so."

"Come *on*, Dad," she insisted, then turned to me, a big grin on her face. "Thank you, Scarlett, for convincing him. After today, he won't be a Muggle anymore."

Chapter Thirty-One

Chad

Over the next few weeks, Bella insisted on baking with Scarlett every morning, and I gave in. How could I not? Then again, I was giving in to a lot of things lately. Guess who ended up watching the first three *Harry Potter* movies? That's right, me. They weren't as bad as I'd expected, but I couldn't muster Bella's or Scarlett's enthusiasm.

The week of Bella's competition, I got a phone call from Sarah as I stepped inside my office. I knew something was wrong before I even picked up because she never called.

"Good morning," I said, putting the phone to my ear. I didn't bother sitting down.

"Hey," Sarah said. "Listen, I want to talk to you about Bella's competition. I need to go to LA for a party this Friday."

I blinked. "What the hell?"

"Spare me, okay. Do you know how much my socialite profile will improve if I go? It's basically work."

"You could've just said no."

"Bella won't even miss me." That was unfortunately very true. She rarely showed up at school events. "Besides, Scarlett will be there."

"What's that's supposed to mean?"

"Nothing bad. I'm impressed, though. I didn't think it would go this far."

"Thank you for the vote of confidence," I said sarcastically. "Have you told Bella yet?"

"I just found out. However, I will tell her when I pick her up from school this evening."

"Anything else?" I asked.

"You're particularly flippant with me today," she said.

"I just don't understand. Why don't you want to be more involved in Bella's life?"

She sighed heavily. "I'm doing the best I can. And she has you and all that huge family."

"You're her mother."

"Yes, I know. As I said, I'm doing my best."

I gritted my teeth because as far as I was concerned, she wasn't, but I was determined to stay on civil terms with her.

"Chad, you know motherhood has never been my thing. We weren't *trying* to get pregnant, remember? It just happened. I'm doing what I can."

"If that's all," I said, "then I have to start my day."

"Sure, sure," she said distractedly. "So do I."

After hanging up, I looked down into the courtyard, but Scarlett wasn't there. I chuckled to myself. If anyone had told me a few months ago that I'd be looking out the window multiple times a day for a glimpse of the woman I loved, I would've told them they were crazy.

I sucked in a deep breath as I replayed my own thoughts. Yes, it was fucking true. I was in love with Scarlett, and I wanted her to know it. I wanted to show it.

The question was how?

Ever since we went to the night market all those weeks ago, I'd been hunting down that painting of Jackson Square that she'd liked so much. I'd assumed the painter would return to the market regularly, but it turned out that he'd only been there for that one evening, and no one knew his whereabouts. That had been frustrating, to say the least. But now more than ever, I wanted to get my hands on the painting.

An idea struck me. Not for nothing, my mother owned a gallery. She'd track it down.

As a rule, I rarely asked my parents for favors. That's what I had all those brothers for. But I'd make an exception this time for Scarlett.

As I glanced out the window again, I called Mom.

She answered after a million rings—as usual. "Darling, so sorry. I couldn't find my phone. It kept ringing throughout the gallery."

I chuckled. "Don't worry, Mom. I understand."

"And to what do I owe the honor?"

"I need a favor."

"Sure, anything."

"I want you to track down a painting."

"That's my specialty. Go on."

"Yeah, I figured I'd go straight to a pro." I debated simply telling her about the painting, leaving Scarlett out of it. But why hide? I didn't mind my mother knowing how I felt. "Scarlett and I were out at the night market a few weeks ago. She saw a painting of Jackson Square that she truly likes, and I went to buy it for her."

"And you can't find the vendor again?" Mom said.

"No. I honestly always thought that most vendors are locals."

"Some are, but the night market is famous. Artists from all over the country come in the hopes of selling. Can you give me more details about what else he had?"

"Paintings!"

She laughed. "Chad, I need details. What kind of paintings? What technique was he using?"

"I have no idea whatsoever."

"All right. Then at least tell me, was he at the start of the market?"

"No. There was a vendor with weird candles right next to him."

"And what night was it?"

I told her the precise date because I remembered vividly.

"How fast can you get it?" I asked.

"Darling, this might take time." I groaned, and she sighed. "Well, I'm sorry, but I don't have a lot of information to go on, and it might take a while to convince the council to give out the names. But I can charm those old bastards if I put my mind to it."

"Thank you. I appreciate it."

"Of course. It's not every day that my second-born asks me for a favor. So, you want to surprise dear Scarlett, huh?"

"Yes," I said. "It's her favorite spot in the city, and she really liked that painting. Fingers crossed that you find it."

"Oh, I will. When I put my mind to something, I don't accept failure."

"That's the family motto, isn't it?" I asked.

"It kind of is." There was a short pause, and then Mom said, "Darling, I can't tell you how happy I am that you have Scarlett in your life and that you've let her in. For the longest time, I didn't think you'd do that with anyone."

"What do you mean?"

I swear to God, if any of my brothers told Mom about my celibacy idea, I'm going to lose it. There was such a thing as too much information, even within a family.

"Just that you were so alone after your divorce. What troubled me was that you seemed to want it that way."

All right, that didn't sound like she knew facts. It was just her mother's intuition at work.

"I thought it was best for Bella," I admitted.

"Ah."

"I didn't want to fail Bella again," I went on.

"My darling, you didn't fail her. Quite the contrary. You're a wonderful father. Look, all we can do in life is keep moving on and put our best intentions behind everything. You did that. Relationships are hard."

"You and Dad have made it work for many decades. So have the grandparents."

"That's true, but if experience has taught me anything, it's that we're the exception. Your dad and I are soulmates, and we were lucky enough to find each other when we were really young. But I think we're all lucky if we find our soulmate at all in our lifetime." She chuckled. "Listen to me. I got all cheesy on you."

I laughed. "That's fine, Mom. Don't worry about it."

"One word of advice. I think gifts are fantastic. And grand gestures in general. But so is being open with each other. Expressing how we feel."

"Not my strong suit."

"Hmmm, maybe that can change. I'll keep you posted about the painting, okay?"

"Sure. I appreciate it," I said.

After we hung up, I managed to go through a good chunk of my to-dos for the day. But my mind was still on her words.

I knew where she was going with this. I usually wasn't a man of many words. I was far better at doing things rather than talking about them. But I wanted Scarlett to know without a doubt how I felt about her. I knew it was early, and that there was a real risk that she wasn't there yet. I'd been divorced for years, but her breakup was recent. Still, I wanted to lay it out for her.

I was going to spoil her even more than usual tonight. I debated taking her out—it was Friday evening, after all—but she was always exhausted in the evening, especially after a full week of work. But that didn't matter. I could take care of her at home as well.

At four o'clock in the afternoon, Joel put a dent in my plan with a text message.

Joel: Hey, boss. Not sure if you're aware, but our chef is super sick. She's barely standing on her feet, but she insists on working.

What the actual hell?

I stood up, grabbed my laptop, and immediately stormed out of the office, hurrying downstairs to the kitchen, where everyone was bustling around as usual.

Scarlett was obviously feeling even worse than I'd thought, because she was sitting. Her face was bright red, and even though she was seated, she was still swaying lightly.

Joel nodded at me, then darted to the opposite side of the room. Scarlett would probably still put two and two together, though.

As I walked up to her, the whole crew moved away.

"Chad," she said and stood up. "What are you doing here?" She swayed precariously.

I put a hand on her face. "You're sick."

"I think I'm coming down with something, but I'm still doing okay. And I'm taking precautions so I don't spread the illness."

"You're not fucking doing okay. Look at you. You're flushed." I pressed the back of my fingers to her forehead. "You have a fever."

"I'm just a bit drowsy."

"I'm taking you home."

She blinked, jerking her head back. "Dinner rush is about to start."

"And you are sick."

Sweat had formed at her temples, but she shook her head. "No, no. I need to be here."

"I'm sure Joel can handle the kitchen."

"Scarlett, we'll manage for the evening. I can do the job," Joel chimed in. "We're all prepped and ready to go. We'll follow your list to the letter, promise."

"You need to rest, woman," I insisted. "Remember what I told you about showing up sick at work? I will throw you over my shoulder, and then everyone and their dog will know what's going on."

She swallowed hard, looking over her shoulder. "You wouldn't." She stopped talking when she saw my stony expression. "Oh, you really would, huh?"

"Yes, I fucking would."

"How did you even know I was sick?" Then she looked over her shoulder again. Joel had been watching us, but he quickly glanced at his chopping board. "Joel blabbed, didn't he?"

"Joel is as worried for you as am I."

"Well, the joke's on you," she said, pulling herself up to her full height, "because I'm not going anywhere."

"Then you leave me no choice." Loudly, I added, "Kitchen crew, turn your back to us."

"Oh my God," Scarlett exclaimed.

"Pretend you're not hearing anything," I continued.

"Chad, you can't do this." Her voice was stern, but the corners of her mouth tilted up. "Fine, fine. I'm coming with you."

"Good." I nodded. "False alarm, crew. Carry on," I said loudly once more.

"I'll go change," she said.

"I'll wait for you outside. Actually, you know what? I might wait for you inside at the entrance."

"Why? You think I'm going to try and sneak back to work?"

"That's exactly what I think."

A few minutes later, she'd changed, and we were heading outside. The fight went right out of her as we left the restaurant. I'd been right, she had a fever. She was so exhausted that she even fell asleep in the car. She only started to stir when we arrived at my house and I shut off the engine.

"Wow, I fell asleep," she mumbled. "My whole body seems like it's made out of lead."

"Don't get out. I'll carry you."

"I'd fight you on it, but I don't want to."

Alarm bells rang in my mind. *Fuck, she's really sick.*

I took her in my arms and headed straight to the master bedroom. She pressed her cheek to my chest. Even through my shirt, I could feel her skin burning.

I'd barely set her down when a phone rang from the living room.

"It's mine," she said.

"I'll get it."

I hurried downstairs, grabbed the phone from her bag—and I accidentally answered. I brought it to my ear, intending to tell the other person that I'd picked up by mistake, but the voice stopped me in my tracks.

"Fucking *finally* you answer."

Who the hell would talk like that to my woman?

"Who is this?" I asked.

"Who is *this*?" the voice replied.

"I'm Chad LeBlanc. I don't know who you think you are, but you don't fucking talk to my woman like that."

"I'm Simon, her ex."

I instantly saw red. "Why are you calling her?"

"That's none of your business."

"I'm making it my business. Actually, you know what? I don't even give two shits about why you're calling her. Just stop doing it."

"Or what?" he snapped.

"Or I'll make your life seriously complicated."

"I'd like to see you try."

"Listen, you piece of shit, you've done enough damage in her life. Unless you want to be a kitchen aide the rest of yours, you'd better stop harassing Scarlett completely."

"I'm a chef," he said.

"I promise you that you won't be for long if you keep this up."

"Who the fuck do you think you are?"

"A LeBlanc," I said easily. "Google us. We're huge in the restaurant industry. So don't mess with me or my woman."

"You dare—"

I hung up the next second. I didn't even care what the guy had to say. I walked back upstairs quickly.

"Chad?" she murmured when I entered the bedroom. "Who was that?"

I cleared my throat. "Simon."

She opened her eyes wide. "Oh my God, no. What did he want?"

"To talk to you. I put him in his place."

She shook her head. "Chad, I'm so sorry you had to deal with that."

I sat on the edge of the bed next to her. "Has he been in contact?"

"He's been going on and on about how I'm ruining his life. He thinks it's my fault that he's at odds with the kitchen team."

"Why didn't you tell me? This is wrong."

She shrugged. "I just try to ignore it. I haven't even replied to any of his threats."

My eyes bulged. I was doing all I could to stay calm. "He threatened you?"

"Just a petty thing, really. Both our names are on the lease of his car. Somehow he thought he could intimidate me into... I'm not even sure what." She shrugged again. "But Simon doesn't always have a reason for the things he does. He just likes to make other people feel like shit for sport."

I moved closer to her. "Listen to me." Cupping her face, I caressed her chin. "You are mine. I'll protect you. I'll shield you from everyone. Never keep things from me, okay?" I smiled.

She raised a brow. "Well, when you put it like that, how can I say no?"

I went to the medicine cabinet and grabbed a package of Tylenol. I also found a cloth and doused it in ice-cold water. When I returned, Scarlett's eyes were open, but she was clearly sleepy. She'd lain down on the mattress.

"Come on, beautiful. Sit up so you can take the Tylenol. It really helps. And I got this too," I said, holding up the cool washcloth.

"Oh, thank you."

"I'll put it on your forehead and—" I paused as she gulped down water with her Tylenol, then put the glass on the nightstand. "—when it gets warm, I'll change it."

"I could do that," she said.

I stared at her. "No, sugar. You'll go to sleep, and I'll take care of you."

She parted her lips. "But why?" she murmured.

"Because I love you, woman," I blurted.

Her eyes widened.

Fuck my life. That was not how I'd planned to declare myself.

"Oh, for God's sake," I groaned.

"What?"

"I'd planned to spoil you properly this evening while I told you how I felt about you. This is not at all what I envisioned."

For the first time since I found her in the kitchen, Scarlett smiled. It lit up her whole face. "You want to stay up and put cold cloths on my forehead. I can't imagine anything more romantic."

I frowned, leaning in to kiss her. She softened against me.

"I do so fucking love you."

"I love you more," she murmured, her voice catching.

I pulled back a few inches, just looking at her. "Are you sure?"

"Yes. I'm just scared."

"Sugar..."

She swallowed hard, shrugging. "I wasn't really expecting this, and..."

"We'll explore this together," I assured her. "It's uncharted territory for me too."

Abruptly, she tried to rise onto her knees, but she swayed precariously and then fell back on her ass.

"What was that?" I asked.

"I was trying to straddle you." She closed her eyes. "Not a good idea."

"Scarlett," I admonished lightly. "This is how tonight will go: You'll just lie on the bed, and I'll take care of you. No argument allowed."

"You won't hear one from me," she whispered as she laid back down, looking at me with eyes full of sleep and also emotion.

Hell yes. This woman was mine, and I was going to take care of her.

And not just tonight.

CHAPTER THIRTY-TWO

SCARLETT

"You're a natural talent," I exclaimed on the morning of the baking competition.

"You hear that, Daddy? I'm a natural!" Bella beamed.

She'd come to LeBlanc & Broussard's every morning before opening, and we'd dutifully baked a pie. She was truly gifted in my... well, not-so-objective opinion. This little girl had wormed her way into my heart.

"The pie looks great, Bella," Chad said, "but we really have to get going now."

She frowned, crossing her little arms over her chest. We'd run a bit late today. Joel was already here, and the rest of the staff were probably going to show up any second now.

"But we still need to make the topping," she protested.

I liked how she always looked for an excuse to stay longer. It had to mean she loved me, too, right?

"I promise you have the topping down perfectly, okay? We've practiced it often enough, and you don't want to be late for school."

"Okay," she said and finally stepped down from the stool. "I'm ready to go, Daddy."

Chad looked at me intently and said, "See you this evening."

Somehow, that one sentence that didn't even have a tinge of flirtiness made me feel warm all over.

After the two of them left, I put a hand on my chest, drawing in a deep breath. I was the luckiest person on this planet, I was sure of it.

As Joel and I started prepping for the day, I checked my email one last time as usual, and I was caught off guard once again by one from Mark. The subject line made me freeze in my steps.

I blinked. *What? Holy shit.* I immediately clicked it open.

Job offer: Chef at Starlight.

Hey Scarlett,

I bet you didn't see this coming, huh? Look, I'm sorry I was so tight-lipped when I came to New Orleans. Some things were still up in the air then, but we've parted ways with Simon. Turns out that he wasn't the chef we thought he was, and without you, his work was subpar.

Hell yeah! I was so happy that I wanted to open a bottle of champagne. Did that make me petty? Sure, but I didn't even care.

I continued reading with a huge grin on my face.

I'm certain that you have a comfortable job in New Orleans, and they clearly value you, but LeBlanc & Broussard's isn't a Michelin-starred restaurant. I'm sure you know how good this would look on your résumé. Besides, you already know everyone here, so there will be no learning curve. Attached is my offer. Let me know how fast you can leave New Orleans. We look forward to welcoming you back.

That was cheeky. Why would he assume that I would just drop my job here in order to go back to Seattle? I was a chef here as well. True, this wasn't a Michelin-starred restaurant, but it was very highly regarded and far more popular than Starlight.

He was right about one thing, though: I certainly didn't see this coming.

So they finally realized that Simon isn't who he bragged he was, huh?

Yeah, I was still gloating about that.

I didn't wish him any ill will, but after the way he'd treated me, I couldn't help but rejoice. I'd worked hard at Starlight for years, hoping for a promotion, but the truth was, I didn't want it anymore. Still, I wasn't going to reply yet. He'd only emailed me this morning, and I wanted him to know that I took my time to consider it. So I put the phone away and went on about my day.

The time passed quickly, especially because I stopped working just after lunch. It felt almost bizarre to skip dinner, but Bella's baking competition had priority. I was so giddy to see my girl baking.

She's not your girl, Scarlett, okay?

It felt like she was, though.

Chad had already gone to the school twenty minutes ago, so I was heading there on my own. I changed at top speed, checking myself in the mirror in the employee bathroom before leaving. I'd brought a dress with me today that was black with a V-neck. It was perfectly decent for a baking competition at a school. At least I hoped it was.

I was wearing flat shoes, though. I loved the French Quarter, but wearing heels around here was mighty dangerous.

I ran my hands through my hair a few times, but it was pretty futile after wearing a chef's bonnet. The best thing I could do would be to pull it up in a cute ponytail, which was exactly what I did.

Then I took out my phone, put the school's address into Google Maps, and hurried there because I didn't want to be late. The competition didn't start until 4:00 p.m., but everyone was encouraged to arrive at least fifteen minutes before. According to my phone, I was going to make it just in time.

As I approached the school, I was about to text Chad to ask him where they were, but then I realized that wasn't necessary because half the family was gathered in one side of the courtyard. My heart was full of joy just watching them. Bella would be so happy that everyone showed up for her baking competition. I especially admired Chad's brothers for being here—let's face it, they were single men, and it was Friday afternoon.

Julian noticed me first. "Ah, the woman of the hour. My niece was talking our ears off about you before she darted inside."

My heart nearly exploded.

Isabeau and Celine were looking at me with kind eyes.

"You're so good to our girl," Celine said.

"She's going to win," I insisted. "She's very good and pays attention closely."

"I do wonder why she didn't want either of us to teach her, though," Isabeau wondered.

"In her own words, it was because you don't follow instructions precisely, and she can't keep up," Xander explained.

Zachary stared at him. "Dude, ever heard of not saying everything that comes into your mind?"

"Young man," Isabeau told Xander, "that's not true."

"It kind of is, though," Celine said. "We're all about precise steps when it comes to mixing perfumes, but we bake by memory. It's not easy for anyone to learn from us, is it?"

Isabeau humphed, giving Xander the side-eye as if this was his fault.

"When's Sarah coming?" Anthony asked.

"She isn't," Chad replied, putting an arm around my shoulders. "She's in LA."

Anthony narrowed his eyes but didn't say anything.

"Really?" Beckett said. "But we've known about this evening for about four months."

"Darlings, let's focus on the fact that we're all here," Adele said.

Hmmm... I figured Zachary had learned the art of "smoothing things over" from his mom.

"It's true. Come on, let's head inside," Beckett said. "I'm determined to get the best spot. I'm in charge of taking pictures. Bella asked me."

Anthony stared at him. "She asked me too."

I tried to keep a poker face, but Beckett immediately caught on. "Scarlett? What's that? You're laughing at us."

"No, I'm not," I said.

"You look smug, so fess up. What is it?" Anthony asked.

"She said she asked both of you because in case one messes up, she'll have a backup."

"She expects one of us to mess up?" Beckett exclaimed. "Which one of us?"

"She didn't say," I replied earnestly.

Xander smiled. "That girl is going places, I'm telling you. She truly remembers everything I tell her."

"Which reminds me," Chad said, "we need to have a word later about the things you teach my daughter."

Xander cocked a brow but didn't reply.

"I wasn't joking before. Let's get inside," Beckett said.

As the group started to move toward the front door of the school, my phone rang. I immediately took it out. "Oh!" I exclaimed.

"What happened? What's wrong?" Chad asked.

We fell back as everyone else went inside. "It's my... Doesn't matter. I'll call him back later."

But he insisted. "Who?"

"Mark, my previous boss."

"What the hell? Why does he keep bothering you?"

"This time I actually do know why. He sent me an offer this morning and probably wonders why I haven't replied."

He stilled. "An offer?"

I looked up at him. "Oh, that's right. I forgot to tell you. Seems Simon didn't work out in Seattle. So they kicked him to the curb and made me an offer."

"As chef?"

"Yes. I didn't want to reply this morning, though, so he wouldn't think I didn't even consider his offer. But let's go inside and I will politely tell him later on that I have no interest in going back to Seattle."

Chad swallowed hard. "Not even for a chef position at a Michelin-starred restaurant?"

"I like the menu at Broussard's so much better. Besides," I said, coming closer, "I'd never want to be away from you and Bella."

His expression softened. "Scarlett, this is a serious opportunity."

"Yes, but one I don't want, so it doesn't really matter, right? And if you don't stop glowering, I'll kiss you right here in the middle of the schoolyard, which would be completely inappropriate."

His frown finally dissipated into a smile. It was a small one, but I counted it as a victory too. I should've told him earlier, but it was hard to think about anything other than cooking once the kitchen was in full motion.

"Come on," I said. "Let's go inside and see what seats Anthony got. And since Bella was so adamant about having a backup for photos, I'm going to snap some too."

Chad stepped forward, kissing my forehead. "You're right. Let's go inside. We can talk about this later."

There was really nothing to talk about, but I didn't reply. I didn't want us to linger outside anymore.

Chad put an arm around my upper back as he guided me through the school to the auditorium.

Hmm, is it my imagination, or is he holding me even more tightly than usual? Well, tight was probably not the right word. Oh yeah—possessive. That was the right one. I wholeheartedly enjoyed it.

Once we reached the auditorium, we noticed Beckett grinning proudly. He was still on his feet. They'd secured the first row.

"This place is impressive. It's so huge. And how many kids are participating?" I asked.

"Not that many, but the school is used to half the family showing up. Well, in our case, the entire family."

I smiled at him. "I think that's amazing. It'll do wonders for Bella's confidence."

"I know," Chad said. "But you know who the most important attendee is tonight?"

"Who?"

"You." He pressed me even closer to him and tilted his head sideways toward me. "You're the most important person to Bella, and to me."

"Hey, you two," Beckett interjected. "Don't just stand there. It's about to start."

Chad

My girl was amazing. I kept my eyes trained on her during the whole competition. She was confident in a way she hadn't been before, and I knew it was all because of Scarlett. The entire family always encouraged her and built up her confidence, but it took meeting Scarlett for this transformation to happen.

My woman was even more excited than Anthony and Beckett to snap pictures. She even took a few videos of Bella when the judges gave feedback. They praised her efforts, but I couldn't fully focus on their words.

My mind was racing, still processing Scarlett's news. Why hadn't she told me before? And why was she so quick to dismiss it? Fucking hell, I should've stayed outside with her for a bit longer and talked this out because it was eating at me. Sure, LeBlanc & Broussard's was ten times more famous than Starlight, but for a chef's career, working in a Michelin-starred restaurant was incredible.

And yet the idea of her going back to Seattle was almost unbearable.

I drew in a deep breath, focusing on the stage again. I was going to talk to Scarlett later. This moment belonged to Bella and Bella alone, and I wanted to be present and remember every detail because I knew she was going to rehash this evening for years to come. I didn't want to be a shitty father.

Once the pies were done, the judges themselves put everything in the ovens they'd brought out specifically for the event.

While they waited for them to bake, they interviewed each kid, asking them about their favorite part of the process and so on. After Bella's interview, I stopped paying attention.

My mind was going around in circles. I looked at Scarlett, but her eyes were glued to the stage. Did she truly have no doubts about rejecting that offer? It seemed almost impulsive, and I wanted to make sure that she'd thought about it.

If she only received it this morning, she worked all day, and then she came here. When would she even have had time to properly think about it?

Fucking hell, I was going insane.

"Dude," Xander said, elbowing me. He was sitting on my other side. "You look like you're not here. Pay attention. They're announcing winners."

Crap. How long did I space out?

Scarlett was on the edge of her seat, eyes trained on Bella. Fucking hell, I couldn't let this woman walk out of our lives.

I kept my eyes glued on the stage, though, as they announced third place, then second place. My girl kept looking at us, and I smiled at her reassuringly. I always made sure to tell her that I loved her no matter what. Her winning first prize wasn't going to make me love her more.

But still, I understood how important this was for her. She'd worked hard.

"And the first prize goes to Bella LeBlanc for a completely perfect pie."

My girl instantly jumped up from her chair, and so did we. It looked a bit like a wave as all thirteen of us rose to our feet, clapping like there was no tomorrow. Scarlett was grinning from ear to ear. Bella was looking at me. No, wait, she was looking at Scarlett, sending her an air kiss.

We only stopped clapping when the presenter gave us a side-eye.

"Now for honorable mentions," he said, and we all sat down quietly.

A few minutes later, they dismissed everyone. Bella came down the staircase on the right side of the stage with the other kids.

"I did it, Scarlett! I did it!" she exclaimed, running straight for my woman, who didn't miss a beat. She lowered herself to Bella's level, taking her in her arms. I couldn't believe that she cared about my girl so much. "Did you see me making that frosting?"

"Yes, you did it perfectly. It's even better than mine."

Bella wrinkled her nose. "That's not true. You're buttering me up."

Scarlett barely stifled a chuckle. "I mean it. I'm not a pastry chef, and you've been practicing so diligently. I'm so happy you won."

She held the medal for me to see.

"All right, everyone," Isabeau said. "Let's head out and celebrate, LeBlanc style."

"Who decided on that? Why isn't it Broussard style?" Celine asked, making us all laugh.

I looked straight at her. "Because I've got the LeBlanc name, don't I, Celine?"

"Yes, but you've both our blood. So does this little one," she said, squeezing Bella's hand lightly. "You did so well. We're all so very proud of you."

"Thank you, Gran. Did you see me when I almost dropped the eggs on the floor?"

"Accidents can happen," Scarlett said in a soothing tone.

"Yes, but not during a competition!" Bella sounded horrified. "Everything has to be perfect."

She looked around at the group and then back at me, smiling. I was so fucking happy that she didn't seem to be upset at all that Sarah wasn't here tonight. Then again, my girl had gotten used to that, as had I.

"We've got a feast waiting for us at home," Dad announced.

"Of cake?" Bella asked, making us all laugh.

Everyone could take their own pie with them, but I knew my girl's priorities. Pie was for the morning, whereas cake was for celebration. And I quite agreed with her.

Chapter Thirty-Three

Chad

Things were even crazier than usual in the LeBlanc-Broussard mansion that night. We ordered enough food to feed a small army, and yet we somehow managed to finish it all. Bella was the center of attention, of course, replaying every moment of the competition for us. And we all listened intently even though we'd witnessed it firsthand.

But the whole time, my mind was on Scarlett. I needed to talk to her tonight. I didn't want to postpone it any longer, but I had to wait until after Bella went to sleep.

After dinner, Bella pulled Scarlett and me to the couches even though everyone was still at the table, waiting for the cake. As Scarlett sat down, Bella climbed onto her lap.

"Scarlett, did I do okay today?" she asked.

"Bella, you were amazing. I'm so proud of you."

"How proud? And how much do you like me?"

Scarlett beamed widely. "To the moon and back. Why?"

"Well... if you like me a lot... would you like to be my week mommy?"

My breath caught. Scarlett froze, then glanced quickly at me. I was completely shocked. Bella had never even broached this subject with me.

"I already have a weekend mommy," she continued, "most of the time, but it's not the same thing."

Scarlett looked at me again, clearly deferring to me.

"Baby girl, this is a big question. I'm sure Scarlett has to think about it."

Bella's shoulders dropped.

"No, I don't. I don't," Scarlett said, and Bella's face exploded in a huge smile.

"So you want to be my week mommy?"

"If it's fine with your dad." Scarlett flashed me a huge smile.

Is this really happening?

Bella buried her face in Scarlett's neck. Scarlett's gaze was fixed on me. I could barely speak past the emotion clogging my throat.

"I love you," I mouthed to her.

She mouthed right back, "I love you too."

Something shifted inside me. Something I hadn't even been aware was out of balance before. For the first time in many years, I felt completely at peace. Completely happy.

"All right, who's ready for cake?" Isabeau called out as Celine walked in with my girl's favorite chocolate cake.

Bella ran straight to the table. I stood up, taking Scarlett's hand and kissing the back of it.

"I fucking love you," I told her.

"Come on, let's head in or we won't get any."

I laughed. "Spoken like a true LeBlanc."

I'd been afraid the sugar rush would mess with Bella's sleep, but I shouldn't have worried. My girl fell asleep the second we got in the car.

"We're heading to the house, right?" I asked Scarlett.

"Shoot, I don't have anything to change into. Can we drop by the studio first?"

"Sure."

We drove in complete silence. My thoughts went to Scarlett's email again. Damn it, I still wanted to bring that up. I was going to do it once we were home.

When we arrived in front of her building, I jumped out and opened her door. Scarlett smiled as she got out.

After I closed the door, she said, "You really don't have to walk me to the door, you know, considering your car is right here. You can see me."

I chuckled. "You're right. Besides, I wouldn't leave Bella alone in the car."

She frowned. "Are you okay? You seemed a bit tense in the car."

"Shit. I didn't realize you'd picked up on it."

Her eyes widened. "Oh my God, so I wasn't just overthinking it. What's wrong?"

I shook my head. "I wanted to wait to talk about it until we got home, but I keep thinking about that email."

She waved her hand. "Oh, please forget it."

"I can't, and I don't think you should either."

Scarlett stared at me. "I don't understand," she said.

"It's a chef's position at a Michelin-starred restaurant."

"I don't understand why you're still pushing the issue if I said no. Especially after tonight and what Bella said."

I inhaled deeply and took her hand in mine. "Because you're young, and you're building your career, and I want you to be sure that you're making the right decision."

"You don't want me to stay?" she asked me.

Fuck yes. That was all I wanted. But instead I said, "I want you to do what's best for you."

She took her hands from mine and crossed her arms over her chest. " I really don't understand why you're being like this."

"Look, I've been mulling this over for hours." The arguments had made more sense in my head. "I wanted to talk to you after Bella went to sleep, not blurt it out like this in the street. We can talk more later."

She glanced over my shoulder. "Bella's up."

I looked at the car and saw her glued to the window, watching us.

Scarlett stared down at her feet. "Do you mind if I stay at my studio tonight?"

My chest clenched. "Fuck, I've upset you."

"I just don't want Bella to pick up on any tension between us," she said.

She was thinking about my girl. Fucking hell, I loved this woman with all I had. I was messing this up, and I wasn't even sure how the hell I'd managed it.

"If you're sure," I told her.

"I think it's best. I'll tell her that I'm super tired, okay?"

"Sure."

As if through a haze, I watched as Scarlett bid Bella good night. She wasn't at all suspicious.

But I was unnerved the entire rest of the night. After I put Bella to sleep, it became clear that I wasn't going to be able to do the same. I paced the living room like a madman, trying to figure out what was going on.

By the time morning came around, I hadn't slept a wink. I was a fucking mess, and I still didn't have a good plan. All I knew was that I wanted to fix this.

To give myself something to do, I began to prep breakfast. Bella liked to sleep in on weekends, so I had some time.

I was midway through mixing the waffle batter when Mom called. I put the utensils down and answered the phone.

"Morning," I said.

"Darling, you sound very exhausted."

"I am," I admitted.

"So, I found the painting."

"What are you talking about?"

"The one of Jackson Square that you asked me to hunt down?"

I instantly felt alert. "That's fucking great news."

"Riiight. I wasn't expecting such an exuberant reply. Is everything all right?"

Usually, I would've just brushed it off by saying, "Fine," but the exhaustion got the better of me.

"No. I kind of screwed things up with Scarlett last night."

There was a pause, and then Mom said, "I honestly don't see how that's possible. You two were adorable."

I ran a hand through my hair. "She got an offer for a job as a chef at her previous restaurant in Seattle."

She gasped. "Oh my goodness. And she wants to take it?"

"No, actually. She insists that she doesn't."

"Then I don't see the problem."

"The problem is that I kind of pushed her by repeatedly saying that she should consider it before saying no."

"That is a trait of LeBlanc men, unfortunately. Thinking you know better than anyone else."

I scoffed. "That was not it."

"Well, it doesn't really matter now, does it?"

"How soon can I pick up the painting?" I asked, finally getting an idea and a plan. Fuck yes, I had a plan.

"Give me an hour or so."

"Perfect. Thank you, Mom." I felt euphoric.

After hanging up, I got another brilliant idea. I was on a damn roll, finally.

Showing, not telling, was my strong suit.

Even though I'd made a massive blunder, I was going to fix it.

I wasn't going to pick up the painting myself or have it delivered. I had something more important to do. It was a good thing my brothers were in town today because this was going to be a group effort.

I called Beckett, knowing full well that he was going to roast my ass for calling him at 8:00 a.m. on a Saturday. He'd gone with Julian to the bar last night after our family dinner.

"Someone better be dying for you to call me at this hour," he said by way of greeting.

"You're not far off," I said. "It's an emergency."

"Fuck. What happened?"

"Nothing."

"What do you mean? You just said it's an emergency."

"Yeah, wrong choice of words. But then again, I am sleep-deprived."

"Are you messing with me?"

"No. I need a king cake. Today. As soon as possible."

"Fucking hell. Are you serious? *That's* your emergency?"

"Yes," I said as seriously as I could muster.

"For Scarlett?"

"Yes."

"You messed up?"

I stopped in the act of picking up the whisk to keep working on the batter. "How did you reach that conclusion?"

"You first got her a cake to get in her pants."

"Beckett!"

"Fine—in her good graces. And now you clearly need it to do the same job again."

"Yes," I admitted. "But with one difference."

"Which is?"

"I'm going to discuss that with your pastry chef."

Beckett burst out laughing. "Well, you know what? I'm up for anything." That was my brother to a T. "And if you want to take this off my hands, then by all means, I'll ask my assistant to forward you the pastry chef's number. She'll tell her to expect a call from you. Knock yourself out. And good luck with whatever it is you're planning."

"Thanks. I'm going to need it."

"Is this a 'go big or go home' kind of strategy?" he asked me.

"You know it."

I was definitely going all out with this plan.

There was one more thing I had to do: wake Bella up.

She and I were going shopping.

Chapter Thirty-Four

Scarlett

I woke up with a headache the morning after the competition. No surprise, considering I'd probably fallen asleep around 3:00 a.m. Even then, I was restless. I practically crawled to the kitchen to make myself the first coffee of the day.

I had a lump in my throat. I'd planned on waking up early today before Bella and Chad and cook breakfast for the two of them. Instead, I was here in my tiny kitchen.

God, I needed to talk about last night with someone or my brain would explode. I needed Ariana.

She was an early bird, but it was Saturday. I didn't want to startle her, so I sent her a quick text message.

Scarlett: Hey, are you up? Call me when you can.

I kept staring at my phone as I sipped a coffee. She didn't reply. I was tempted to call my parents, but why worry them? I'd only told them bits and pieces about my relationship with Chad, so this would feel very out of the blue for them.

I was on my second cup of coffee when Ariana called.

"Hey! Good morning," she said.

"You sound full of energy. So I didn't wake you up?"

"No, I was out for my morning jog."

My eyes widened a bit at that. "You have all my respect. I couldn't do anything first thing in the morning."

"So, what's up? How was yesterday?"

I couldn't believe that everything had only happened yesterday.

"It was great," I replied.

"So why the sad voice?"

"Because... well, remember how I told you that my ex-boss, Mark had been in contact?"

"Yeah."

"He actually sent me a job offer yesterday."

She gasped. "Are you serious?"

"Yeah. As a chef, no less."

"Oh my God." And then she said, "So Simon's out—no surprise. Oh, wait, I can't get too excited, because I'm betting you're turning it down, huh? For that hunk and his adorable daughter."

"Exactly. That's what I want. But Chad is insisting that I think about it thoroughly because it's a great opportunity."

"Huh. You believe that's actually his way of saying he doesn't want this to get any more serious?"

My stomach fell. "I didn't really think that far into it."

"Sorry. I don't want to put crazy ideas in your head. It's just my experience with guys. As soon as I even hint at taking things to the next level, they get cold feet."

"Oh, I didn't think about that. Maybe he feels pressured. Like... if I stay here, it means I want more. And..." I took in a deep breath, remembering Bella's question. I'd completely melted at the time, but what if it had pushed him over the edge?

"What?" she prodded.

"Last night, after the competition, we went to his family's house, and Bella actually adorably asked me if I want to be her week mommy."

"Oh my God, the cute girl. The *week mommy*."

"Yeah. I thought it was adorable and said yes. But what if it was too much too soon?" I was almost afraid to voice that fear.

"And Chad told you about considering the offer right after that?"

"Yes, but we started that conversation before going to the competition." I pressed my palm to my forehead. "I'd hoped that if I talked this through with you, I'd get some clarity, but now I'm even more scared and confused."

"You know what? Forget all the crazy things I've told you. It's only my experience, and it's not relevant right now."

We were both quiet for a moment before Ariana went on.

"Look, Chad is not like the deadbeats I'm dating. I can't see him getting cold feet now either."

"No," I admitted. "But it seemed so sudden." My chest constricted, and my throat clogged.

"I can feel you panicking through the phone," Ariana said.

I didn't have the energy to pretend I wasn't. "I just... I'm not even sure what to do right now."

"Talk to him, maybe?"

"But what if we're right?" *No, damn it. Why would my mind go there?*

"I'm here for you no matter what, okay? Maybe he doesn't want you to have regrets. You two are at completely different stages in your life. He's a bit older. He's got a daughter and a very successful business. He's a CEO. You just got your first position as a chef. Maybe he figures he'd be holding you back from achieving your potential or something."

"But I am living my potential. This is all I've dreamed about. To be a chef in a great kitchen and have someone to love and take care of." My eyes watered.

"Oh, hon. And you're sure he knows that?"

I blinked. "Sort of. I haven't exactly come out and told him."

"Maybe you should," Ariana suggested softly as I took a sip of coffee. "So he knows exactly where you stand."

I took another sip, my heart starting to beat faster. "You know what? You're right, I should. I kept repeating that I don't want the position, but I should've just laid out what I *do* want."

"Exactly. See? We're making some progress even though I'm really not the one to give you advice, considering my shitty history."

"You're the best person in the world, Ariana. I love you so much."

"Oh, I love you, too, bestie. Now, is it okay if we chat later? I want to do some abs, too, before I start the day."

I laughed. "You go, girl."

After we hung up, I was in a much better mood. Was I full of anxiety as well? Yeah, but apparently the two feelings could coexist.

I stood at the counter as I sipped the rest of my coffee. I really needed to wake up, so I hopped into the shower, letting the water soothe me. I'd just finished shampooing my hair when I heard the doorbell ring.

Oh shoot. I bet it's one of the million Amazon orders I've made.

I stepped out of the shower and quickly put on a robe. I had soap all over my neck as well, but it didn't matter. My hair was piled up, and my shampoo was keeping it in place. I hurried to the front door and pressed the button to let the delivery person into the building. Shortly after, my doorbell rang. I looked through the peephole. I couldn't see who it was, but he was carrying a huge package.

Whoa, what did I order? I tried to mentally go through my last few shopping sprees, but it was futile. I'd ordered so many things lately, getting settled in my new hometown, that I typically forgot about them until they arrived.

I opened the door. The person carrying it lowered the box, which I realized wasn't a package at all. It was huge, all right, but it was also very thin.

"Julian," I said, instinctively pulling my robe tighter, even though he couldn't see anything.

He looked at me with a huge grin. "I caught you at a bad moment?"

"Yeah, I was washing my—what is this?"

"I can't say."

I frowned. "Huh?"

"I'm just delivering it."

"I don't understand."

"Honestly, neither do I. Neither Mom nor Chad wanted to give too many details. My instructions are to give this to you, no questions asked."

I cocked a brow at him. "But you're not one to follow instructions."

He chuckled. "Usually I don't, but I suspect that today, it's actually important. Where can I put this?"

"Wherever you want. Just leave it here by the entrance. Would you like something to drink, a coffee or tea?"

"Scarlett," Julian said after putting down the package, "you still have shampoo in your hair. You just got a gift from my brother. I think the only thing I'm supposed to do is take a hike and let you enjoy the day. By the way, I've also been instructed to tell you that you should open that as soon as you get it."

"Okay." I laughed nervously. I couldn't wait to be alone with my gift. "Thank you, a lot, for bringing it over."

"Sure. Whatever the family needs, I'm there. Especially if I happen to be in the neighborhood and they involuntarily make me their transportation mule." He winked at me. "But still, my pleasure."

On that mysterious note, he left, closing the door behind him.

I immediately darted to the kitchen to get a pair of scissors. What could it be that was so large? I carefully cut the brown wrapping paper so I wouldn't damage whatever was inside. And then my heart leaped in my chest.

Oh goodness. It was *my* painting. The one I'd fallen in love with all those weeks ago. *Jackson Square.* I beamed from ear to ear as I took in all the colors, especially the delicate shades of the sky. I loved it. I'd loved it at first sight anyway, but this was different. I felt like this painting was meant for me.

Belatedly, I noticed there was an envelope too. It had fallen to the floor. I picked it up, seeing there was nothing written on either side and that it wasn't sealed. Opening it, I took out a piece of paper. It simply said, **Meet me in Jackson Square at our beignet bench at eleven o'clock.**

It was Chad's handwriting. I was overjoyed.

I grinned, shaking my hips, and then realized that was only an hour away. And as Julian had well pointed out, I was a mess.

Even though all I wanted to do was call Chad and look at my painting some more, I darted back to the bathroom and finished washing my hair. Then I blow-dried it as fast as I could. It usually took me thirty minutes to get it completely dry, but there was no chance of that right now.

Oh, who cares, Scarlett? The humidity will do its thing anyway.

I put on a cute summer dress because New Orleans was starting to heat up pretty early on in the day. I kept glancing at the clock as I went through the motions, slowly starting to panic. I only had twenty minutes to get there. No way in hell could I rely on my streetcar. Instead, I ordered an Uber. The nearest car was five minutes away, but I was too anxious to wait inside, so I headed out of the building.

After I got outside, I looked at my phone, intending to check the Uber app. But my screen lit up with a call.

It was from an unknown number, but I had a hunch about who it was. Simon had called from an unknown number when Chad had answered. I'd wanted to call back to give him a piece of my mind once I got better, but I couldn't. This time, though, I wasn't going to back down.

"Hello, this is Scarlett," I answered.

"You bitch." His voice was enough to make my skin crawl. "You thought I wouldn't know that he offered you my job?"

"It's not really your job anymore, is it? Word on the street is, he threw you out even though he hasn't gotten a yes from me."

"Turn it down. He'll come crawling back to me. You'll be no good. You don't have what it takes to be a chef."

I bristled. "You listen to me, Simon. You put me down for years, trying to make me feel small. I'm ashamed to say that you even succeeded on occasion, but no more. I'm strong. I'm very good at what I do. I am a chef, and a damn good one. You losing your job has absolutely nothing to do with me. You lost it because you are a piece of shit."

God, it felt so good to say that, so I kept going. "You've got rage issues, and you're simply not a good person. No one wants to be around someone like that."

"Tell Mark you're not taking the job."

"I shall do no such thing."

I had zero plans to take it, but he didn't need to know that. For now, I was simply basking in the satisfaction that he was tearing his hair out, thinking I'd gotten his job.

"Have a nice life, Simon," I said before hanging up on him. I felt victorious and utterly free. I should've had this conversation with him a long time ago. But I was proud that I'd finally done it anyway.

My Uber arrived right on time. I was a complete basket case during the drive, going through everything that had happened in the past hour and trying to process it all.

What's this about? It has to be something good, right?

I couldn't believe he'd actually tracked down my painting. I loved him even more for that.

"Is this okay?" the driver asked when we reached Jackson Square. "The drop-off pin is farther away, but I can stop here. It's gonna be trickier farther down the street."

"This is fine. Have a great day."

I practically jumped out of the car, grinning as I walked into the square with quick steps. We'd only met here once, but I knew exactly what he meant by "our beignet bench." That evening was branded into my memory.

When I got there, I saw Chad had already arrived. He was sitting down with a small box next to him but rose to his feet when he saw me.

"Good morning. I see everything worked out flawlessly." He grinned.

I chuckled, playing with a strand of hair between my fingers. "Except for the fact that I didn't get to dry my hair, and your brother saw me in my robe with shampoo still in my hair."

I decided not to tell him about Simon's call right now, as I didn't want to ruin this moment. But I would eventually. I didn't want any secrets between us.

Chad growled. "He didn't tell me that. Were you naked?"

I couldn't believe he was actually asking this.

"No! And your brother probably didn't tell you because he's a gentleman."

He barked out a laugh. "No, he's not."

I pointed at the small box bearing the Broussard & LeBlanc Bakery logo. "Is that for me?"

"Yes," he said, "but later."

"What do you mean, later?" I asked as we sat down.

"First, we need to talk."

"Oh my God. Yes, we do. Thank you so much for that painting. How did you get it?"

"My mom pulled some strings."

I giggled. "I can't believe you asked your mom to do that."

"Why not? It's her area of expertise. I talked to her last week, and she surprised me this morning."

"It's gorgeous. And my favorite spot in the city."

"I know."

He held his hand out palm up, and I knew what it meant. I put my hand in his, and he closed his fingers tightly around it.

"Scarlett, last night didn't go the way I planned. I never for one second want you to think that I don't want you here, okay? Because I do. It's all I fucking want."

I opened my mouth, but he shook his head. "Just hear me out."

"Okay." I pressed my lips together.

"Bella and I both love you. We'll always love you, and whatever you choose to do, we can make this work. You taking that job doesn't mean we're not together."

"But that's not what I want," I cut in, making him frown. "I'm sorry, but I can't help myself anymore." I started to move closer to him on the bench, then stopped, picked up the package with my free hand, and put it on my other side so I wouldn't squish it in my desperation for this man. Sliding up against him, I said, "I've already got everything I want. You and Bella and New Orleans. I love working at the restaurant. I've never had aspirations to be some globetrotting chef. All I ever wanted was to have my cozy spot where people treat me right, and I've got so much more here. It's everything I need to be happy."

"Fuck, woman." He cupped my face. "I want to devour you right here."

"We're in public," I murmured.

Taking a deep breath, he pressed his forehead to mine. "I just want to stay like this with you, just for a moment."

"Okay," I whispered, and I could've sworn it was the most romantic moment of my life. I was here in Jackson Square with this man all wrapped up around me.

When he finally pulled back, I batted my eyelashes. "Can I open my goodies now?"

"Sure."

I immediately took the package and placed it in my lap, opening it carefully. "King cake! How did you even manage to do that? The dough needs a few hours to rise."

"It does, as the pastry chef reminded me multiple times. But she said she used the dough she'd prepped for something else. Be careful when you bite into it, though."

"Did you hide a baby Jesus inside it?"

He smiled. "Just be careful."

I heeded his advice. In fact, I didn't even bite into it. Instead, I carefully ripped off a piece and then a second one.

Huh. Disappointment roiled in my stomach. If there was a baby Jesus inside, it was tiny.

I continued to rip off big chunks, and then I hit something hard!

Then I stilled, because my middle finger went through something that was unmistakably a ring.

I held it up, and Chad took it from my finger before I even had time to process what was happening. He went down on one knee, holding the gorgeous ring. It was a pristine white diamond, and I absolutely loved it.

"Chad," I whispered.

"I woke up this morning wondering what the hell happened last night. Then I remembered why I don't talk much. Judging by last night, I should keep to my strengths, which is showing you how I feel." His hand was shaking slightly. I was fighting tears of joy, though I wasn't sure I could hide them much longer. "You're perfect in ways I couldn't have imagined."

I put a hand on my stomach. *Deep breath. No tears, Scarlett. No tears.*

"I love you with everything that I am, and I'm yours, Scarlett. Not just today or for now. I want you to be mine forever." He took my hand, kissing it quickly. "I want you to be my wife. Will you marry me?"

"Yes. God, yes. Of course I'll marry you." My voice cracked on every second word.

"You're mine, baby," he whispered as he put on the ring. "And I am yours. Only yours."

He kissed my hand again. "And right here in your favorite spot in the city, I want to promise you that my entire life, I will strive to surprise you, spoil you, and protect you on haunted tours."

I chuckled. "Especially that."

"And to forcefully take care of you when you're sick. Although, I might use my husband privileges and not let you go out of the house in the first place."

"Like that could stop me," I murmured, no longer bothering to hide the tears. "I love you."

"And I love you."

He rose to his feet, and I did the same. He wrapped his arms around my waist and kissed me right here in Jackson Square for all the French Quarter to see. Chad LeBlanc gave a new meaning to the term *PDA*. We only stopped when someone cleared their throat.

We pulled apart and saw there were two guys right next to us.

"Erm, can I help you?" I asked.

"Right," Chad said. "I forgot."

The man closest to us grinned. "Awesome proposal, man. You didn't give us your number so we could send you the pictures."

I barely stifled a laugh, but then my mouth fell open. "You have a picture of us? Oh, that's so sweet."

Chad rattled off his number, and they immediately sent the pics.

"I've got them," Chad confirmed. "Thanks a lot."

They congratulated us before leaving.

I turned to Chad. "Why did you ask two people?"

"Bella's instructions. In case one of them messed it up."

I started to laugh and then realized... "Oh my God. Bella knows."

"Of course. We went ring shopping together." He cupped my face, pressing one thumb against the corner of my mouth.

By the glint in his eyes, I knew he wanted to devour me again, but that wouldn't do.

"What do you think about going to the house?" he asked.

"Sure. Is Bella there?"

"No. Xander took her out for the day. And you know what that means?" He wiggled his eyebrows. "We have the house all to ourselves."

Chapter Thirty-Five

Chad

We didn't linger in the Quarter. Instead, we went straight to the house. I was always hungry for Scarlett, but right now, I was downright desperate. I needed this woman with every fiber of my being. I kissed her without any restraint, walking her directly up to the master bedroom.

"You smell so damn good," I said, and she giggled. I straightened up. "Why are you laughing?"

"No reason." Her secretive smile told me different, but I wanted to explore her too much to press her about it.

"I bet you taste just as good."

She swallowed hard as I sank my fingers into her hair. Turning her around, I closed my eyes while I took in a deep breath, then kissed her neck.

"This dress is fantastic," I murmured against her skin.

Her upper back was exposed. The lower was covered. Wanting to trail my mouth all the way down, I kissed down her spine. When I reached her lower back, I lowered the zipper past her ass. Then I pushed her panties down and licked the base of her spine. She shuddered in appreciation, and I trailed my hands down her legs before clasping her ankles. She moaned, dropping her head back. I slowly moved my hands back up, pressing both thumbs into the backs of her knees while I nuzzled the base of her spine with the tip of my nose.

"Chad," she whispered.

Her reaction only fueled my desire. I moved one hand farther up and drew circles on the back of on knee with the other one.

I reached between her thighs and tugged blindly, needing to touch her pussy. I quickly realized I'd used more force than necessary, because her panties ripped. Scarlett gasped as I felt for the elastic band, then pulled them down her legs, wanting them out of the way completely. Sure enough, they were torn.

I thought I'd be content with touching her bare skin, but no. I wanted to see more of her too.

I started to yank down her dress, but she protested. "Chad, no! The other way round."

I pushed her dress over her ass and to her middle. She grabbed it from there, pulling it over her head.

Hell yes. I wanted to watch this woman get naked for me every single night, forever.

When she started to turn around, I said, "No. Stay like this."

Stepping closer, I pressed two fingers along her opening. She was wet and so damn ready that I almost pulled her down on me right then, but instead I kissed her ass cheeks. I reached her pussy from behind, nudging her clit. At first, I only used the tips of my fingers, then the entire length of them, drawing out the movement. I felt her muscles contract with every passing second. Her moans resounded through the room.

I loved hearing my woman cry out in pleasure, but if she continued like that, I wasn't going to be able to wait until she came to sink inside her.

"Chad," she whispered. "Please, please, please, please."

It was more than I could bear.

I kept rubbing my fingers up and down, feeling her get wetter and then wetter still until her body started to jerk. They were slight movements at first, but I could tell the exact moment when her climax started to course through her body because they became more instinctive, almost animalistic. She was riding my hand, and I fucking loved it. But it wasn't enough. I wanted her to ride my face while she came, so I stopped touching her pussy and stepped around her.

"Chad...," she began, her eyes widening as I kneeled in front of her, pushing her against the wall so she could comfortably rest her back against it.

I put one of her legs on my shoulder and licked her clit, enjoying the way she pressed her thighs against my ears. A few beats later, I pushed two fingers inside her. She needed them there right now, and she needed them hard. I moved them in and out of her while I focused on her clit with my tongue. Then I pulled it into my mouth just as I curled my fingers inside her. She jerked forward, crying out loudly.

I slowed the pace of my fingers while she calmed down, though I was still fixated on her clit. She seemed to prefer the flat of my tongue, so that's what she got.

I pressed my tongue against her until her breathing slowed and she ran her fingers through my hair. I pulled back while looking up at her. Her eyelids were hooded.

She licked her lips. "I want to taste you now," she said.

I felt a stirring below my belt. The thought of her mouth on me... Fuck yes. It was exactly what I needed.

I put her leg down from my shoulder and rose to my feet, kissing her breasts and then her neck before going straight to her ear. "I want you so damn much," I said, and she sighed.

"I know, but I want to taste you first."

Fucking hell. My cock turned from semihard to a full-on rock in the span of a second.

Stepping back, I took her hand and led her to the bed. I had an idea. I wasn't done tasting her either, and this way we'd both be happy.

"Lie on top of me," I said.

The saucy grin she gave me told me that she understood exactly what I meant, no explanations or further instructions needed.

I laid down on the mattress as she climbed on all fours over me, putting her pussy right over my face. As I tilted my head forward, she clamped her lips around the tip of my cock. I sank my head back into the pillow.

"Fuuuuuck!" I exclaimed, and then she took me in even more. She moved her mouth on me at a rapid pace, and pleasure was already coiling toward me.

I pressed down on the base of her spine, so she lowered her pussy over me, and then I pushed my tongue inside her. I brought a hand between us so I could touch her clit too. Having her mouth on me while she was also wide open for me was fucking fantastic. Her moves became more frantic as she became even more sensitive to the strokes of my tongue. Her breasts brushed against my legs, her nipples rock hard, and when I pressed two fingers on her clit, she broke into a sweat.

This woman was going to drive me crazy. There would never come a day when I'd have my fill of her. I'd always want more and more. I'd want everything.

I increased the rhythm of my fingers on her clit, and I felt her lips clamp tighter around my cock. Then she pulled her head back.

"Chad... oh my God, you can't—" Her breath hitched. "I can't focus anymore."

"That's okay, babe, because I need to be inside you right now."

"But I wasn't done."

"I want to be inside you when I come."

Goose bumps popped up across her ass. I gave it a light slap, and she pushed it toward me even more.

"Turn around," I commanded. She looked at me over her shoulder and then rose onto her knees. "Actually, I changed my mind. Just move farther away and lean backward."

She shifted until her feet were at the outsides of my thighs. Then she leaned backward. This angle was going to be fucking perfect.

I didn't even need to position my cock. She lowered herself onto it the next second, all the way down.

"Fuck!" A cold shudder raced through my entire body. She'd brought me too close to the edge with her mouth, and I knew she needed a bit more until she reached a climax after the first one.

So I didn't move at all, just simply held her over me. When she started to slide up and down, I gripped her hips tightly. "No, stay still."

"Chad...," she protested.

"Just stay like this and take all the pleasure I'm giving you. You're only allowed to move when you can't take it anymore. Do you understand?"

"Yes," she said in a breathy voice.

I pushed myself into a sitting position to make sure she wasn't moving at all. Then I kissed along her back, feeling her pussy clench and then relax around me as I teased her clit with my fingertips.

Our bodies were so in sync that I felt every single wave of her building orgasm as if it was mine. Her back spasmed, then softened. The muscles in her belly clenched. I knew when she'd reached the point of no return even before she said it. I felt it by the way her body shuddered and her head lolled backward.

"Chad..."

"I know, sugar" was all I replied. My own voice was strained because the effort of not climaxing was taking every ounce of willpower I had.

"Can I move now?" She was pleading, and it was my undoing. Even if she hadn't been this close, I couldn't possibly have resisted.

"Yes, you can move."

She rose up and down my cock the very next second. Lying back down, I grabbed her hips and thrust forward relentlessly, and she braced her palms on the bed. Then she lowered herself onto her elbows before finally turning completely soft and resting her back against my chest. Her head almost reached my shoulder.

"That's it, babe." I said. "Surrender to me. I promise I'll make you come."

"Chad, oh my God," she whispered.

I pinched my eyes tightly together, focusing as hard as I could on my woman's pleasure. I alternated between pushing inside her and circling her clit. She was too close to stand both at the same time, but when I felt her squeeze me harder than ever, I knew she was right there, nearly over the edge. I slapped her clit, and she climaxed instantly, writhing on top of me.

The vortex of sensations grabbed me, too, and I let go this time. There was no need to stay in control. I could relent to this woman who'd claimed every part of me. I was ready. I was going to spend the rest of my life with her.

I thrust and thrust until we were both spent and had relaxed. Then she was complete mush on top of me. I wrapped my arms around her belly.

"I kept thinking I might fall off you," she said.

"Oh, babe, I'm keeping you right here. Don't worry."

"I'm not because you're my rock."

Yes, I fucking was, and I was going to be her rock for the rest of our lives. And she was mine.

"I love you so much. I'll make sure every day that you don't doubt that."

"I don't."

I chuckled. "I'll remind you several times a day anyway. You might get visits from the boss now and again."

She jerked her head back. "You're serious, huh?"

"Hell yes. Now that you're my fiancée, I have a good excuse."

"I want to play coy, but why should I? I totally grant you that fiancé privilege."

"I plan to make sure you never lack coffee or beignets."

She sighed. "See, you can just send me gifts all day long. You don't even have to be there yourself."

I laughed, pulling her closer. "But I will be. I can't wait for us to build our life together."

"One coffee and beignet at a time?" she asked with delight.

"Exactly."

EPILOGUE

SCARLETT

"To Scarlett's first Christmas with the LeBlanc-Broussard clan," Isabeau exclaimed.

I smiled from ear to ear as we all clinked glasses of eggnog. "I'm super happy to be here."

"Thank you for inviting us too," Mom said.

She and Dad had arrived yesterday. We were spending Christmas Eve at the LeBlanc-Broussard mansion and were going to have a second celebration tomorrow in a smaller format. My parents still looked shocked at the sheer size of the house even though they'd been here for an hour already. I was wearing the sweater Mom knitted for me all those months ago.

"All right, everyone," Isabeau said. "Once we drink our eggnog, it's time to start bringing out the goodies."

"Hear, hear!" chorused around the room.

Chad put an arm around my waist and took me a few feet away from everyone. "Everything okay? Your parents overwhelmed?"

"Yes, but in the best sense," I assured him. "We're used to quiet Christmases, just the three of us. This is absolutely beautiful."

The house looked like something out of a movie. I'd never seen so many decorations in one place, but it wasn't overwhelming. The fireplace was crackling, and there were a million stockings hanging on the mantelpiece, one for each of us. They were stuffed to the brim. There were also four huge trees. At least, I only counted four. Who knew how many others there were on the upper levels? One was in the hallway, one in the sitting area, one in the dining room, and one closer to the kitchen. Each had a different color scheme, and they all fit together.

"Do you always celebrate Christmas in grand style like this?" I asked.

"That's an absolute yes." Chad looked at me with warmth and love, and I truly couldn't get enough of him.

"Hey, Scarlett," Bella said, jogging up to us. "I have an idea." She wrapped her arms around my middle.

I looked down at her, running my hand through her hair. I loved being Bella's week mom, although lately I was being her weekend mom, too, because she was requesting to spend more and more weekends at the house. Sarah wasn't against it. In fact, she seemed to prefer it, as it enabled her to travel more. Bottom line, as long as Bella was fine with it, so were Chad and I.

"Aha," Chad exclaimed, eyes trained on Bella.

"What?" the little one asked a bit too innocently.

"Nothing. You've just got that grin."

I braced myself.

"Have you noticed that the grandparents have four trees?" Bella asked.

"Yes, and I love them."

"They're different colors too."

"I know, right? Very festive."

She bit her lower lip. "So I was thinking, maybe next year, we can decorate four trees at home too: green with silver on one tree, gold and red on another one, blue and white on the third one..."

"And yellow and black on the last one?" I guessed.

She burst out laughing. "Yes."

"I don't get it," Chad said.

We both looked at him.

"Dad, we watched the first three movies together, and you're still a Muggle. It's the colors of the Hogwarts houses."

"Right," he murmured.

"I love that idea," I exclaimed.

Chad shrugged. "I don't have anything against it."

Bella grinned. "Great! And then maybe we can negotiate with Dad so we can watch one more movie. At least one."

Oh shoot. Why didn't I see this coming? Bella would be one year older, but still not old enough for *Goblet of Fire.*

I glanced at Chad, then back at Bella and said, "We'll see."

Bella's mouth hung open.

Chad started to laugh. "Bingo, kid. She's on my side on this."

Bella straightened up, letting her hands drop by her sides. " I'll convince you. I have time."

Chad opened his mouth but didn't say anything. And who did Bella run to straight away? *Xander.*

"We've got a little fighter on our hands," I said.

"Yes, we do," Chad replied. Then he took me by the waist, pulling me into him. "You've got to promise me that you will not switch sides."

"There *is* a small risk of that, but you're pretty persuasive about getting me to see your point of view."

"That's right, I fucking am."

"This is the best Christmas ever," I murmured.

"I'm glad you think so."

"I love all the traditions your family has, especially the stockings over the fireplace. I can't believe they added some for me and my parents too."

"Maybe we'll add one more next year."

I raised a brow. "Oh? Who else do you want to invite?"

He smiled at me. "A baby?"

My whole body instantly softened. "You really mean that?" I asked.

"Yes. Of course, we'd also have to decide on the wedding day between now and next Christmas."

I laughed. "Is this another ruse for you to convince me to set a date?"

We'd been debating this ever since he proposed, yet somehow we hadn't reached a consensus. I wanted a summer wedding, but he insisted it was too hot. Spring was looking good, though.

"As you pointed out, I'm excellent at finding ways to convince you."

I couldn't believe I was lucky enough to be here with this amazing man. I was utterly and blissfully happy.

I had a permanent contract at LeBlanc & Broussard, and the kitchen was thriving. I'd declined Mark's job offer as politely as possible. I'd half expected him to get Simon back, but whatever happened between them must have been really bad, because he didn't. In fact, I'd done a bit of stalking on Facebook with Ariana's help. What would I do without her? Simon wasn't even a sous-chef at his new job. He was simply a kitchen assistant. I was trying really hard not to rejoice, but hey, I couldn't help it. I felt a bit vindicated.

Shortly after our engagement, I'd told Chad about Simon's last call. We were both glad Simon was finally getting what was coming to him.

"I guess we're getting married next year, then. As long as it doesn't fall during any rush weeks at the restaurant."

He groaned. "Woman, you're marrying the boss. He can pull some strings."

"Yeah, but I don't want him to. That's the point."

"We'll discuss this later at home."

Yeah right. He was going to use his sexy skills to win me over.

"All right, everyone. First round of snacks is on the way," Celine announced.

"Coming!" I said, but Chad put a hand firmly on my waist.

"No. You're not going in the kitchen, remember? Mom made that a rule."

The LeBlancs and their rules. "Okay. I'll stay put."

As we went to the table, Chad said, "I wonder what's up with Julian."

I followed his gaze to his brother, who was chatting softly with Anthony and Beckett. "He seems in a bad mood," I said.

"I know." Chad sounded stunned.

"I didn't know Julian could be in a bad mood," I confessed.

"Neither did I. I wonder why that is."

"Let's go find out," I said, and we headed their way.

"Is there a crisis at the office?" Chad asked without further ado.

The three brothers stared at him.

"Why would you think that?" Anthony asked coolly.

"Julian, you seem to be in a foul mood, and it's unusual," I said.

His eyes bulged. "You picked up on it?"

"Um, brother," Beckett said, "I'm sorry to disappoint you, but I think aliens could've picked up on it. You have no poker face."

"Right," Julian said. "No, I'm just... I got a rude email from someone we used to work with. She just won't take no for an answer."

Beckett grinned. "It's a woman, and she seems like a force to be reckoned with."

Julian stared at him. "That's what you got? After everything I just told you?"

"Sounds like she's giving you a run for your money instead of simply surrendering to the power of the LeBlanc and Broussard names."

"It's not about surrendering," Julian replied. "She's simply rude and hardheaded for no reason."

"Is she attractive?" Anthony asked.

"I've never met her in person. And anyway, that has nothing to do with anything," Julian replied. There was a bit of an edge to his voice.

"Is that so?" Celine asked. She was carrying a tray of pralines.

"You should've let them talk for a little longer," Isabeau tsked. She had a tray of dates wrapped in bacon. They smelled amazing. "Then we could've gotten more details."

Julian shook his head. "There's no need for that. Let's head to the table." He looked pointedly at Anthony and Beckett, who followed him over.

"You two eavesdropped?" Chad asked.

"Well, but you weren't exactly keeping it quiet," Celine said.

"You know, we could find out who that lady is. We'll see if we can give her a nudge with the lilac," Isabeau said.

I started to laugh. Chad looked at his grandmothers incredulously.

"Oh no. We have to see if she's worthy first," Celine countered.

Huh. They'd thought I was worthy when they'd really only met me a few times? That was something, wasn't it?

"We should just let things unfold. The lilac only works if the two are meant for each other. It doesn't work miracles," Celine went on.

"That's true," Isabeau confirmed, and the two of them looked at us with unmistakable pride in their eyes. "You two are perfect for each other. Your brothers will be lucky if things go the same way for them."

Chad chuckled. "I think my brothers would disagree with you."

Isabeau waved her hand. "All in due time." Then she took my arm, walking with me to the table. "Your perfume should be running out about now."

"Yes," I said, surprised she knew that.

"You can come back for more anytime."

"Grandmothers, why are you trying to lure Scarlett back to your store?" Chad asked.

"Oh, we're not luring her anywhere, boy," Celine said.

"We just want to spend some time with her on her own. Find out what plans you two might have for the future. Regarding babies," Isabeau said.

I gasped as Chad laughed and shook his head. "You know, usually I'd say it's none of your business. But we were discussing it earlier."

"Excellent," Celine said. "Bella needs a sister or brother—maybe both—and it's been a long time coming."

"Well, Celine, he had to meet the right one," Isabeau commented. "And we all knew Sarah was not that, though I'm pleased she's not making an issue out of anything."

On the contrary, according to Chad, Sarah just wanted to have as much time as possible for herself. That was fine, really—I planned to shower Bella with love forever.

Celine turned to me then. "Scarlett, dear, we can try out a new perfume for you." She winked. "We've been told it does wonders."

I opened my mouth, then closed it again. I'd been skeptical about the lilac too. But now I was almost a believer.

Chad put an arm around my waist. "Let's go to the table. Who knows what these two are up to," he said, looking at Celine and Isabeau.

"Whatever they have in mind, they have my full approval," I informed him.

As we gathered around the table, I noticed Chad's parents talking to mine. I was grateful for that because it was helping them relax.

"All right, everyone. Since we do everything a bit differently in this house," Celine said, "we actually decided to start with some pralines—from our family's confectionery, of course—and dates."

Chad and I each took a praline from the center of the table.

I smiled at him and said, "Your family does everything their own unique way."

"And that's why you fit. Merry Christmas, sugar."

"Merry Christmas, Chad."

We ate our pralines at the same time. It was an explosion of flavor in my mouth, sweet but not overly so. I immediately reached for another one, devouring it just as quickly. Such a perfect way to start dinner, by having dessert first.

I was happy and simply complete. I couldn't wait for every Christmas yet to come.

Dear Reader, this is the end of the book. For a full list of Layla Hagen's books, please visit laylahagen.com

Made in the USA
Las Vegas, NV
21 April 2024

88959136R00184